STEVE WHITE

THE DISINHERITED

Copyright © 1993 by Steve White

A Baen Books Original

Baen Publishing Enterprises
P.O. Box 1403
Riverdale, N.Y. 10471

ISBN: 0-671-72194-1

Cover art by Paul Alexander

First printing, November 1993

Distributed by
SIMON & SCHUSTER
1230 Avenue of the Americas
New York, N.Y. 10020

Typeset by Windhaven Press, Auburn, N.H.
Printed in the United States of America

HIS COURSE WAS SIMPLE ENOUGH—
NOT EASY, BUT SIMPLE

DiFalco, like everyone else, was confined to his acceleration couch, so he couldn't even pace as the first of the Korvaash missiles began to arrive. . . .

❖   ❖   ❖

Seivra was under attack. Impossibly, someone had gotten into the system! He couldn't imagine how, but he knew one thing, and as he was hauled up through the hatches by the other humans, he could see they knew it too: Someone was attacking the Korvaasha. Someone was *hurting* the Korvaasha.

The astonishing thought immobilized him for an instant. And one of the Korvaash guards rounded on him. "Move! We must close the hatch!" Before his victim could respond the guard's neurolash slashed out.

Aelador gasped as the jag of hideous pain shot through his nervous system. Then, as he fell forward into the arms of one of the other humans, suddenly something seemed to lift from him, leaving nothing except the certain knowledge of what he must do.

As he staggered erect, Aelador took one backward step to the lip of the hatch and met the eyes of the other humans for an instant, with an odd little smile. Then, before the startled guards could react, he tilted over backwards, and fell toward the glowing mass of wiring below.

With a crackling roar and a blinding, spark-showering flash, he vanished, and the chamber filled with the stench of burned meat. And electrical systems began to die.

❖   ❖   ❖

"Colonel!" Farrell sounded puzzled. "Something's happened to the incoming missiles. There are just as many of them, but it's as if their fire control has suddenly become a lot less effective."

Baen Books By Steve White

Insurrection (with David Weber)
Crusade (with David Weber)

To Sandy,
for encouragement, love,
and proofreading

CHAPTER ONE

Tareil had set, and Norellarn was a city of light. The pedestrian slidewalks were streams of mercury, the soaring crysteel-and-glass towers were a blaze of illumination, and, barely visible in the far distance, this hemisphere's orbital tower was a string of light rising impossibly up, up, up into infinity.

Yes, Norellarn seemed constructed of light. And to Varien hle'Morna, viewing the dazzling cityscape from the balcony of his private office, it was as insubstantial as the massless photons of that light, for he knew it was doomed.

The great city in the last days of its greatness, its civilization a ghost that does not yet know it is dead! Varien shook himself irritably. *And how many more banalities shall we dredge up from bad historical fiction?* He rubbed the tip of his right index finger across an area of skin on the back of his left hand, activating the imprint circuits, and consulted the tiny chronometer that glowed to life. Yes, it was time. He squared his narrow shoulders, turned his back on the city and strode purposefully inside.

He paused to look around the familiar office, seeing its architecture and furnishings with new eyes. It

1

was like a showcase for a tradition of understated
elegance that had had centuries to refine upon
refinement . . . a showcase about to be smashed by
a steel truncheon.

*Yes, perhaps one could do worse than historical
novels as a source of inspiration just now. History
has started happening to this world of Raehan again,
and it's been so long that we've forgotten how to
react. Better cliche than speechlessness.*

Enough! He lowered himself into a Taelieu-period
recliner and took a set of wraparound, ear-covering
goggles from the small matching end table beside it.
He then attached a few tiny movement sensors to
his clothing at various points on his upper body, put
on the headset, and spoke a short numeric code.

Tarlann and Arduin were already seated at the
plain conference table. Sitting and talking was, of
course, about all that the three of them, located in
as many continents, could do; nothing more was
required at the moment, and it would have been too
much trouble to don the full suit and helmet that
would have enabled them to interact physically, with
all the appropriate sensations. *Never really liked the
things anyway,* Varien groused to himself. *If they get
much better, how will we keep track of what is and
isn't real?* At least, this shared line was as secure as
Varien's resources, and the military ones at Arduin's
disposal, could make it. And the stark, utilitarian
meeting room that the program simulated was appropriate to the subject at hand.

"Well," Varien began without ceremony, addressing
Tarlann. "Is everything in readiness?"

His son nodded, his unease palpable as the computer faithfully reproduced all the outward signs of
human emotions it would never feel. "Yes, father. I
know it's useless to try to talk you into changing your
mind. . . ."

"Then don't bother trying," Varien cut in. "Our
time is limited." He instantly regretted his curtness—

he might never see his only son again. He softened his tone, which had always represented his very best effort at apology. "Our plans have already been set in motion, son. And you've been running our enterprises on a day-to-day basis for years now, so the company shouldn't go into shock. Besides, It's not as if I was leaving permanently!" Which, he gibed at himself, might even turn out to be true. He turned to Arduin. "And at your end?"

His old friend and colleague nodded, looking even more miserable than Tarlann. Varien understood; as a senior officer in the new Raehaniv military, Arduin was experiencing a conflict of loyalties with which his open and honorable nature was unfit to cope. Varien's arguments had persuaded his intellect, but his conscience remained stubbornly unconvinced. Of course, Arduin's misery might also have had something to do with the sheer discomfort of the uniform he was wearing. The Raehaniv had remembered enough of their history to think, uncritically, of uniforms as something soldiers were supposed to have. And for their desperately improvised military, they had naturally looked to the most recent examples of such things: the consciously archaic (even then) confections used by the rival states of the Fourth Global War in their efforts to reignite their despairing populations' nationalism.

So we made our defenders look—and feel—like buffoons, Varien reflected. *Ah, well; we did everything else wrong, so why not that too?*

"Yes," Arduin amplified. "The last of the supply caches is in place. And I've managed to arrange for the transfer of the remainder of the units whose commanders I can be sure of. There'll be a resistance fleet operating in the asteroids when you return." A fresh wave of anguish crossed his blunt features; he was discovering what it was to serve two masters, and it was anathema to him. When he spoke, it was to blurt out the final appeal that Varien had known he must make. "Varien, you don't need to do this! Turn the new drive over to the government! Maybe we can still put it to use, stop the Korvaasha before . . ."

"We've been over this ground already, Arduin," Varien interrupted, his voice unwontedly gentle. "Many times, in fact. I put it to you: has the situation changed since our final decision was reached? Do you have any new information that invalidates the logic of that decision?"

"No," Arduin admitted.

"Then," Varien went on remorselessly, "our conclusions still stand. The Korvaash fleets are advancing at a rate limited only by their own caution—I imagine they still haven't fully grasped how feeble their opposition is." He raised a forestalling hand. "Forgive me, old friend, but the time for good manners is past. No one doubts the courage of your young men and women. They will go on till the end, trying to shelter Raehan behind a wall of their own corpses. But they are, quite simply, amateurs—products of a society for which war has been nothing more than the fading memory of an old nightmare. And they are fighting an enemy who sees himself as being permanently at war and organizes his society accordingly, and who commands resources that dwarf ours."

"But," Arduin argued stubbornly, "our technology is more sophisticated than theirs! Given your new drive . . ."

". . . We could do far more damage to them than we otherwise would," Varien finished for him. "Maybe even provoke them into making exceptions to their usual guidelines for dealing with newly conquered planets—exceptions we wouldn't like. But we could not stop them. No technological advantage can win a war without a viable military force to take advantage of it. To give the drive to our government now would merely make it part of the spoils the Korvaasha will take when they occupy Raehan." He paused for breath, and then gazed somberly at the other two.

"I haven't used this argument until now, partly because"—a wintery smile—"it is so out of character that you both would have suspected I was up to something. But I ask you to consider this. We now know we are not the only intelligent race in the cosmos. So we are acting not only for ourselves, but for all that lives and thinks! To give the Korvaasha the secret of faster-than-light interstellar travel without recourse to displacement points—and, I repeat, that is precisely what turning it over to our government would amount to—would be to remove all limits to the militaristic expansion their ideology commands them to pursue. Their capabilities would become as unbounded as their aims. I will see Raehan go down into the dark rather than permit my work to be so perverted!"

He stopped, as astonished at his own vehemence as they doubtless were. Tarlann finally broke the silence.

"The Korvaasha will eventually discover it for themselves. You yourself have said it is a logical outgrowth of gravitics. In fact, you've admitted the concept wasn't original with you—you merely found a way to make it workable."

"Which is precisely why I have no intention of leaving them in peace to discover it," Varien replied, his normal asperity reasserting itself. "The entire purpose of our plans is to secure allies. Raehan cannot be saved—but it can be liberated."

"And what makes you so sure the Landaeniv will be able—or inclined—to do so? You've learned enough about them to know that their technology is laughable compared to ours or even the Korvaasha. . . ."

" 'Far behind' I will grant," Varien interrupted his son. "But not 'laughable'. Aelanni's people at Lirauva have concluded that we are looking at a civilization at least as advanced as ours was at the time of the Third Global War. And it seems probable that for the last

several generations they have been advancing about as
rapidly as we did during that era. So constant change
has become an expected part of their lives; they are
intellectually ready to accept the notion of a still higher
technology, and not just fall down and start babbling of
magic. They will be able to understand, utilize, and
even—with certain exceptions—manufacture the
devices we will explain to them. And as for why they
will be willing to ally themselves with us . . . well, you
seem to have answered your own question. We can
offer them a technological quantum leap. We can offer
them the stars!" He paused, then continued more
matter-of-factly. "Of course they'll have to be
approached in the right way. That's why I have to go
myself; I don't trust anyone else to manage the critical
first-contact stage. . . ."

Arduin barked laughter. "Right! You're just what
we need when tact and diplomacy are called for!
Varien, you never change. Always the Indispensable
Man!" The big engineer-turned-admiral paused
reflectively. "Still, you may be right about their ability to help us. They still live with the threat of
war—they have professional soldiers. And they'll be
able to enter this system from a totally unexpected
direction." The other two nodded unconsciously; it
was their other great secret, and they knew what
would have to be done to preserve it. "You may also
be right about their willingness to help us against the
Korvaasha, given . . . what we now know about
them."

His voice trailed to a halt, and no one broke the
silence. They were all rationalists, children of a culture for which rationalism had been beyond debate
for centuries. Faced with the rationally inexplicable,
they were intellectually lost. In his circumlocution,
Arduin was as one with the most superstitious of his
forebears, fearful to speak aloud the names of
unknowable, ill-omened things.

We must face what we know to be fact, Varien

thought bleakly, *and not let our inability to explain it paralyze us. Later—if there is a later—we will have time to try and account for the manifestly impossible. In our present pass, we can only seek to take whatever advantage we can from it.*

"Well," he spoke briskly, "at all events, my mind is made up. I will depart on schedule." He spoke a command, and a holographic image-of-an-image appeared, suspended above the table. It showed stars, identified by glowing labels in the uncial Raehaniv alphabet and linked to each other by narrow bands of pale-blue light representing the connections between displacement points—those gravitational anomalies which were, as far as nearly everyone knew, still the only way to evade the lightspeed limit. Four of the luminous bands branched out from the star Tareil, on whose second planet they sat; every other such display on this world of Raehan showed three. Varien reached out and indicated the series of displacement connections reaching outward from the fourth point through three intervening star systems to the glowing star-symbol of Lirauva. His eyes lingered over another such symbol floating close to Lirauva in isolation, unconnected to any other star, with the name "Landaen" beside it in letters of light.

"The Lirauva Chain," he declaimed, giving it the convenience-label by which it was known to the few who knew of it at all. "The knowledge of its existence will, after tonight, vanish from every record in this planetary system . . . except, of course, your living memories. And you both know what must be done if you are in danger of being interrogated." The others both nodded, and for an instant Varien gazed at Tarlann and knew irreparable loss. Tarlann—brilliant student, efficient executive, the father of his grandchildren . . . but, somehow, never fully a son. Never enough time for that. *Where did all that grey at his temples come from?* All at once Varien wished they had, after all, donned the full virtual reality gear. A virtual embrace would have been better than none at all.

                    *   *   *

The next day, the global datanet interrupted the daily war news with the announcement that Varien hle'Morna, fabulously wealthy manufacturer of spacecraft and related technologies, holder of numerous scientific honors, discoverer of the displacement points that had given humankind the stars (and the Korvaasha, some muttered, though all admitted that the aliens' inexorable expansion would eventually have carried them to the Tareil system anyway) had died in a freak aircar accident. The body fragments found in the wreck made the identification certain—as they should have done, having been cloned and force-grown expressly for the purpose.

Raehan's great loss was duly remarked upon, suitable obsequies were uttered . . . and the world went back to awaiting its end.

                    *   *   *

In the outer reaches of the system, beyond the orbit of the outermost gas giant, where Tareil itself was little more than a yellow zero-magnitude star, a heavily stealthed ship rendezvoused with a small fleet of like vessels. In a little while, the ships began accelerating still further outward. Each of them, upon reaching a certain location in the void, suddenly surrounded itself with a momentary, space-distorting pulse of artificial gravitation . . . and vanished.

Presently, only two ships were left. They remained, with only the occasional absentminded flare of thrust needed to keep them on station near the region of nothingness that had swallowed their fellows, and monitored the reports of the robotic proxies that kept watch on the distant inner system of Tareil.

                    *   *   *

Again it was night. *And I had so looked forward to seeing once again a living world's daylight,* Varien thought, pulling his cloak tightly around his old body against the chill. But this was the night of a different world. And it was a different sort of night, here on the third planet of Lirauva's primary stellar component. The planet's sun—a yellow-white star somewhat more massive and luminous than Tareil—had set, but the secondary star of this binary system was in the sky, currently almost halfway out on its long elliptical orbit but still a bright orange flare that illuminated the coastal plain below the bluffs on which this base was built and dimmed all but the brightest stars in the sky—such as Landaen, at which he now gazed.

Not really a very luminous star, he knew—slightly less so than this planet's primary, in fact. But it was so close that light could travel the distance in just under six of Raehan's years. And it was the goal that had brought him here tonight, and that previously had lent urgency to his quest for a means of outpacing light where no displacement points existed. For his earliest outpost here at Lirauva, scanning the nearby stars, had detected the extravagant outpouring of patterned radio waves that could only represent the signature of a fairly advanced civilization, so tantalizingly just beyond this final terminus of the Lirauva Chain.

A patch of blackness flanked by running lights suddenly occluded a few stars, growing rapidly as Aelanni's drop shuttle fell groundward until it reached a sufficiently low altitude for its atmospheric drive to take hold. It then swooped around in a landing pattern that avoided areas of the base where electronic equipment might have been disrupted by the annoying side effects of grav repulsion. *Must do something about that*, Varien entered in his mental filing system as the shuttle settled onto the landing platform, its hatch wheezed open, and, for the first time in over two years, he saw his daughter.

Varien, and Varien alone, had never really seen her beauty. Features that were merely sharp in himself and Tarlann were, in Aelanni, chiseled by a sculptor of genius. Such a sculptor would have been inspired by the body her form-fitting light duty vac suit revealed, moving with unself-conscious grace as she descended the shuttle's ramp in a gravity eight percent less than Raehan's. Her long, thick dark hair held a fascinating reddish glint now brought out by Lirauva's secondary sun; it harmonized with reddish-brown skin, made even more coppery by long exposure to this planet's wind and sun. Her great deep-brown eyes also had a faintly reddish, almost mahogany tone . . . and Varien did, at times, see those eyes, for they were the eyes of his long-dead wife. But mostly he saw a mind as whetted as his son's, and an adventurousness that Tarlann would never possess.

They embraced with the restraint enjoined by their culture, which taught that to display personal passion was to crack open, ever so slightly, a door behind which roared the flames of total war. Still, it was more than the small, formal bows Varien's parents would have exchanged.

"Sorry I was at the orbital station when you arrived," she greeted him. "Miralann is sure he's onto a fundamental breakthrough in . . . well that doesn't matter now, does it?" She withdrew a step and looked him over. He had aged. "How bad is it?"

"Worse than you think . . . however bad that may be. When the last courier was sent here, we thought Raehan couldn't hold. Now we're certain of it."

"So." She gazed somberly around her at the base, and the world, that had been her home for two years. For a moment, it was so quiet that the faint, hissing roar of the distant surf was audible. She then looked upward at the tiny point of yellow-white light. "Then we must all go to Landaen?"

"Oh, not everyone. This base can remain in operation with a skeleton staff—I'll leave the choice of who remains up to you. But if our observers at Tareil ever come here with the news that the Korvaasha have discovered Tareil's fourth displacement point and the

Lirauva Chain, it will be necessary to *immediately* obliterate every indication that we ever knew of it. We destroyed all the robot stations in the intervening systems on our way here." (*So much still to learn in those systems!* Aelanni looked as sad as Varien felt.) "And we've brought a fusion device which can be triggered with a minimum of fuss, and is powerful enough to wipe out every trace of this base.

"But," he continued more cheerfully, "for now we'll keep the base operating. I'll need you at Landaen, of course, and certain others . . . notably Miralann."

Aelanni smiled impishly. "For his professional expertise, Father? Or could it be that you also expect his hobby to be useful?" Varien smiled back. The brilliant linguist had made the initial breakthrough that had enabled them to crack the primary Landaeniv language sooner than anyone had expected. But they both knew that Miralann's hobby was the truly eccentric one of military history.

"Well, possibly," Varien allowed. "But I can certainly appreciate his professional achievement. Throughout the voyage here, I've been force-feeding myself that awful language. Of course, sleep-teaching devices are no substitute for actual practice. . . ."

And, Aelanni knew, they exacted a price. She looked again at Varien's haggard face. "Father! At your age . . . !"

"There's no alternative," Varien said harshly. "I must be able to communicate with them. So must we all . . . although the rest of you can take it at a saner pace. And there is no time to be lost. As soon as your ships can be ready, we must depart for Landaen."

Aelanni's gaze drifted upward to the bright yellow-white star again. She had been there, almost a year before. "Yes, Landaen," she said somberly. "It's seemed to dominate our destinies, hasn't it? I remember when you were almost ready to make it, and the entire Lirauva Chain, public knowledge. But then we found out about the Landeniv, and we all agreed that the secret would have to be kept a little longer. There was no predicting how people would react to the news that we had discovered the one, single thing that we had *known* we would *never* discover: another race of *humans!*"

Silence descended again. Trust Aelanni to say it openly and unflinchingly, Varien thought. She was right, of course. The social consequences of blurting out upon the datanets the great contradiction their earliest probing of Landaen had revealed—the starkly impossible which was also starkly factual—were unpredictable. Varien and the group of brilliant people he had gathered around him might think of themselves as fearless iconoclasts; but they were, inescapably, Raehaniv. Uncontrollable, unmanageable change was, simply, bad. So it had been for centuries.

Varien also looked up at the yellow-white star, and the skin at the nape of his neck prickled.

"Well." He spoke a little more loudly than necessary, straightening his cloak. "Whatever my reasons—and I seem to recall hearing the term 'childish secretiveness' from you at the beginning—it is fortunate that I kept the knowledge to myself. For it is now the one advantage we have over the Korvaasha. We must make what use of it we can—for we, here, are now acting for our entire race. As quickly as possible, we must depart Lirauva . . . but no." He smiled, seeking to lighten the mood. "I must practice my Landaeniv, and broaden my vocabulary. What do the Landaeniv call Lirauva? They must have a name for this system—it's one of the brighter stars in their night skies."

"Oh, yes. Let's see . . ." She frowned as she struggled with the impossibly strange syllables. "*Alpha Centauri*, I believe they call it."

Varien nodded, and practiced the words as the two of them walked toward the waiting ground car.

CHAPTER TWO

"Colonel, we've got something very odd on the scope."

Lieutenant Colonel Eric DiFalco, United States Space Force, hesitated a moment—Lieutenant Farrell, the duty officer, could be overconscientious at best and excitable at worst—then sighed and thumbed the intercom switch.

"I'm listening, Lieutenant." He wasn't sure he had gotten just the right warning note into his voice. The news from home wasn't exactly something he resented being torn away from. Even Farrell's latest attack of the jitters would be a welcome relief from a detailed analysis of just how the lunatics were going about taking over the asylum.

"Well, sir, it appears to be a spacecraft of unknown origin. Its performance parameters don't check with anything we know about. And . . . it's on a course that should intersect ours in . . ."

DiFalco came out of shock. *Please, God, don't let Farrell be seeing a UFO! And don't let him have already logged it!* He concentrated on making his voice soothing.

"All right, Terry. You were correct to report this. I'll be right up. Keep tracking it." He turned off his digital reader—plenty of time later for a masochistic reading of the Social Justice party's latest gains in the off-year elections—and stood up. It took only two long-legged strides to exit his tiny cabin and step out into the passageway that ran around the outer circumference of USSFS *Andrew Jackson*'s spin habitat. People stood aside for him—about as far as military punctilio was carried in a spacecraft under way—as he proceeded to the hatch. He reached up, grabbed the rail, and pulled himself up and over into the weightless central access shaft, compensating with practiced ease for the Coriolis force. With an occasional assist from the railings, he shot forward past the shuttle docks to the control room.

The contrast between the dim chamber with its glowing instrument panels and the starry firmament beyond the wide-curving viewport seldom failed to affect him. But now he made a preoccupied beeline for the command acceleration couch. Motioning to Farrell to remain seated, he settled to the deck, magnetized soles clamping gently to its surface.

"All right, Terry. What's the status?"

"Unchanged, sir. It's on a ballistic course—a very flat hyperbola, almost a straight line. The computer has projected it backwards, and it seems to have come from a region of the asteroids where we've never had anything." He gestured at a screen showing the simulation of the unknown's orbit, and DiFalco sucked in his breath. That ship had come a long way . . . but then he glanced at its velocity figures, and realized that it could have covered the distance in a reasonable length of time after all. "And as for where they're going . . . well, Colonel, the only explanation that makes sense is that they want to intercept us." Farrell's voice was steady. *At least he has the balls to lay his opinion on the line*, DiFalco admitted to himself.

"No possibility that it's Chinese, I suppose," he asked. It wasn't much of a hope, anyway; they had no reason to be in this particular segment of space outside the orbit of Mars.

"Negative, sir. That was the first thing we checked. Nothing of theirs has been in a position to have gotten into that orbit, even if they had anything that could manage that many sustained gees." He glanced at the time. "By the way, Colonel, enough time has elapsed from our initial hail for us to have received a reply from that ship, if they'd sent one."

DiFalco glared at the offending blip. A UFO. Just fucking beautiful.

The term had originated in the second half of the twentieth century, when many people had looked skyward in search of a substitute for religion and persuaded themselves that they had seen alien spacecraft performing impossible feats in pursuit of no intelligible objective. It had died out in the early decades of the present century, as space flight had settled into routine and the we-are-alone arguments of Tipler and others had fossilized into dogma—the scientific establishment had come to reject the possibility of extraterrestrial intelligence with such unanimity that the concept hardly even appeared in science fiction any more.

But over the last few years, curious reports had begun to appear. They never seemed to have any unambiguous instrument corroboration, and DiFalco had always been inclined to write them off as a product of the general lunacy of the times. (The California school system had recently required that astronomy texts give equal space and respect to the flat-Earth theory, for to do otherwise would be "elitist"; the Social Justice party was expected to write a similar requirement into its national platform.) Only . . . *these* reports had come, not from the Great American Majority of functionally illiterate drones, but from space crews, all of whom were very competent people—the only kind that anyone could afford to send into space, which was why the new civilization growing up outside Earth's atmosphere had less and less in common with the collapsing society at the bottom of the gravity well. And *these* UFOs, although decidedly high-performance, hadn't reversed direction without loss of velocity or otherwise violated physical laws.

Still, such reports were not noted for furthering the careers of those who made them.

Just had to take command of the last of the Washington *class ships in Mars orbit for the evacuation to Phoenix Prime, didn't you?* DiFalco gibed at himself. *Couldn't make the trip in cryo hibernation, could you? Couldn't even travel awake on a ship commanded by one of your juniors and spend the trip dumping words of wisdom on the younger generations!* (He was all of thirty-five.) *Oh, no! Perish the thought!*

He reached a decision. "All right, Terry. Have Gomez do an EVA with her photo equipment. The UFO"—there, he had said it—"is within ten million klicks, and she might be able to get something we can analyze. And laser a message to RAMP HQ at Phoenix Prime, in Level Three code, for General Kurganov personally." Sergei had ridden the *Boris Yeltsin* out to the asteroid base earlier, hibernating like a gentleman and leaving DiFalco as acting military CO of the Russian-American Mars Project. But now he was awake and back in command, at least until DiFalco relieved him early next year when the top spot rotated back to an American. He needed to be told . . . and he would have the sense to sit on the information until they had learned more.

"Give him," DiFalco continued, "all the data we now have on the UFO. And tell him that I intend to continue to try to communicate with it. If it attempts a rendezvous with us"—no need to even check the figures to confirm that it was strictly up to the UFO to do so; *Andy J.* was committed to this Hohmann transfer orbit and lacked the reaction mass for any funny business, at least if it wanted to be able to choose an attainable destination afterwards—"I will do whatever seems indicated." And, he knew, Sergei would back him to the hilt. He unclipped his perscomp from his belt and consulted it. "It will take a few minutes to get a reply. Ask Major Levinson to join me in my cabin as soon as he can get away from Engineering. And buzz me as soon as you get any response from the UFO, or from General Kurganov . . . or when Gomez has some usable imagery for us."

"Aye aye, sir." (Funny, the way naval usages were surfacing in a service descended from the Air Force. The ex-squids in the Space Force had to be threatened with bodily harm lest they call the control room the "bridge.") Farrell looked up, and for an instant he seemed even younger than he was. When he spoke, his tone was almost beseeching. "Colonel, what is that thing?"

"I think we're going to find out, Lieutenant. Like it or not."

*   *   *

DiFalco's cabin was too small for pacing, and he soon found himself turning the news update back on. It was a link with familiar things, with home . . . and he needed that, however much he hated what home was turning into. He was up to the latest synagogue burning in New York (the state's Social Justice governor hadn't quite winked at the cameras as he had condemned the act "despite centuries of terrible provocation") when Jeff Levinson arrived. He switched it off hurriedly.

"Oh, that," *Andy J.*'s executive officer indicated the reader. He smiled wryly at DiFalco's palpable embarrassment, creasing his dark features—his mouth, like his nose, belonged on a larger face. "Why do you think there are so many of us in space? Out here, you can get away from some things. Not all, of course." He took out the plastic Ethnic Entitlements Card that every American citizen was required to carry at all times—white, with a large yellow Star of David, in Levinson's case. DiFalco's was brown; his mother was one-quarter Cherokee, which, despite all her Swedish, Scots and English genes, and the Italian, Irish and additional English ones on his father's side, made him a "Third World person" and helped account for his rank. (Levinson had risen as high as he probably ever would, especially if the quota structure was further stacked against him as seemed likely after the next general election.) DiFalco was old enough to recall when the cards had been introduced . . . strictly as a temporary measure, of course, to "enable the proper authorities to readily identify the victims of past discrimination until its effects have been compensated for." Ex-officials of the former South African government had been hired for their experience in administering a similar system; those who had commented on the irony had been prosecuted for the misdemeanor of "inappropriately directed laughter."

"But," Levinson continued, "you didn't call me in to discuss the political situation. What's up, that couldn't wait 'til after Fraser and I were done with the fuel feed?"

"Well," DiFalco drawled, "how about little green men? Terry seems to have spotted some, doing their damnedest to intercept us."

"*Oy vey!*" Levinson sagged down onto DiFalco's bunk. "What does the kid think he's seen now?"

"It's no bullshit, Jeff," DiFalco assured him, turning serious. He accessed the data on his perscomp and handed it to Levinson. The XO studied it with frowning concentration, then looked up.

"Eric, just what the hell is going on here? *Nobody* has anything like this, and extraterrestrials . . ."

" . . . don't exist," DiFalco finished for him. "Everybody knows that. I'll tell you what I told Terry: we'll find out the answer soon enough, so all we can do now is assess our own capabilities—which, I know, don't include either attempting or avoiding a rendezvous. Our weapons"—the missiles, the antimissile lasers, and the big spinal-mounted particle accelerator—"are in working order." Levinson nodded emphatically. "But I don't intend to use them except in self-defense. For now, we'll continue to try and communicate with them. We simply don't know what we're dealing with here. . . ."

The intercom beeped, and DiFalco acknowledged. "Colonel, Gomez is ready for you," Farrell reported.

"Good. Tell her the XO and I will be in the lab ASAP."

* * *

Afterwards, neither DiFalco nor Levinson was ever sure how long a period of utter silence they had spent staring at the blowup. No fine details could be made out, of course, even with deep-space photography using mid-twenty-first-century equipment. But two things were very clear about the spacecraft. The first was that it *was* a spacecraft, an inarguably artificial construct. And the second was that it was a product of no known design philosophy, nor even any known concept of a viable spacecraft; there was no room for doubt that it had originated elsewhere than Earth.

Finally, Levinson looked up, his engagingly ugly face wearing a lost expression DiFalco had never seen there.

"Colonel, what are we going to do?"

"We are going to wait," DiFalco stated firmly.

* * *

The Unknown lay a few kilometers off, a clearly visible affront to DiFalco's sense of reality.

It had matched vectors with *Andy J.* so smoothly that DiFalco was somehow sure that it wasn't showing off, merely executing a routine maneuver. It certainly had the thrust to do it . . . he had tried to calculate the power required for that kind of sustained maneuvering by a ship massing what that one must, and given up. And it produced all that thrust with no great display of flaming exhaust; its drive was evidently too efficient to waste much energy on such things.

"Well," Levinson broke the silence in the control room, "we know one thing about them."

"You mean besides the fact that they're very god-damned advanced?" DiFalco, like the XO, spoke in a hushed voice, for no reason that stood up to logical analysis.

Levinson nodded. "They don't need weight."

DiFalco nodded in reply. He had already thought of it himself. That gleaming bluish-gray shape—rather like a cigar with the small end forward, with four elongated blisters spaced evenly around the hull near the stern, alternating with what was obviously tankage—was a seamless unity without any segment which could plausibly be a spin habitat like *Andy J.'s*. If its occupants had wanted to use angular acceleration to counterfeit gravity while in free fall, they would have to spin the entire ship, which was patently impractical. Humans were unsuited to prolonged periods of weightlessness. Drugs coupled with regular exercise now enabled them to live indefinitely in low-G environments like Luna, but some weight was still required to prevent fluid imbalances and atrophy of the bone tissues and muscles, and all interplanetary spacecraft designs reflected this. It was the final piece of evidence that the UFO's crew were not human. Were they even organic?

One thing they definitely were: damned uncommunicative. He had stopped paying attention to Farrell's endlessly repeated hails and requests for acknowledgment up and down the frequencies—they had become a meaningless ritual of some forgotten religion.

So, like everyone else in the control room, he jumped when the hush was shattered by a screech of static, dying down to a faint roar overlaid by a voice speaking in careful, faintly accented English.

"Calling United States Space Force Ship *Andrew Jackson*. We urgently request that your commanding officer come aboard our ship for consultation on matters of the highest importance."

In the stunned silence, DiFalco was the first to find his tongue.

"This is Lieutenant Colonel Eric DiFalco, commanding," he rapped out, pleasantly surprised that his voice didn't crack. "Who am I addressing? Can we have a visual signal?"

"I am afraid not," the voice resumed. "All your questions will be answered here. You will, of course, find our shipboard environment quite safe. Please enter through the airlock we have illuminated." Levinson touched his arm and pointed at the magnified image of the UFO. A blinking exterior light had awakened on that unbroken surface. He was gazing at it when Farrell looked up.

"The signal has been broken off, Colonel. They're not accepting any further transmission."

"Damn!" DiFalco turned to the XO. "Jeff, could that voice have been artificially generated?"

"In theory, yes," Levinson replied judiciously. All state-of-the-art computers could accept vocal input, and the more sophisticated ones could provide simple "spoken" output. But you knew damned well it was a machine talking, and there was no question of carrying on a conversation. Chatty computers still belonged to the realm of science fiction. For that matter, so did UFOs.

DiFalco gazed a moment longer at the image in the screen, with its somehow impudent winking light. Then he unstrapped and shoved himself up from the acceleration couch.

"XO, have GP shuttle number two readied. And have Sergeant Thompson meet me at the docking bay."

"Holy shit, Eric!" This was pushing the limits of informality even for the Space Force, but Levinson

looked like he was past caring. "You're not actually
going over there, are you? I mean, we don't
know . . ." He sputtered into speechlessness.

"That's right," DiFalco said quietly. "We don't
know *anything*. And we're not going to find out, sitting here staring at them and hoping they'll resume
radio communications. And I want very badly to find
out, Jeff. Call it curiosity or anything else you like,
but there's no way I could *not* accept this invitation.
Anyway," he continued with a slight smile, "if they
wanted to zap us, I have this strange feeling that
we'd all be dead by now." He moved toward the
hatch. "You have the con, XO."

Levinson made one last try. "Colonel, we only
have the word of some robot or some bug-eyed
monster that it's safe in that ship! How can they
even know what's safe for us?"

DiFalco turned toward him with an odd expression. "You know, Jeff, that's one of the things that
makes me so curious about all of this. Remember
when he told us that?" Levinson nodded. "Well . . .
why should the suitability of their environment for us
be an 'of course'?"

*   *   *

Andy J. was still visible as an elongated dumbbell
(DiFalco had vetoed Levinson's suggestion that the
ship be realigned so as to aim the particle accelerator at the alien) when the lighted airlock became
visible as a faint outline on that curving wall of
unidentifiable alloy.

Piloting the little interorbital shuttle toward it,
DiFalco stole a glance at his companion's black face,
frowning with concentration as he checked out, not
for the first time, his recoilless launch pistol. Not
that the little rocket gun would be likely to do much
good, even if the colonel let him use it. Since he
had no real intention of doing so, he wondered why
he had even brought the sergeant. Purely as a ceremonial bodyguard, he supposed—the Marines

performed shipboard duties for the Space Force similar to those they always had for the Navy, although their EVA role was a new wrinkle for them. Anyway, having him along made DiFalco feel better.

Gunnery Sergeant Joel Thompson, USMC, was not a particularly huge man. In fact, he was only slightly bigger than the six feet and one hundred eighty pounds maintained by DiFalco, who worked at keeping in shape—largely, as he admitted to himself, because he was reaching the age at which a flat stomach was an emblem of self-discipline. But vanity had nothing to do with the sergeant's unrelieved musculature, without an ounce of efficiency-impairing fat. He was not an easy man to know, but he was as formidable and dependable as he looked. And his stubbornness was a force of nature.

A faint boom sounded through the shuttle as it made airlock-to-airlock contact with the UFO's hull and instruments confirmed magnetic seal attachment. For a moment, the two of them sat in silence as if awaiting something, then exchanged quick, sheepish smiles and proceeded to don their vac suit helmets. DiFalco's mounted a videocam whose continuous transmission to *Andy J.* would, he guessed, be of some interest to Levinson and everyone else who could contrive an excuse for being near a screen. Like their helmet communicators, it would be relayed by the shuttle's more powerful comm equipment; they shouldn't be out of contact with the big ship, barring intentional jamming by the . . . aliens, he supposed he had to call them. Concentrating grimly on the the concrete and the routine, he led the way to the airlock.

Decompression completed, their outer door slid open to reveal, as he had more than half expected, the UFO's airlock similarly open to vacuum. They floated from one chamber into the other, and the strange door sealed behind them. There. That was it. *Shouldn't I have said something historical before stepping across?*

"Can you hear me, XO? Are you getting this?"

"Barely." Levinson's voice came faintly. "The transmission sucks. Swing a little to your left, will you . . . there! I wanted to get those instructions, or whatever they are, on the wall . . . shit!" The light that awakened just above the odd, cursive lettering startled DiFalco almost as much as it did Levinson, whose picture it momentarily overloaded like a flash bulb.

Immediately, DiFalco began to feel the return of outside air pressure.

Sergeant Thompson studied a readout on the bulky equipment he was carrying. "Skipper"—it was one of the things DiFalco had stopped trying to break him of—"pressure is almost up to one bar. And the initial reading shows nitrogen and oxygen in the right percentages."

"Did you copy that, XO?" Levinson confirmed, and Difalco continued. "All right. I am going to open my faceplate." Ignoring Thompson's disapproving frown, he did so, holding his breath. The air was a little warmer than *Andy J.*'s. He was preparing to take an experimental breath when the light went out and the inner door slid open. Lightheaded as he was, nothing else seemed to register. He expelled his breath and pushed himself across the threshold into the passageway beyond. . . .

The universe fell on him, slamming him to the deck.

Lying there, he heard Levinson's shouts and Thompson's bellows as if from a great distance, for reality had, for him, suddenly narrowed to two impossible facts. One was that he had just floated directly from free fall into a gravity field that had absolutely no business being there. (How strong was it? Two gees, surely. No, make it three.)

The other was the pair of feet, in utilitarian-looking boots of some unfamiliar material, planted on the deck a few inches from his face. His eyes travelled up the legs and body, the videocam travelling with them . . . and Levinson's frantic voice trailed off. DiFalco got slowly to his feet (maybe the gravity was only around one gee after all), groping for something to say.

He finally managed it. "You . . . look human." So much for history.

The elderly gentleman—he reminded DiFalco of one of his maternal uncles—looked miffed. "Thank you," he said dryly. "So do you."

One of the group behind him, a striking-looking young woman clad like all of them in a kind of jumpsuit, stepped forward and spoke rapidly to the oldster in an utterly unfamiliar language of many liquid vowel combinations and few hard consonants. DiFalco knew a scolding when he heard one. The man smiled in acknowledgment and turned back to his guest.

"Forgive me," he said with his faint accent. "I should have warned you about the internal artificial gravity field. One takes things for granted. Oh, by the way, ah, Colonel—is that it?—could you possibly speak to your subordinate?" He gestured rather fastidiously toward the airlock. DiFalco turned and saw that Sergeant Thompson had also entered the passageway but had managed to land in a crouch, from which he now had the scene covered with his launch pistol. His hand and his expression were both rock-steady, but beads of sweat were visible on his brow behind his faceplate.

"Sergeant," DiFalco spoke carefully, "stand up and lower your gun. I think we're among friends. And you might as well open your faceplate—I seem to be doing okay, under the circumstances."

"Aye aye, sir." Thompson grimly obeyed. He still looked very watchful.

DiFalco turned back to the man who had no more right to be here than the gravity that kept them both standing on the deck. He didn't really look much like Uncle Dick, or any other member of any of Earth's racial groupings, although he could probably have walked down a street in any large Western city and attracted no more than occasional glances of mild curiosity as to his origin. He was tall and spare, his hair and thinnish VanDyke-like chin beard of a silvery gray that contrasted with his skin, which was a rather coppery brown. His cheekbones were wide, his nose prominent and straight, and his eyes a brown so dark as to be virtually black. The people behind him showed about as much individual variation in size, features and coloring as you would expect in a group made up of members of one moderately heterogeneous nationality on Earth. The common denominators seemed to be a tendency toward height and slenderness, and a coppery quality to the skin tone.

"I trust I was telling the sergeant the truth," DiFalco said. "About being among friends, that is."

"Of course, Colonel. And I apologize for our seeming secretiveness. Let me begin to try to answer some of the questions I know you must have. My name is Varien hle'Morna. My companions and I come, as you have undoubtedly surmised, from another planetary system. And you may rest assured, the fact that you belong to the same species as ourselves is as inexplicable to us as it is to you. We have merely had a little longer to become accustomed to it. We—"

"Excuse me," Di Falco cut in, about to OD on unreality, "while I communicate with my ship." Varien made a gesture which presumably signified gracious assent. "XO, are you getting all this?"

"Affirmative." Levinson's faint voice came after a slight pause. "I've been keeping quiet because I didn't want to distract you—and because I'm in a state of shock like everybody here."

"You and me both," DiFalco muttered. "I'm just coping from second to second. Stand by." He raised his voice. "Uh, Mister . . ."

"Simply 'Varien' is sufficient, Colonel," the stranger said indulgently.

"All right, uh, Varien." DiFalco plowed grimly ahead. "You obviously know a lot more about us—our language, for starters—than the zero we know about you. Your radio message was less than informative. . . ."

"Again, I apologize for that, Colonel. That message was sent using specially constructed equipment which was not up to visual transmissions—our own communications devices are incompatible with yours. And, candidly, we were also motivated by security considerations; we wished to minimize signalling that might possibly be picked up at random." He paused thoughtfully. "I know this is all very overwhelming for you, Colonel," he continued in a slightly patronizing way. (Was it DiFalco's imagination or did the young woman roll her eyes heavenward?) "But I am going to have to decline to answer many of your questions at present, in order to avoid repeating myself later, when we reach the asteroid I believe you call 'Phoenix Prime,' your present destination. You see, I have approached you to solicit your aid in arranging a secret meeting with whoever is in ultimate authority there."

"So," DiFalco said faintly, "you want me to . . . take you to our leader?"

Varien brightened. "Yes. That's it. Well put. If you wish, I will gladly accompany you back to your ship, as a gesture of good faith." *Does he think we primitives are into giving and taking hostages?* DiFalco wondered. Varien motioned the young woman forward. "Or, if you prefer, I will send my daughter, Aelanni zho'Morna, who has full authority to make all arrangements."

DiFalco heard a low moan from his helmet comm. "What is it, XO?" Varien and the others politely did not listen.

"It had to happen," Levinson groaned. "Why am I even surprised?"

"What are you talking about, Jeff?"

"The mad scientist has a beautiful daughter!"

CHAPTER THREE

The potato-shaped asteroid known as Phoenix Prime turned slowly on its long axis. Its interior, hollowed out by lavish use of clean, laser-detonated fusion devices, was little more prepossessing than its rugged surface—none of the parklike spaciousness visualized for asteroid habitats by space-colonization advocates of the last century. It merely provided the basics of habitability for those who labored, in shifts, to prepare the large ice asteroid called Phoenix for the journey that was its destiny.

DiFalco had often reflected that Phoenix was misnamed. The Phoenix of myth had arisen from the ashes. Its namesake would descend to the surface of Mars at interplanetary velocity and impact with the force of a billion average fusion bombs, blasting the planet's original atmosphere into space and triggering the seismic and volcanic cataclysms that would give it a new, dense one. In less than a generation, after the molten surface cooled, oceans would form and microorganisms would be introduced by the humans who would again be able to set foot on the surface. After another generation, a major human presence, and some oxygen-producing plants, would have taken hold and terraforming would enter a new stage. Less than a century after the initial impact, atmospheric oxygen should suffice for the formation of an ozone layer and large-scale soil fertilization would be underway. After another half-century, oxygen pressure would have reached Earth-like levels and simple genetically engineered animals would be released.

So, he reflected, maybe the name wasn't so inappropriate after all. A new, living world would arise from the wreck of the old, lifeless one. It was incomparably the greatest engineering project in human history, conceived in the heady decades after the turn of the century when Communism had fallen and free enterprise seemed to have taken a new lease on life in the young republics of Eurasia and on the high frontier of space.

It was the era into which DiFalco had been born—the full high tide of the Third Industrial Revolution—and he had often wondered, with an uncomprehending inner hurt, what had gone wrong with it.

*   *   *

With a beard and the right clothes, Brigadier General Sergei Konstantinovich Kurganov would have looked like an Eastern Orthodox saint. He was a Russian of the tall, slender sort, with a long, triangular face and a broad brow from which the gray-brown hair was beginning to recede. His English was only slightly accented—indeed, he spoke it better than most victims of American public education. And it was a source of constant embarrassment that he knew far more of the history of DiFalco's own nation than the American himself.

He came aboard *Andy J.* with full military formality, after which they proceeded to DiFalco's cabin and cracked a bottle from the latter's private stock of Scotch. (The general had once admitted, in strictest confidence, that he had never liked vodka.)

"Well, Eric," Kurganov began, "what is it you have brought me?"

"I can hardly wait to find out," DiFalco replied feelingly. "Believe it or not, what I sent you before our arrival represented all I know. This Varien—he's the only one of them I've actually spoken to except his daughter, and her English isn't as good as his—is playing it very close to his chest. He came over to this ship for part of the trip, and was insufferable about how delightfully quaint it all is, but told me essentially nothing." He shook his head slowly. "I'll never forget the first time he and I left his ship to transfer to our shuttle; he just stepped into the airlock wearing the skintight one-piece outfit they all wear shipboard. I was sure he was mad as a hatter. Then he proceeded to put on gloves and pull this clear plastic hood over his head from a flap behind the neck . . . and opened the airlock! The hood puffed out into a fishbowl helmet, but otherwise the suit still looked like a body stocking. He must have seen the look on my face; he condescendingly explained that they have heavy-duty vac suits for long-term or hazardous-labor EVA, but that this thing suffices for brief jaunts." He shook his head again and took a pull on his Scotch.

"But now," Kurganov prompted after a moment, "he wants to meet with both of us aboard his ship?"

"Right. It's parked in easy shuttle range, behind an asteroid—God knows why. Their stealth technology . . . well, the only reason we detected that ship was because they wanted us to. They can't defeat the Mark One Eyeball, but you know how much use that is in deep space."

"Indeed." It was Kurganov's turn to muse and sip. "Clearly, Varien is being very circumspect about approaching our governments. Thank God for that. It makes me wonder if he may have some inkling of what is happening on Earth." He turned grim, and set his glass down. "I must tell you, Eric, that we just received word that the Social Justice Party in America has held a special mid-term conclave in the wake of the recent Congressional election, and announced its intention of terminating the Project as the first stage in eliminating all private-sector activity in space . . . and, eventually, all activity of any kind. The resources are, it seems, to be turned to 'socially useful' ends."

DiFalco was momentarily without the power of speech. *So this is what it's like to go into shock*, he thought with an odd calmness.

"'Socially useful'?!" he finally exploded. "Jesus H. Christ! What do they call the powersats that provide eighty percent of Earth's energy without polluting anything? What's going to replace them? And do they plan to go back to strip-mining Earth for the minerals we're now getting from the asteroids?"

"I doubt if the irrationality of their proposal will prevent the victory that the media has decreed for them in the presidential election year after next," Kurganov said dryly. "Any more than will their declaration that the election after that may have to be postponed, and the Constitution suspended, 'until the political process has been cleansed of capitalist and Zionist influence.' There was a time when that statement would have made them unelectable in America. Not now, of course. And Russia will, as always, follow along."

For a long moment, DiFalco sat stunned. When he spoke, his voice held a plaintive tone that no one but Kurganov was ever permitted to hear.

"Sergei, what the hell happened? How did we screw up? It wasn't supposed to be like this, you know. When you people kicked out the Communist regime two generations ago, everybody thought the Totalitarian Era was over!"

"Oh, yes; the collapse of the old Soviet Union *should* have permanently discredited coercive utopianism. But its Western followers and apologists—who, like the Bourbons, had learned nothing and forgotten nothing—retained their strongholds in academe and the media. And their opponents, for reasons I have

never been able to understand, continued to be morally
intimidated by them. So now they have, against all
expectation, staged a comeback . . . hastened by their
masterstroke of adding anti-Semitism to their
repertoire." His blue eyes, usually mild, took on a hard
glint, and his faint accent roughened. "The perfect
selling point in my country, of course. I fear the
Russian peasant is eternal in his follies." He sighed
with infinite sadness, and took another sip of Scotch.
"We wanted freedom so badly—my grandfather led his
tank regiment to the defense of the Parliament
building during the coup attempt of 1991, when we
thought we had finally won it. And now we're willing
to throw it all away the instant someone screams
'Death to the Jews!' "

"So," DiFalco asked bitterly, "all we're doing out
here is pointless? We're readying a new world for
mankind just when mankind begins to stampede back
into the Dark Ages?"

"Oh, not altogether pointless, Eric Vincentovich."
He smiled gently, and DiFalco snorted; it was a
long-accustomed form of needling, and they both
followed the well-worn grooves of habit. "Eventually—in generations or centuries—the Gods of the
Copybook Headings will come crawling out from under the rubble and try to explain it all again."
(Strange, the way Kipling was best remembered in
Russia; most people there thought he had *been* a
Russian.) "And if we and our successors are allowed
to carry the terraforming process to the point where
it becomes irreversible, then a living Mars will be
ready when humanity—including recognizable Russians, I like to hope—is ready to come into its
inheritance."

"But how can we? We've had to become
self-sufficient in some things out here, but we're still
dependent on Earth for a lot of what we need to
complete the project. If they really want to do a
Proxmire on us, they can."

"Who knows?" Kurganov shrugged eloquently. "The civilian management council has asked for an emergency meeting with the two of us to decide what our response should be. Of course, they don't know yet that a rather large new factor has just been added to further complicate matters!" He finished his Scotch, set his glass down with a click, and stood up. "Shall we go, Eric? I'm looking forward to meeting your rather surprising extraterrestrial!"

*   *   *

Hand-shaking was not a custom of Varien's people, but he bowed gracefully when Difalco introduced his commander.

"Welcome aboard my ship, General Sergei."

"Actually," the Russian smiled, "the conventional usage is 'General Kurganov.'"

"Yes, of course." Varien shook his head in annoyance, whether at his own forgetfulness or at the peculiarities of Earthly forms of address was unclear. "So, General Kurganov, Colonel Eri . . . DiFalco informs me that you are the senior government official here in this system's asteroid belt."

"I am," Kurganov explained, "the senior military officer in charge of the Russian-American Mars Project, a joint effort by my government and Colonel DiFalco's to terraform . . . ah, to render habitable our system's fourth planet. Much of the actual work is being carried out by a consortium of private corporations and research institutions, but no civilian governmental structure has ever been set up in the asteroids; Phoenix Prime, our base, is still legally a military installation. So you are correct; I represent the ultimate government authority short of my superiors on our home world—which you must know is the third planet, inasmuch as you know so much else. In particular, you have me at a disadvantage with your knowledge of the English language." He smiled again. "It is, I suppose, too much to hope that you also know Russian."

"I am afraid, General, that puzzling out even one of your languages from a study of your broadcasts was the limit of our capabilities. Let me introduce Miralann hle'Shahya, who was largely responsible for that achievement—and who I am sure would be fascinated to be introduced to 'Russian.'" The man who bowed in response was younger than Varien, a little shorter and plumper, and he did, indeed, look intrigued. DiFalco couldn't avoid the impression that what intrigued him were the service dress uniforms they had donned for the occasion—his own USSF black and Sergei's dark bottle-green, both with the red-and-gold RAMP shoulder patch.

"And my daughter, Aelanni zho'Morna, who is already known to Colonel DiFalco," Varien continued. Kurganov did a small bow of his own, complete with a soft heel-click, and she smiled tentatively. *Alright, Sergei, enough with the Old World charm*, DiFalco found himself thinking.

"And now," Varien said impatiently, "if you gentlemen will be seated, I will finally satisfy your curiosity." He indicated a semicircle of chairs around a slightly raised platform on one side of the spacious chamber. (At least it *seemed* outrageously spacious to DiFalco, considering that they were aboard a space vessel.)

"I will be most interested," Kurganov said as he took a seat. He had the look of a man trying to delicately impart a painful and embarrassing piece of news. "You see, Varien, I must tell you that from our standpoint you are, ah . . . impossible."

"So I have been told." Loftily: "I have chosen not to take it personally."

DiFalco squirmed uncomfortably in the chair that insisted on trying to conform itself to the contours of his butt. "Look, Varien, it goes beyond the fact that you people are human, which you've admitted is a stumper—one of our science fiction writers once compared the chances of the same species evolving on two planets to the chances of one locksmith making a lock while another locksmith working independently on another planet makes a key that fits it, and I imagine he was understating the improbability by several orders of magnitude. But aside from that, our scientists have decided that we're the only technological civilization—and probably the only tool-makers—in the history of the galaxy."

"Whatever led them to this extraordinary conclusion?" Varien was frankly curious.

"Well . . . for one thing, we've never been visited by anybody else."

"But you have. Now. By me." Varien spread his hands in a gesture of bogus self-deprecation. "*Someone* had to be the first, after all."

"I think," Kurganov put in, "that Colonel DiFalco is referring to Fermi's Paradox: the fact that our planet has never been colonized during all the hundreds of millions of years it has existed as a life-bearing world—which seems inexplicable if civilizations are as numerous as they *ought* to be if life is a normal occurrence in a galaxy of four hundred billion suns."

"But," Varien said with an air of fully stretched patience, "the same objection applies: there has to be a first. Even if no star-travelling race has existed heretofore, the fact dosen't logically preclude the possibility of one or more now. And your astronomers must be aware that your sun, like ours, is an exceptionally old star of its generation—which is the first stellar generation to have formed from a medium enriched with heavy elements by numerous supernovae. Planets suitable for life are very common, and in the normal course of events they will give birth to it; but relatively few are old enough to have done so to date. Highly-evolved, sentient life is a recent galactic phenomenon."

"Okay," DiFalco resumed doggedly, "so there was nobody around to colonize Earth during the

Precambrian. But what about the total failure of our SETI programs?" Seeing Varien's blank look, he amplified. "Search for extraterrestrial intelligence. For almost a century, off and on, we've been 'listening' to the stars for broadcasts in the radio wavelengths, and the result has been consistent: zilch point zip!"

For the first time in their acquaintance, Varien's jaw fell. *I've finally managed to astonish him,* DiFalco thought, just before the older man almost doubled over in his efforts to contain the loud belly laugh that was an impossible gaucherie in his culture. Miralann was undergoing similar contortions, and Aelanni was trying to look sternly disapproving of the other two while sputtering just a bit herself.

"*Radio* broadcasts?!" Varien gasped when he had gotten his breath. "Why should you have detected radio broadcasts, of all things?" He finally recovered his composure and explained in his usual condescending way. "Use of radio transmissions for large-scale, long-range communications is a transitional phase in the history of technology, rather like fission power. We've been communicating by neutrino pulse for centuries. Radio broadcasts! Why didn't you watch the stars for smoke signals while you were about it?" DiFalco and Kurganov looked crestfallen. "You can be sure that we haven't been generating anything at Lir . . . Alpha Centauri that you could have detected."

Kurganov pounced. "You're from Alpha Centauri, then?"

"No, we're merely based there. Our home sun is called Tareil. You have no name for it—understandably, as it is somewhat less luminous than your sun and is roughly a thousand of your light-years away."

"You've come a thousand light-years?" DiFalco asked faintly, thoughts of suspended animation and Einsteinian time dilation running through his head.

"Not in the sense you mean, Colonel. Perhaps I'd better explain." He spoke a command in his own language, and a holographic display appeared over the raised platform. To his two guests, it suggested a stylized molecular diagram with golden atoms linked by pale-blue lines.

"Is your civilization aware of the true nature of gravity, General?" Varien asked with seeming irrelevance.

"Well," Kurganov spoke hesitantly, "in the present generation, Hartung's theory has reconciled Newton and Einstein . . . two of our greatest physicists. The first, three and a half centuries ago, postulated that gravity was a force that causes material objects to attract each other. The second, in the last century, described gravity as a curvature of space in the presence of large masses." Varien nodded repeatedly, as if approving of the orthodoxy with which Earth's knowledge had progressed. "Most recently," the Russian continued, "Hartung has demonstrated that both were right: a force inherent in matter and carried by massless subatomic particles—and hence instantaneous in its propagation—is what *causes* the Einsteinian curvature of spacetime."

"Precisely! But I gather you have not yet carried the concept of curved space to its ultimate conclusion: the fact that a curve implies a circle, and that given the right conditions—involving a sufficient number of large masses, such as exist in the galactic spiral arms—space curves back upon itself in patterns caused by the interrelationships of those masses. Wherever the pattern is interrupted by a stellar mass, the local curvature of space causes a break in the pattern, which we call a 'displacement point' because of an effect which I discovered when I was considerably younger." He indicated the hologram. "This depicts, in very crude terms, the situation in our galactic neighborhood. The gold lights are stars that have one or more displacement points associated with them. The blue lines indicate the relationship between each such point and the next such break in the pattern. This all becomes of practical interest with the discovery of how to artificially simulate gravity. You see, if a ship heads into a displacement point at a heading identical to the bearing of the imaginary line, as plotted in realspace, to the next displacement point—normally, nothing happens. But if the ship generates an artificial gravity 'pulse' which warps space still further at the displacement point, then it experiences an instantaneous transition to the next displacement point, in the vicinity of another star."

"Then," DiFalco breathed, "you're saying you can travel faster than light?"

"Of course not," Varien snapped. "For a material object to exceed the velocity of light is not merely impossible . . . it is a mathematical absurdity! What I am describing is, to repeat myself, an instantaneous transposition without crossing the intervening realspace distance, possible only at certain locations determined by the gravitational patterns—the 'shape,' if you will—of space. So, for example, it is possible to transit from Tareil"—he aimed a wandlike instrument at one of the golden star-symbols, from which four of the blue bands radiated, and a bright white dot appeared in mid-air beside it—"to *this* star system." The cursor, as DiFalco decided to think of it, flashed along one of the blue light-bridges to another sun. "One then proceeds via normal space to another of the second star's displacement points, and transits to *this* star . . . and then *this* one . . . and finally to the one you know as Alpha Centauri." He held the cursor steady at the indicated star.

Kurganov leaned forward raptly. "So you came a thousand light-years in only the time it took to travel between the various displacement points in these star systems. But," he continued, perplexed, "Alpha Centauri appears to be a cul-de-sac; where is the further displacement connection that enabled you to come to this system?"

"Well," Varien spoke apologetically, "I'm afraid there isn't any." He raised a forestalling hand as the Russian and the American both tried to talk at once. "As I have indicated, displacement points only occur under rare conditions; all of those we know of are at least a hundred light-years apart, usually much more. So the vast majority of stars are without them. Including yours."

"So," DiFalco spoke very slowly and deliberately, "how did you come here?"

"Ah, well, that's another story, which will also provide the answer to the related question of *why* I came here. Attend, please.

"As I mentioned, some time ago I discovered the secret of interstellar travel via displacement points. Subsequently, my planet—called Raehan, by the way—began exploring rapidly." A quick sentence in his tongue, and arrowlike lights moved illustratively from Tareil along three of the four spokes of blue light extending from it, through star after golden star. "Too rapidly, in fact. Permit me a digression on the history of Raehan.

"Five of your centuries ago, Raehan was almost as advanced as it is now, following two centuries of explosive technological development accompanied by constantly escalating war and social disintegration. At that point, what was left of our people came collectively and spontaneously to the conclusion that change in general must be halted to allow civilization to recover and unify. Over the centuries, there was much refinement but virtually no innovation. Finally, in my parents' time, the strictures began to give way; the chance discovery of artificial gravity set unstoppable changes in motion. I imagine our exuberant and headlong exploration through one displacement point after another, without pausing to consolidate, was partly a release of impulses too long pent up. Also, we could

imagine no danger in the stars—we were firmly
convinced, on the basis of our own history, that any
civilization advanced enough to constitute a potential
threat must surely have given up military aggression in
order to survive.

"We were wrong."

He spoke a command, jarringly harsh for the language of Raehan, and the star-diagram vanished, to
be replaced by something that brought the two
Earthmen to their feet in horror.

"That," Varien stated somberly, "is a life-sized
image of a Korvaasha. One of our exploration ships
blundered into an outpost of their empire . . . an
empire that has been slowly expanding for more centuries or millennia than we know, dedicated to
imposing its own kind of unity on all the accessible
galaxy. It is expansionism that has nothing to do with
greed or glory, ambition or anger—rather, it has
taken on a dour and leaden life of its own, and con-
tinues long after it has ceased to be profitable or
even practical. Dismiss any thought of decadent over-
lords living in luxury on the labor of slaves. In fact,
they've impoverished themselves to maintain a centralized state over a range whose frontiers take years
of travel to reach even through the displacement
points. Their empire is nothing more than a vast
logistics base, a means that has become an end."

DiFalco, like Kurganov, couldn't tear his eyes from
the startlingly lifelike hologram. It wasn't precisely
ugly, for ugliness implies deviation from an accepted
and recognizable standard. Rather, there was a fundamental and indefinable *wrongness* about the thick
two-and-a-half-meter image.

"I assure you that you're seeing the species at its
best—that is, at its most natural. This is a
non-specialized leader type. The lower orders are
bionically enhanced to make them efficient modular
units of the runaway machine that is Korvaash
civilization, and no resources are wasted on disguising

the artificialities." Varien restored the star-diagram, to DiFalco's relief.

"When they captured our scout ship, they captured our complete body of astrogational data—the concept of computer security was, of course, foreign to us. It was a windfall for them: all those displacement points we had already surveyed, plus our highly advanced civilization to be welded into the machine. Their unvarying rule mandates planetary extermination as the penalty for attacking or successfully rebelling against the Empire, but not for merely encountering it; we're earmarked for enslavement instead." Varien actually smiled. "The odd thing is that they're fair-minded by their own lights. Unfortunately, by our standards their lights are few and dim."

Baleful red flares moved along one of the blue displacement-chains, branching off onto others as they made their cancerous way toward Tareil.

"Their technology evidently stopped developing as soon as they discovered the secret of displacement points, for it is less sophisticated than ours—though more so than its apparent crudity would suggest. And the defender of a displacement point enjoys the advantage of knowing where the attacker must emerge, and at what heading. These factors have enabled us to delay their advance, even though we had to improvise defense forces after five centuries of peace. But their resources are effectively limitless, and their orientation military to the last detail of their lives. The result is not in doubt. We cannot stop them."

For a long moment, they all sat in funereal silence. Then DiFalco finally decided what had been bothering him about the display.

"Hey," he spoke suddenly. "All these little lights—your white ones and the red Korvaasha ones—haven't come anywhere near that route you pointed out earlier, the one that leads from Tareil to Alpha

Centauri. What's the matter with *those* displacement points?"

"The matter with them, Colonel, is that no one—Raehaniv or Korvaasha—knows about them. Except, of course, myself and my friends. Again, perhaps I'd better explain.

"You'll remember that I invented the technique of displacement point travel. I also pioneered other applications of artificial gravity, although I hadn't originated it. Our economy is what I believe you would call liberal-capitalist: society has no objection to vast personal wealth as long as it is acquired by the rules, particularly the rules against technological innovation—but this latter restriction, as I mentioned, had been breaking down even before I came on the scene. To be brief, I am what you would call a multibillionaire several times over. Private explorers in my employ discovered Tareil's fourth displacement point. I decided to investigate the systems beyond—the 'Lirauva Chain' is the term we use—for potential opportunities before making it public. I established a base on a habitable planet of Lirauva . . . excuse me, Alpha Centauri. There, we became aware of your civilization. It was in order to come here and study you that I invented a new interstellar drive, which evades the light-speed barrier without recourse to displacement points."

"So you *can* travel faster than light!" DiFalco declared triumphantly.

"No, no, no! What is involved is a series of very short instantaneous displacements, which can be repeated millions of times a second, allowing our most efficient ship to date to transit from Alpha Centauri to this system in just over six of your days. Most of our ships take five times that."

DiFalco looked mulish. "Well if that's not travelling faster than light, I'd like to know what is!"

Varien visibly controlled himself. "If I may continue," he said frostily, "I will come to the purpose of my presence here. You see, my discovery of the new drive coincided with the beginning of the war . . . no, let us be honest: the annexation. I have special sources of information which enabled me to see, more clearly than most of my compatriots, that we were doomed. So instead of turning my secrets over to the Raehaniv government, I faked my own death and came here." He paused portentously. "I am here to offer your governments all our scientific knowledge, the entire panoply of our technology—to offer you, in fact, the stars—in exchange for your help!"

"Our help?" and "Our governments?" came, faintly and simultaneously, from Kurganov and DiFalco respectively.

"Yes! Remember, the Korvaasha know nothing of Tareil's fourth displacement point. Once they are settled into their occupation of Raehan, a liberating fleet could enter the system from an entirely unexpected direction—an unheard-of occurrence and a shock to their hidebound professionalism! And once we have captured some of *their* astrogational data, the new drive—which I have also kept secret, lest it fall into Korvaasha hands—can be used effectively to counterattack!" His enthusiasm suddenly waned. "Used effectively, that is, by *you*. The Raehaniv have been strangers to war for centuries too long; our new military barely qualifies as a joke. I can show you how to build weapons and equipment, and provide you with those components your technological base cannot yet manufacture, but your people have abilities mine have lost. It is for these that we are prepared to pay you very well indeed. Due to our ignorance of the nuances of your politics, I have approached you first, rather than announcing our presence directly and publicly to your home world." He looked proud of himself for this uncharacteristic subtlety; Aelanni's expression suggested that she might have had something to do with it.

The Russian and the American looked at each other, neither trusting himself to speak.

"Varien," Kurganov finally said, carefully, "we must have time to consider this. We and certain of our colleagues are already scheduled to meet on Phoenix Prime in connection with . . . political developments on Earth, our home world. I believe your proposal will be very relevant in this context."

"Of course, General."

CHAPTER FOUR

The conference room was a buzz of talk, with ugly undercurrents, when Kurganov, DiFalco and the others entered. These were not military people and Phoenix Prime was not a warship, so there was no coming to attention. But the hubbub subsided as the officers took their seats at the head table and Sergeant Thompson came to parade rest beside the door.

DiFalco had Levinson in tow, and Kurganov had brought the pair who headed his intelligence section, an organization whose real function was more and more the accumulation of information and analysis on the increasingly unpredictable governments which were the Project's sponsors. Major Arkady Semyonovich Kuropatkin was short and stocky, with a thick black mustache and small, sharp eyes; Captain Irina Nikolayevna Tartakova towered over him and had straight, dark-brown hair hanging past a narrow, severe face. Levinson, who had a perverse fondness for pre-computer-enhancement twentieth century animated cartoons, had dubbed them "Boris and Natasha." They had been told what lay behind a certain nearby asteroid, and still wore stunned looks which did nothing for the half-dozen civilians' collective state of mind.

"Thank you for waiting, ladies and gentlemen," Kurganov opened. "Colonel DiFalco and I have been occupied with an unexpected development."

"Haven't we all, General," George Traylor of Trans-Orbit Developments growled. His voice, like a rock-crusher at full throttle, went with the rest of him—in earlier stages of his career, he had needed something more than his array of degrees in bossing construction crews. "The question is, what are we going to do about it?"

"Actually," Yakov Lazarovich Rosen of the St. Petersburg Institute of Planetology put in, "the first question is how seriously to take what we've heard. Well, Arkady Semyonovich?"

Kuropatkin scowled with concentration as he dragged his thoughts away from his new knowledge. "Ordinarily, I would discount it as mere political bluster. But now . . . ?" He shrugged. His English was heavily accented but fluent. "Economic reality means nothing to fanatics—we Russians know that. And American media has created a climate of opinion which can only be described as arrogant hysteria; rationality has become morally suspect." He gave an apologetic shrug which took in all his American listeners.

"Ha! So what the hell else is new?" Traylor snorted explosively. "Okay, then; we have to assume that these people aren't just blowing hot air out their asses but really mean what they say. And we all know that Russia won't—can't—continue the Project on its own if America pulls out." None of the Russians in the room looked happy, but none of them contradicted him. "If they did, I'd have to think about going to work for them myself," Traylor continued grimly. "But it's just not in the cards.

"But," he went on, sweeping the room with a glower, "I'd like to remind everybody that we're not entirely powerless. We represent some very wealthy organizations on Earth. We need to use our contacts in those organizations to get them off their numb butts! They have to start using their influence in ways that count politically, before it's too late!"

"But shouldn't we wait and see what happens?" Elizabeth Hadley of Consolidated Astronautics didn't quite wring her hands, but her face and voice held a note of anguish that had been there more and more of late. She spoke up to override the chorus of groans. "Yes, I know what we've heard sounds bad. And I know a lot of mistakes have been made Earthside. But maybe it will all blow over if we and others who feel as we do will just avoid being provocative. . . ."

"Jesus Christ, Liz!" Traylor's face was even ruddier than usual. "Do you really believe this shit, or do you just need to pretend to yourself that you do? Haven't you figured out *yet* what we're dealing with?"

Kurganov rapped the edge of the table with a stylus as Hadley started to open her mouth. "If we could have order, ladies and gentlemen, there is an additional factor we need to consider." He didn't raise his voice, but it held a note of command that Traylor and Hadley obeyed, even thought they were neither military nor Russian. But then, DiFalco reflected, the latter made less difference than would once have seemed possible; more and more, RAMP was these people's nation and Kurganov, like a constitutional monarch, was its embodiment.

"I must caution you," the general continued, "that this information is classified 'Most Secret.' In fact, I have assigned it a military security classification whose name you haven't even heard. But I have, on my own responsibility, decided to share it with you. You all have a need to know which, in my view, overrides the legalities involved. None of it must go beyond this room." That sobered them still further. "Colonel DiFalco, you may begin."

DiFalco stood up and fed a disc into the wall viewer, which he then linked with his perscomp. "The video you are going to see," he began, "was

recorded during *Andrew Jackson*'s transit from
Mars. . . ."

*   *   *

DiFalco finally concluded, his last words falling
like pebbles into a well of silence.

They had been remarkably quiet, with neither the
clamoring questions he had expected nor the hysteria
he had feared. Aside from an occasional hiss of
indrawn breath or quickly stilled murmur, they had
sat, stunned, as the fundamental assumptions of their
lives were demolished.

"As you can see," Kurganov finally spoke with
studied understatement, "this changes things. Varien
wishes to make his offer to governments which,
unknown to him, are about to turn their backs on space
as part of a general retreat into the kind of statism we
had all thought lay safely in the last century."

"And which could now become permanent if he
does," Traylor continued for him. "Before the collapse of Communism, a lot of people thought the
modern totalitarian state was invincible because of
the gap that had opened up between the leading
edge of weapons and thought-control technology and
what was available to private individuals. That nightmare turned out to be premature—but what kind of
stuff do Varien's people have? If it's anything like
we've just seen and heard about . . ."

"But," Hadley interrupted him, "maybe the obvious
possibilites here—the stars, for God's sake!—would
turn our governments around, weaken the anti-space
elements. Remember," she went on earnestly, "we're
dealing with people who, however misguided some of
their policies, are basically idealistic and
well-meaning. . . ."

"Yeah," Levinson snapped, leaning forward and
raising his voice over the general rumble of scorn,
"like the well-meaning idealists who publicly cas-
trated that old Hassidic rabbi in New York last
month while the cops looked on? And the idealistic,

well-meaning governor who made excuses for it?
Something about an 'understandable reaction by the
historically disempowered,' I think he said."

"You *know* what I think of that kind of stuff, Jeff!"
Hadley's features twisted as they reflected her inner
conflict. "You know I've never condoned it! But we
can't give up hope in our country because of an
occasional aberration!"

"It is more than an aberration, Ms. Hadley," İrina
Tartakova spoke coldly. Her accent was almost as
thick as Kuropatkin's. "It is predictable outcome of a
trend of long standing. Almost exactly a century ago
your country got into habit of pursuing faddish social
ends by socially destructive means. And by the 1980's
anything, including anti-Semitism, was excused by
opinion-makers as long as it was rationalized in fashionable terms by representatives of fashionable
groups."

Hadley's long-accumulating torment spilled over in
bile. "You bitch!" she yelled. "You don't understand
the background . . . the, uh, social problems . . ."

"Hold on everybody!" DiFalco's deep baritone held
considerable force when he let it out. He let it out
now, and they shut up. "Aren't we all forgetting a
couple of points, which have nothing to do with
what we think of the Earthside governments? This
opportunity—whether or not we think those governments can be trusted with it—carries with it a
terrible danger. Remember what Varien said about
the Korvaash policy on worlds that attack them?"

"Planetary extermination," Rosen breathed. It
sounded loud in the sudden silence.

"Right. And he also said that the Korvaasha are
people who believe in doing things by the book! So,
what if our governments accept Varien's offer, carry
out his plan . . . and lose? We're talking about the
life of our entire world, not just some political
sleaze-balls!"

"But," Traylor began with uncharacteristic hesitancy,

"isn't Earth safe from them? I mean, even if they discover this 'Lirauva Chain' of displacement points, it stops at Alpha Centauri! How could they get here?"

"The same way Varien did: his continuous-displacement drive, which works anywhere outside a major gravity well if you just know how to do it. Remember, we'd be committing the thing to battle for the first time; if we lost, it could easily get captured. As would knowledge of the Lirauva Chain. They'd know where we came from, and how to get there. Come to think of it, we wouldn't even have to lose—all it would take would be one of our ships falling into their hands!"

"So, Colonel," Rosen asked after a moment, "are you proposing that we tell Varien, as I believe you Americans put it, 'Thanks but no thanks'? And, perhaps, tell him the truth about what is happening on Earth, to discourage him from bypassing us and contacting our governments directly?"

"Not necessarily. Because my second point is this: Varien's not saying so, but he must know that the USA and the Russian Federation aren't his only possibilities."

The silence became complete. China's had been the last Marxist regime to fall, and afterwards the giant country had become more and more closely tied to a Japan which was being frozen out of Western markets. Now the partners, of which Japan was increasingly the junior, were united in a kind of corporate Confucianism, capitalistic but not individualistic. Long active in orbital and cis-Lunar space, they had now begun ranging further afield, and the solar system had been tacitly split, leaving them the inner planets. Talk had been heard of mining Mercury and terraforming Venus, but to date nothing had been done.

"I'm sure Varien would rather deal with us, if only because we still have the biggest and most highly developed deep-space capability," DiFalco went on.

"But if need be, he can always turn to the Chinese. And if they accept his offer . . . well, everything I said earlier about the danger to Earth would apply equally. We'd be in just as much jeopardy, but with none of the benefits. I somehow doubt if the Korvaasha would be inclined to draw fine distinctions based on our Earthside political alignments!"

"But Eric," Hadley wailed, "we can't let Varien approach the Chinese!"

"Just how do you suggest we stop him, Liz?"

Kurganov let the silence last a few heartbeats before rapping the edge of the table again. "I think a recess is in order," he said, glancing at his wrist chrono. "We will reconvene in one hour. Remember, none of this is to be discussed with anyone . . . no one at all."

* * *

DiFalco and Levinson were deep in muttered conversation when the general and Kuropatkin entered the almost-deserted refectory and proceeded to their corner table.

"As you were, gentlemen," Kurganov said, polite as always but clearly preoccupied. "Have you arrived at any suggestions to offer the meeting?"

"I'm afraid not, General," DiFalco admitted. "We keep coming back around to the basic dilemma: irresistable benefits carrying unacceptable danger."

"Well, Eric, not that it matters to that dilemma, but I've just viewed a new report that came in during the meeting. It's not part of the official message traffic; it comes directly from Major Kuropatkin's Earthside sources." He gestured to Kuropatkin to proceed.

"*Da*, Konstantinovich." The Russian spook leaned forward and spoke in a low voice. "American Social Justice party and its Russian counterparts have been in communication. It is now clear that they mean everything they have been saying—and more." He avoided the two Americans' eyes. "Next American election will be last one. And they are absolutely determined to terminate Project. Afterwards, they have secretly agreed that all military and civilian personnel connected with it—and their families—are to be 'politically re-educated' at camps in isolated areas. All memory of Project is to be expunged."

After a long moment, Levinson sighed deeply. "Well, let's look on the bright side," he said with a crooked smile. "At least this knocks Liz Hadley's arguments into a cocked hat and settles the whole question on what to do with Varien. Putting him in touch with our governments is *not* an option!"

"Isn't it?" Three heads turned to face DiFalco as he spoke like an automaton. "Even if we could get rid of him and keep him away from the Chinese, it wouldn't solve the problem. It would just postpone it. Sooner or later, the Korvaasha are going to discover the Lirauva Chain for themselves. And they're also going to discover the continuous-displacement drive! Varien admits that it's a natural outgrowth of Raehan's technology, which the Korvaasha are busy appropriating. Face it: the Korvaasha are going to arrive here eventually!"

"And when they do," Kurganov said slowly, "we will need Varien's technology if Earth is to have any hope of defending itself from enslavement. But he won't give it to us unless we agree to use it to attack the Korvaasha, and thus expose Earth to the danger of obliteration!"

"Enslavement by the Korvaasha might not be that much worse than what Earth is getting ready to do to itself," Levinson said savagely. "It might even be hard to tell the difference!"

"But destruction . . . ?" DiFalco let the question trail off into silence as thoughts that had nothing to do with politics filled four separate minds. The Colorado Rockies above Aspen . . . a forest of slender white birch trees south of Lake Ladoga . . . Indian Summer in New England and a little covered bridge . . . Red Square and the inspired Tartar madness in brick that was St. Basil's . . . and faces, faces, faces. . . .

All a desert of windblown radioactive ash, it tolled in DiFalco's head. *No. We can't risk that.*

But . . . maybe we don't have to!

He grew aware that the others were staring at him. He took a deep breath and began, improvising as he spoke.

"Look, there may be a solution after all. . . ."

* * *

Kurganov still hadn't recovered his mental equilibrium when Kuropatkin finished revealing his new information to the reconvened meeting. Afterwards, Liz Hadley sat twisting a lock of hair as if she wanted to pull it out. The others just sat.

"In light of what we have just heard, ladies and gentlemen," the general began, "Colonel DiFalco has a proposal to offer the meeting. Colonel, you have the floor."

"Thank you, General." DiFalco looked around grimly. "First off, people, let's begin by being honest with ourselves. Otherwise, we're just pissing into the wind. What Major Kuropatkin has told us proves what most of us already suspected: there's nothing for us or our families on Earth any more." Not even Hadley contradicted him. But then, she, like many others, had a family here. Sergei had once remarked that RAMP's people were in a position not unlike that of the British in India before steamships—their tours were, of necessity, years-long ones. Those with families brought them to Phoenix Prime; spouses not directly involved in the Project worked in support services. When this was unacceptable, families broke up or people declined positions with the Project. The result was a kind of natural selection: there was no one here who wasn't emotionally committed to RAMP.

"Nor is there anything for us out here," DiFalco continued remorselessly. "We're not going to be allowed to continue the Project after another two years." They all visibly winced, but again no one argued.

"Having disposed of all wishful thinking," he resumed, "let's turn to the question of how to respond to Varien's offer. There are two reasons for *not* accepting it. First, governments such as ours are becoming shouldn't be given the kind of technology he offers." His eyes swept the room, challenging anyone to disagree. No one did, although Liz very nearly dislodged her lock of hair. "And second, the penalty for failure: destruction of our world by the Korvaasha." Heads nodded affirmatively at this.

DiFalco paused for an interminable moment, then drew a breath and spoke with the force of absolute, bridge-burning commitment. "But neither of these arguments applies if *we* accept his offer. Not our governments . . . *us*! RAMP! Think about it," he hurried on, before the disjointed shock in their faces could congeal into opposition. "We have a fair-sized fleet of deep-space-capable ships here, and we've had to develop a substantial industrial capability. We can refit our ships with Varien's stuff, while continuing to keep his existence secret, and then depart the solar system along the Lirauva Chain—*after* wiping our records and our ships' computers of every scrap of data that could be used to identify the star we came from! If our attack on the Korvaash occupiers of Raehan succeeds, fine. If it doesn't . . . well, the Korvaasha will have no idea of where this attack on them originated. And neither will anyone on Earth; where we went will be the biggest unsolved mystery since the Lost Colony! And . . . I think I'd rather die in battle, fighting for the long-term defense of Earth, than rot in some goddamned concentration camp!"

His voice had risen in volume until it was a rolling thunder. Its echoes died away, leaving the room in a silence of total shock. Liz had actually stopped twisting her hair.

"But," Traylor finally broke the silence, "win or lose, we'd be cutting ourselves off from Earth for all time. . . ."

"Hell, no! Look, Varien and his people know the locations of the displacement points that make up the Lirauva Chain. After we defeat the Korvaasha and Earth is out of danger, we can just proceed back along the Chain to Alpha Centauri. From there, Sol's the brightest star in Cassiopeia . . . we could find it with our eyes closed! We can go the last four-and-a-third light years of the trip on continuous-displacement drive and arrive back here bringing a whole new order of technology and the news that we've got allies—*human* allies—among the stars. That ought to really do the trick Liz was talking about and turn Earth around!"

He surveyed the room and saw much the same look on every face. It was the look of people who had been offered an escape from an insoluble dilemma . . . and were terrified of it.

"But Colonel," Tartakova spoke hesitantly, "how could we keep this a secret? Surely not every one of the hundreds of people here and at Phoenix will agree!"

"Of course not. We'll have to restrict all knowledge of what's really going on to people we've sounded out and know we can trust. I know you and Arkady already have a pretty comprehensive list of the people we definitely *can't* trust. They, and everybody else who isn't involved, will just continue to rotate back and forth between here and Phoenix as before. In the meantime, we'll be doing the crucial work at Varien's outpost, protected by his stealth technology. Only one of our big ships would have to be there at a time, and we'd only have to have our people in a few key positions to be able to cover for those absences. I'm willing to bet that we can be ready within the two years the Project's got."

His eyes swept the room again. Relief still warred

with fear on every face, but relief was winning. And it was being joined, here and there, by sheer awe at what they—just possibly—had in their power to do.

Kuropatkin, who had been prepared, recovered first.

"Colonel," he began, "I know you and General Kurganov have not yet discussed this . . . alternative with Varien."

DiFalco and Kurganov exchanged glances. "No, we have not," the Russian admitted. "I believe another visit to his ship is in order!"

CHAPTER FIVE

Varien was uncharacteristically silent after they had finished. Then he sighed and shook his head slowly.

"We really had no conception of the political climate we were dealing with, you know. Some of the broadcasts we picked up merely led us to question the depth of our understanding of your language. In particular, when we heard someone—evidently a prominent public figure and not a character in some comedy—declare that the government should guarantee *every* citizen an *above-average* income, we decided that our translation *must* be at fault!"

"I'm afraid not," DiFalco admitted. "That's been part of the Social Justice Party's platform for years. You were probably hearing a speech by the governor of New York . . . who, barring a miracle, will be my nation's head of state two years from now."

"Dear me! I begin to see why we've always had difficulty differentiating the political news from the popular comedies in your broadcasts; both are farcical but neither seems particularly funny." Varien had almost entirely lost his Raehaniv accent by now, and it was clear which linguistic role models had been influencing him; he had come to speak a variety of English that Levinson characterized as "acting-class British."

Aelanni, on the other hand, still spoke with a liquid accent which should have kept the asperity out of her voice but didn't. "What kind of lunatic asylum do you come from, anyway?" she demanded. "And how did the inmates ever manage to get into interplanetary space?"

DiFalco felt himself flush. Criticism from outside the family never makes comfortable listening, even—especially!—when one agrees with it. "Things were better a generation ago," he insisted, a little defensively. "That was when we started to get into space in a big way. But there were a lot of problems left over from the last century. . . ." *Shit! I'm starting to sound like Liz Hadley!* "The simple fact is, our system of public education had stopped educating the public. It was possible to get a first-rate education . . . but it was also possible to become a certified graduate without having learned anything except the right ideological slogans to parrot." He smiled sadly. "Standards had been lowered to the lowest common denominator in the name of 'equality'; but the end result was rigid social stratification, with an educated minority—including the people who took us into space—sitting precariously on top of a vast majority that was, by any meaningful definition, illiterate."

"By now," Kurganov added, "the literate minority has become so small as to be politically and culturally ignorable. And it is about to cease to exist altogether. The Social Justice party is pledged to eradicate all non-public alternatives in education. 'Equality' requires that illiteracy become universal!"

Aelanni shook her shining reddish-black head. "Incredible!"

"Not really," Miralann disagreed. "Something of the sort very nearly happened to our society between the Second and Third Global Wars, during the Trelalieuhiv ascendancy. . . ."

Varien waved him to silence. "This is all very interesting, I'm sure. But the immediate problem is this: we came seeking help from an advanced society which, it turns out, is busily reconverting itself into a primitive one." He clasped his hands behind him and began pacing. "And now, if I understand correctly, you are accepting my offer on behalf of your Project, without reference to the governments that sponsor it and whose uniforms you both wear." He paused and gave them a long look with those dark, dark eyes. And all at once, without any tricks of technological wizardry, he was no longer just a supercilious old fart.

"It goes without saying," he resumed, "that those governments would regard your actions as treasonous. But I am more concerned with how *you* will regard them. Will you be able to act wholeheartedly against all your training, all your conditioned loyalties? I must know, before we proceed one step further!"

DiFalco and Kurganov looked at each other for a moment, and then the former spoke. "I don't think there is a conflict, Varien. I still consider myself loyal to the United States of America—at least to what it *was*, and what the memory of it still means to any-one who believes that individual human beings have the right, and the responsibility, to rule themselves. As for our nations . . . well, all of us out here are about to become outcasts to them, by their own decision. But we'll be defending them, without their knowledge, against a threat they never dreamed ex-isted. And we mean to return to them, one day. Whether they're prepared to welcome us then, only time will tell."

Kurganov spoke slowly. "Colonel DiFalco is right—probably even more right than he knows—about what his country once meant to everyone on our world who longed for what its people had but took for granted. That they have betrayed that memory does not in any way diminish it." He flashed his wry smile. "Any more than the *rodina* is diminished by all the tyrannies it has submitted to in the past, as it is about to submit once again. And as for me, personally . . ." He sighed. "In two months, my tour of duty here is over, and Colonel DiFalco assumes military command of RAMP. I will return to Earth and become director of the Russian branch of the Project's administrative structure. From there I will be able to expedite the supplying of whatever is needed to prepare for the departure. I will also be able to safeguard the secret. I will not, however, be able to depart with the fleet myself." DiFalco's eyes lowered. He had not yet cared to face up to this, though he had known it intellectually all along.

"You can be sure, however," the Russian continued quietly, "that the secret will continue to be kept." He and DiFalco exchanged a quick look; neither of them spoke, or needed to.

"Yes!" Varien resumed his pacing, oblivious to what had just passed. "With Colonel DiFalco in command here, and you so strategically positioned on Earth, it might just possibly work—especially if, as you say, practically everyone in this asteroid belt is as alienated from your rulers as you yourselves are. And I myself have—ahem!—some small experience in the art of bureaucratic concealment. Yes! I actually believe we can do it! At least," he added, brow furrowing with sudden worry, "we can do it in the two years you say your Project still has left. How can you be sure that this 'United States' won't withdraw its support before then?"

"The current administration, and the Libertarian Party that still controls the White House—the executive branch—have too much of a stake in it," DiFalco explained. "They'll continue to back it to the hilt. You see, the 'launch window' for Phoenix—the time we *have* to move it out of its orbit and start it on the parabolic transfer orbit that will intersect with Mars—happens to occur just before the next American general election. The administration is hoping that event will give it a political shot in the arm; they'll give us whatever we need to meet the deadline without too many questions asked, which is what makes the whole thing possible."

"You know best about these matters, of course," Varien said with a rather offhand graciousness. "But the greatest problem will be the melding of our technologies in those systems—notably the various applications of artificial gravity—that require components beyond your current ability to fabricate. Fortunately, I anticipated this when equipping this expedition. Our superconductors, for example—" He stopped abruptly, realizing he was rambling. "But there's no time to waste! We can begin at once to form an initial impression of what will be required. Aelanni, show Colonel DiFalco our engineering spaces while I discuss specifics with General Kurganov."

* * *

DiFalco emerged from the engineering hatch, drew a deep and shaken breath, and leaned on the railing below the wide viewport of transparent plastic that was nearly as strong as the molecularly aligned crystalline alloy of the hull.

"I trust you are favorably impressed, Eric," Aelanni said with a slight smile as she exited the hatch behind him. He reminded himself that the use of the given name alone did not carry an implication of familiarity for the Raehaniv; it was simply the usual way of addressing people. But her smile seemed genuine, and her voice held a warmth that the musical accent alone could not entirely account for. It somehow went with her coloring—against the backdrop of space, her hair seemed a warmer blackness. . . . He forced his mind back to practicalities.

"Yes, you might say that," he acknowledged. "This kind of fusion drive is only a theoretical possibility for us. The system we're building on Phoenix is a crude, brute-force approach—essentially an ongoing series of laser-detonated fusion explosions. So far, controlled fusion power has only been possible in huge installations; even our larger spacecraft still have fission powerplants. Earth itself mostly uses orbital-collected solar power." He paused with a preoccupied frown as he recalled what lay in store for Earth's space effort and, by extension, its civilization.

Aelanni sensed it. She spoke formally. "I wish to apologize for what I said earlier about your world, Eric. As an outsider, I have no right . . ."

He grimaced. "Oh, no. You were right on target. Which reminds me of something I've been wondering about. What do you Raehaniv use for a government?"

"Ever since the end of the Global Wars, we've had a world state presided over by what I believe you would call a constitutional monarch. The world was turning its back on change, and people were looking for continuiuty, for a sense of permanence. All our nations but one, Tranaethein, had expelled their old royal houses by then; but the Arathrain, or king, of Tranaethein, was related to all the principal old dynasties and had some sort of claim to many vacant . . . thrones? And he was a remarkable individual, after a series of nonentities his family had produced—'natural constitutional monarchs' someone unkindly called them. He was a charismatic leader of the move toward global unity, and one nation after another decided to restore its monarchy and declare him the heir to it. This became the legal basis for the unification. The actual legislating is done by the assembly of . . . well, the name would mean nothing to you. It's not an elected body in your sense, but a nominated one." She stepped to a nearby computer terminal, moving with unselfconscious grace in her skintight shipsuit (it was a light green now; he had seen her change it to other colors with a touch of a finger to a certain spot). She spoke a lilting sentence, and the liquid crystal screen displayed a deep-blue hexagon divided by golden lines into six triangular segments, each containing a stylized representation in gold of a different object or group of objects.

"We don't use 'flags' like yours," Aelanni explained. "But this is the emblem of the Raehaniv state. It shows the symbols of the six principal national dynasties that the first world-Arathrain succeeded to." She pointed. "Like the eight-pointed star of Tranaethein, and . . ." She saw the look on his face and stopped. "What is it, Eric?"

He pointed an unsteady finger at one of the heraldic symbols. "That," he stated positively, "is a horse."

"A . . . yes, I believe that is what you call a *rhylieu*." She gazed thoughtfully at the rearing quadruped surmounted by a kind of coronet. "I see what is troubling you. But," she shrugged, "there are humans on both worlds, so why not . . . horses, as well? Impossibility, like infinity, cannot be multiplied."

"Granted. But what the hell is *that*?" He pointed at a crouching beast that looked more reptilian than anything else but really looked like nothing ever seen or even imagined on Earth. An oddly shaped sword lay under its forepaws.

"The *mneisafv* of Trelalieu. Why?" She gave DiFalco a sharp look. He seemed more shaken than she had ever seen him.

"Is the *mneisafv* a mythical animal?" He spoke slowly and deliberately, each word like a footstep into a minefield.

"No. Much rarer than they used to be . . . they almost became extinct. But . . ." She paused. "So you don't have them on your world? Well, then, not all species on Raehan are duplicated on Earth. But we already knew from your broadcasts that you have some animals we don't."

"But," DiFalco persisted, "unless I'm going blind, that sucker's got *six legs!*"

"Why, yes. So do all its relatives, and certain other families of animals, such as the . . ."

"Don't you get it?" He stopped and took a deep

breath. "Look, Aelanni"—might as well follow the local conventions; "Ms. zho'Morna" didn't even make
sense in Raehaniv—"I'm no biologist, but I know
that *all* vertebrates on Earth have four limbs, even
though it's less obvious when one pair of them are
specialized—for flying, as with the birds, or for tool-
using in the case of humans. I also know there's a
reason for this. We've fantasized about worlds where
species have all different numbers of legs and
arms—remind me to tell you about Edgar Rice Bur-
roughs sometime. But it's evolutionary nonsense. All
the higher animals on Raehan should have six limbs
like this *mneisafv*, or else they should all have four
like you!"

Aelanni looked with fresh eyes at the . . .
Americahiv? No, "American." It was so hard to know
what to make of him. He was undeniably
attractive—about average height and very solidly built
on Raehaniv standards (this "Earth" had a stronger
gravity than Raehan's), his features and coloring exotic
but somehow not as much so as most of his fellows.
Likewise, his eye color (the Landaeniv word was
"hazel," she reminded herself) was unusual but not
beyond the Raehaniv pale. No, the problem wasn't his
appearance. Partly it was the sense that here was
someone who lived the way people had in the days of
the   Third   Global   War—barely   above   the
transistor-electronics level!—and actually survived such
conditions. (Had people really been tougher then, as
writers of historical fiction insisted?) But mostly it was
the way he acted, always so careful to conceal, except
in moments of excitement like this one, the trenchant
native intelligence that had cut through in an instant to
the heart of one of the classic paradoxes of Raehaniv
science. Was it the culture into which he had been
born? However much he might consciously reject its
egalitarianism fetish and its anti-intellectualism, he
could not escape the guilts they had programmed into
him, making him need to act like a—she searched her

memory before recalling the Landaeniv word "roughneck"—except in unguarded moments.

"Yes," she finally replied. "Of course we've thought of it. The fact of evolution became inescapable long ago . . . even before the First Global War. But we've never been able to fit ourselves, and many other Raehaniv species, into it! The fossil record cannot be denied: there is no evidence of four-limbed animals on Raehan before"—she paused and spoke a sentence in Raehaniv, and her eyes seemed to focus on a point a few inches in front of her; DiFalco recalled Varien's offhand comments about data displayed directly through the optic nerves by an implanted micro-computer communicating with more sophisticated computers—"about thirty-two thousand of your years ago. None of our clever attempts to account for this have held up."

DiFalco felt a prickling at the nape of his neck. "But *homo sapiens* was already around on Earth by then! Do you realize what this means? Humanity, and all those quadrupedal animals, must have evolved on Earth! They can't be native to Raehan!"

"But how did they get to Raehan?" she challenged. "Is there any evidence of a space-travelling civilization on Earth in that era?"

"No," he admitted ruefully. "And there *would* be! As we've found out, high-tech civilization produces by-products that are *permanent*; you can't get rid of them if you want to! All our legends of advanced prehistoric civilizations like Atlantis are bullshit." (Aelanni recalled the vulgarism without recourse to her infallible implanted memory.) "And the notion of an ancient nonhuman starfaring civilization doing it is at least as silly. Such a civilization would have left the same kind of traces. And it should still be around! I mean, even if it collapsed on one planet, it would have others to fall back on . . . and I've never bought the notion of a far-flung interstellar civilization chucking technology and going back to the home planet and becoming philosophy professors! And, finally, just why should super-advanced star-farers be chauffeuring stone-age humans around the galaxy in the first place? No, it just doesn't make sense."

"You have just summed up centuries of Raehaniv scientific speculation," Aelanni said solemnly. "Our conclusions are essentially the same as yours: it doesn't make sense."

They looked at each other for a long moment. Then, wordlessly, they walked side by side toward the briefing room, past the viewport and its suddenly sinister stars.

CHAPTER SIX

Sergei Kurganov finished the report and leaned back with a deep sigh. The selection process still took up more time than he had to give it, but it had reached a point at which he was not so much choosing the fit as weeding out the unfit—a simpler job, given the dossiers that Kuropatkin and Tartakova had accumulated. It could, he reflected, have been far worse. There were no political commissars here. The people who would have been interested in such a job were the very people who viewed the entire concept of spaceflight with revulsion, if not with the ideological equivalent of holy horror, and were scarcely inclined to inflict it on themselves for a period of years. And they were also people without the kind of skills and training which could have justified the transport and life-support costs of sending them past Mars. So Kurganov and his predecessors had successfully resisted the never-very-intense pressure to assign a *zampolit* to RAMP.

And there weren't even many party stooges. The growing social rift between Earth and its space colonies, and the unattractiveness of the Social Justice ideology to competent people, saw to that. Oh, there had been a few in the past—that fatal accident several years ago, under General Carlson, had seemed awfully odd, but

the investigation had pretty much died on the vine.
Kurganov remembered it well; as second-in-command,
he had been in charge of the investigation. . . .

He shook off the thought and turned to another
report. Yes, the personnel problem was becoming quite
manageable. Soon he might be able to get away more
often to the heavily stealthed site, not far away in the
Belt, where the work of refitting had commenced
under the direction of Varien and his people and where
every moment was a new encounter with the unknown.
He allowed himself an instant's envy of DiFalco, now
out there with *Andrew Jackson*.

                    *   *   *

It was like being inside a multistory Christmas
tree ornament, gazing out through wide-curving
transparency at heaven. Fleecy wisps of cloud
drifted past in the brilliant blueness here above the
low cloud cover the passenger module had passed
through earlier in its ascent up the orbital
tower—the beanstalk, as he still thought of it,
although explaining why to Aelanni had taken some
doing. Below, through rifts in that cloud cover, vivid
tropical greenness blended with vast swathes of
cityscape. Above, where the geostationary spaceport
facility that was their goal and the tethered asteroid
beyond (where, surely, the giant lived!) were still
invisible, the intense blueness shaded to royal and
then to navy, and the brighter stars winked.

He dragged his gaze inside and looked around at the
lounge, bathed in the intense (if, to his eyes, slightly
yellow-hued) sunlight of these altitudes. A throng
dressed with colorful but somehow restrained elegance
conversed in low tones, a musical murmur which
conveyed nothing to him. In the background, unfamiliar
instruments played a tune that was stately, highly
abstract and, he thought, slightly atonal. He would, he
decided, probably never grow to like Raehaniv music.

A figure detached itself from a group, back toward
him—a woman, tall and slender like most Raehaniv

but more muscular than most, in a clinging dress of some intensely emerald-green material that included a kind of hood. She set down her oddly shaped wine glass and pulled back the hood as she turned to face him, smiling impishly. Aelanni!

"Have you had enough for now, Eric?"

DiFalco nodded reluctantly, feeling slightly foolish, and reached up and fumbled with the wraparound goggles. Aelanni's smile was unchanged, though she was sitting behind a desk in her small shipboard office and wearing her usual shipsuit.

"That," he said accusingly, "was sneaky!"

She laughed softly. "One tries to come up with something more original than a message that seems to float in midair—and the computer isn't programmed for written English anyway. Besides, it was fun setting up the illusion; I haven't had a chance to dress like that in years! Of course, it isn't perfect, or you would have recognized me before I turned around."

"Oh, it'll do until perfection comes along," he assured her, running a hand through his dark hair (touched with gray at the temples, to her surprise inasmuch as he was less than fifty Raehaniv years old). "We've experimented with virtual reality ourselves—the concept has been around for some time, but neither the software nor the sensory input are up to it yet." He shook his head slowly. "You sure can't beat it for a travelogue! But . . ." He hesitated, embarrassed. "I imagine *anything* can be simulated. And you've mentioned that there's a suit-and-helmet rig that allows the sensation of full physical interaction. Doesn't it become, well, a problem?"

"Oh, yes, virtual reality addiction became a very real social problem in the era of the Fourth Global War—one of the many in those days. I gather it practically put an end to drug abuse among the affluent; how could chemicals compete? And escape from the real world was an irresistable temptation in those days." Somberness crossed her face like a cloud-shadow. "Since the Unification, of course, social pressure has worked against excessive and self-destructive indulgence in anything. It is a source of . . . guilt? No, that's not it. I think the English word is 'shame.' "

It occurred to DiFalco that the Raehaniv might have found more in common with the Sino-Japs after all, but he decided nothing could be gained by saying so. "Well, at any rate it's given me a feel for your world. It's as if I've been there. I can come a little closer to appreciating what you've lost . . . at least for now," he added hastily.

"Yes: for now. Just as you are preparing to lose your world for now." She sighed. "We never risked a landing; I have no . . . feel for your Earth. Of course you've told me of your memories of it. Indeed, you've made them *live*. But you've never really said anything of your own life there. What—or, perhaps, who—will you miss personally?" She stopped as if annoyed at herself. "Forgive me. I had no wish to pry into what you may consider inappropriate subjects. . . ."

He waved a hand absently. "Oh, no offense taken. There's just not very much to tell. Those of us out here generally don't have many deep attachments Earthside. . . ." He trailed to a halt, as a long-shut door swung open to reveal memories that were dappled with late-afternoon sun like his grandmother's kitchen. Then, too late, he remembered why he always kept the door shut. As always, he could recall for just a fleeting hurtful instant what it had felt like with Nicole . . . at first. And from there it was always the same futile, compulsive quest for the precise point at which it had gone irretrievably wrong—not when he had stopped trying but when he had admitted to himself that he no longer *wanted* to try. It must have been after Erica arrived, of that he was certain. Erica, who according to hallowed cliche was supposed to "bring us closer together" and had, in fact, merely been another thing to bicker over. Erica, who to Nicole was just one more weapon with which to exact vengeance for all her dreary little grievances . . . no, that wasn't fair. *Fuck fairness! I did my best, even when I no longer really thought it was worth it—when I couldn't even ask her a question without getting the "what's-that-supposed-to-mean?" look, and all I really wanted to know was . . . why didn't she ever smile anymore?*

He blinked once, and gazed across the desk at the woman from another star. "Not very much," he repeated. "A daughter, back on Earth, by a previous marriage. Seven . . . no, eight years old. Calls somebody else Daddy now. How about you?"

She shook her head. "I had a few relationships when I was younger, of course. But our customs discourage lasting attachments at an early age—a long history of overpopulation, you see." (She was, he recalled, slightly over forty Earth years old; he would have guessed late twenties—maybe thirty, tops.) "And more recently I haven't had the time. My father can be . . . demanding. Not that I can complain; he's given me opportunities beyond the dreams of most. And, to be honest, the men I've known have been . . ." She stopped, at a loss for words. "Our culture encourages a certain uniformity, possibly even blandness; we've always seen it as part of the price of peace, a price we've gladly paid. Still . . . every one of the men I've known as an adult has seemed like a book I've already read." She reached across the desk and placed a hand lightly over his, and their eyes met. "Am I making sense at all?"

He started to speak, cleared his throat, and tried again. "Yes, I think I understand. But look on the bright side." His lips quirked upward. "You can't say you're not in a position now to find . . . exoticism. Novelty."

"Yes, I believe I've found that, Eric."

Her hand didn't move. And, belatedly, he remembered how much more physical intimacy, even on the level of a touching of hands, meant to the reserved Raehaniv than to his own people.

Moving as if with a dream's protracted time-scale and lack of volition, he took her other hand and stood, raising her to her feet. Their eyes were almost level.

This is crazy! It's a complication we don't need! I'm not a goddamned horny teenager anymore! And even if we're technically the same species, the cultural differences . . . ! And isn't there something in Leviticus . . . ?

None of which seemed to matter very much. . . .

The door chimed a request for entry. It seemed very loud. Abruptly, time resumed its accustomed pace, and their hands snapped apart as if from an electric shock. But their eyes held each other for a bare, knowing instant before Aelanni spoke a Raehaniv word and the door slid soundlessly open.

"Ah, Colonel DiFalco! So glad you're here!" Varien smiled benignly as he bustled in. "I need both of you. Your Major Levinson has run into a problem with computer interfacing. It seems that certain problems are proving thornier than we had originally anticipated. He needs a command decision from you on structural modifications. And, Aelanni, you are far more up-to-date on cybernetics than I am. . . ."

"Of course, Varien. Lead the way." He turned toward the door, then stopped and faced Aelanni. "Oh, and . . . thank you again for the orientation regarding your world."

"Think nothing of it," she spoke just as emotionlessly. But they held eye contact just an instant longer. Varien still looked bland to the point of obliviousness as the three of them left the office.

*   *   *

"It is becoming increasingly apparent," Varien spoke briskly to the half-dozen people in the briefing room a few weeks later, "that not all our Raehaniv ships are needed here at any one time. Security requirements limit the number of American or

Russian ships that can be here for refitting simultaneously. Even after General Kurganov arrives on Earth and begins to expedite our arrangements at the highest levels of RAMP, there will be only so many absences that can be plausibly accounted for.

"I have therefore decided that two of our ships equipped for survey work can, for the time being, be better employed investigating the nearby stars known locally as Sirius and Altair." He turned to Kurganov and DiFalco, clearly in lecture mode. "The nature of displacement points is such that the more massive stars are more likely to possess them than the relatively small main-sequence stars which can have life-bearing planets." His expression suggested a certain annoyance with the universe. "So these two stars are the most likely possibilities in this stellar neighborhood. The Sirius and Altair expeditions will be commanded, respectively, by Nuraeniel and—" the briefest of pauses "—Aelanni."

"But, Varien," Kurganov inquired, slightly puzzled, "I recall you saying that displacement points occur at great distances from each other—normally a minimum of a hundred light-years. How likely is it that there would be others so close to the one at Alpha Centauri?"

"Actually, General, I said that displacement *connections* are that far apart. But it is not unheard of for unconnected pairs of displacement points to be relatively close to each other in realspace. You see, the displacement network is a product of the gravitational interrelationships of stellar masses . . . oh, yes, you already know that, don't you? Well, as a result the long displacement chains tend to run more or less parallel with each other, up and down the galactic spiral arms where most such masses are found; and they sometimes intertwine."

"Still, Varien," DiFalco spoke more stonily than was his wont, "what is the probability of these particular stars having any displacement points?"

"Quite small, actually," Varien replied with disarming frankness. "But if there are any accessible displacement points that might give alternative access to Raehaniv space, it would certainly be worth our while to find out. And, since it can be done without delaying our work here . . ." He let his voice trail off, and his eyes held DiFalco's for just an instant.

You know, you old buzzard! And you've found an excuse to send her out of harm's way, light-years from the primitive savage! Wouldn't do to let her get sacrificed to a volcano or something, would it? And she could never face the relatives with a bone through her nose!

No, let's be reasonable. He's just thought of all the same arguments against it that I have. And he's probably thinking more clearly than I am.

Still, Varien, may you roast in hell!

His eyes slid away from Varien's and met Aelanni's across the room. She knew.

*   *   *

The docking area that was the largest open space with life support in Phoenix Prime was full to capacity for the change of command. The honor guard dressed its ranks repeatedly under the eyes of Sergeant Thompson and his Russian opposite number, as the technicians counted down to the playing of the two national anthems. And beyond the spectators rested the shuttle that would take Kurganov to *Aleksandr Kerensky* for the voyage to Earth. They'd had some bad moments when the Earthside brass had wanted to change plans and have him take *Yeltsin*, which was in the process of refitting. A little creativity in accident reports had turned the trick, and the general confusion had enabled them to transfer several unreliable people to *Kerensky*.

Behind the sliding access doors, Kurganov and DiFalco awaited the signal to make their entry and mount the podium, unconsciously checking each other over. DiFalco's mood had not been improved by the older man's ribbing: surely, if he *really* tried, he could get his new full colonel's eagles even shinier!

Now, though, Kurganov had turned serious.

"No, Eric," he said quietly, "it is impractical. There would be no conceivable excuse for me to come back here just for the ignition of the Phoenix engine. And you will have no way to approach Earth; if one of Varien's ships came into detection range it would defeat our entire purpose of secrecy. And what about the pickup itself? Are you going to land a fusion-drive shuttle in Red Square? No, I must remain on Earth."

"To hell with that! I'll think of a way to take you with us."

"Ah, Eric, never stop being an optimist! I wouldn't recognize you." The general glanced at his wrist chrono. "It's almost time. I think this must be our real farewell. Remember me, however far you travel—you, and Varien, and Aelanni."

DiFalco blinked a few times—some damned crud in the air system! "Farewell . . . Seryozha."

Kurganov turned mock-pompous. "I've told you a thousand times: the familiar form is *not* used by a junior to a senior! And for another minute or so I'm still in command of this great ugly rock!" He shook his head sorrowfully, eyes twinkling. "You Americans have no respect—no sense of the proprieties."

"Just maybe," DiFalco heard himself say, "that's what will save us yet."

Kurganov looked at him for a long moment. "It always has in the past, Eric, but . . . I think not this time." His smile seemed to hold all the world's sadness. "In my grandfather's time, I could have watched with equaminity what your country is doing to itself. I might even have been tempted to indulge in what I believe Americans call the 'horse laugh.' But now my country has become a cultural dependency of yours, and if you go down into the dark you'll take us with you." He gripped his friend's shoulders, hard. "Come back, Eric! You must come back, carrying the stars in your hand! That's all that can save us now."

On his last word, the intercom crashed into the Russian anthem—first, for the outgoing CO—and there was no time for a final embrace. The doors slid open and they strode, shoulders aligned, to the podium.

* * *

It was off-watch, and no one disturbed the solitude of the wide-curving corridor outside the engineering spaces, bathed in starlight from the viewport where DiFalco and Aelanni stood, gazing alternately at each other and at the ship that she would, in a few watches, take to Altair.

The journey to the type A giant star was almost eight months' round trip under continuous-displacement drive. (The survey ship was not one of those that was built for speed and little else; she could only manage the equivalent of slightly better than fifty times lightspeed.) That, plus God knew how long surveying that star's vicinity for displacement points. *Yeah, Varien, I can tell you put some thought into this.*

And it was more than just the time factor. Varien had found the perfect rival for him: new frontiers. She hadn't admitted it, but while she contemplated the separation with genuine bleakness, it was clear that her excitement at journeying to yet another new star was equally genuine. The very qualities that had caused him to recognize in her a kindred spirit made it impossible for her to feel otherwise. Any nascent rebellion she might have felt had been a casualty of this war of emotions.

"I wonder how your father knew?" he wondered aloud.

She gave one of the expressive Raehaniv shrugs that Sergei had always said made him homesick. Which, in turn, reminded him of the Russian and deepened his melancholy. Soon Aelanni would be gone too, and he would be alone with the enterprise he had conceived and must now carry to completion.

CHAPTER SEVEN

The American election of 2060 drew closer, and with it Moving Day for Phoenix.

It had been, DiFalco reflected, over a year and a half since Kurganov had departed—a year and a half marked by unprecedented poor planning in the Project. Design change after wasteful design change, bungled components requiring replacements, flawed supplies and equipment . . . astonishing amounts of money pissed away to a rising chorus of protest Earthside. The protests would have been even louder if anyone had known that the "rejected" materials had been taken to a nearby region of the asteroid belt and used to jury-rig devices whose like no one on Earth had ever seen and whose very functions few could have recognized.

The administration had backed them to the hilt through it all, as it continued to hope for a political miracle. It had no choice anyway; it had been identified with the Project from its inception, and couldn't admit a mistake of such magnitude. So the supplies had continued to arrive while the political situation Earthside had continued to crumble. And they were all too aware that their own machinations had hastened the crumbling by discrediting the Project—a realization that posed a morale problem no one had anticipated. (Liz Hadley in particular had come close to an emotional collapse.)

But their morale had merely suffered erosion; that of the Raehaniv had received a hammer blow when one of the picket ships had arrived from Tareil after setting a new speed record for traversing the Lirauva Chain, bringing the news that the home system had fallen even sooner than expected. Raehan had surrendered when the Korvaash fleets had filled her skies and further resistance could only lead to planetary devastation. Certain local authorities had doubted the seriousness of the aliens' threats, on the grounds that dead populations and atomized industrial plant would be no economic asset to the conqueror; they had not lived to regret their miscalculation, and neither had some millions of people under their charge. (The Korvaasha clearly subscribed to the half-a-loaf philosophy.) And the effect of a falling orbital tower on the planetary surface was something no one had wished to contemplate. So Raehan's surviving cities now lived in the threadbare, hungry twilight world of occupation, a bleakness varied only by the occasional mind-numbing horrors inflicted with machinelike emotionlessness by the silent cyborgian giants who stalked their now-shabby streets.

It wasn't unexpected, of course; its very inevitability had originally driven Varien and his followers here on their desperate quest. And it didn't invalidate their plans, which had been predicated from the first on the assumption that no help could be looked for in the Tareil system save from whatever tatters of the Raehaniv space fleet continued to wage a guerrilla resistance in the system's asteroids (and, indeed, some had escaped there, under Arduin's leadership). But none of that helped. For a space of days the Raehaniv had withdrawn into themselves, as was their way in the face of the grief for which they had no acceptable outlet, and the Terrans had spent an embarrassed time—what can you say? Even Varien, knowing nothing of the fate of his son and grandchildren, had seemed inadequate, almost broken.

He had gotten over it eventually, of course, and become his old self. (DiFalco had surprised himself by being relieved.) But then the realization had grown that their estimates of their ability to raise the American and Russian warships to the technological level at which the Raehaniv and the Korvaasha waged war had been too optimistic; if the initial breakthrough into the Tareil system was followed by a long-drawn-out campaign, it was well that they would have access to the resources Varien had secreted in Tareil's asteroid belt, and the help of the free Raehaniv fleet there. So Varien's enthusiasm had been dampened, but never extinguished . . . until now, when he looked across the desk at DiFalco with eyes as empty of life and hope as they had been the day he had learned of the fall of Raehan.

"I fear, Colonel, that I bear heavy tidings," he sighed after lowering himself into the chair. He was acting every day of his age—almost ninety Earth years, DiFalco now knew—and the vitality that Raehaniv medical science could partly but not entirely account for was in abeyance. Under some circumstances, DiFalco would have felt sympathy. Today, he leaned forward and spoke with a self-conscious cruelty normally foreign to his nature.

"Oh? I suppose you mean that there's still no word of any ship returning from Altair."

Varien visibly flinched, as if from a sudden jag of pain. Nuraeniel had returned from Sirius when expected, reporting that binary star's lack of displacement points. But from Aelanni there had been no word. Ample time had passed for her to locate any displacement points Altair possessed, or to satisfy herself that there were none to be found, and return to Sol. Then still more time had passed. And now, with Moving Day less than three months away, there was no question of sending a rescue mission to Altair. Aelanni and her crew were presumed lost.

"No, there is not," Varien said slowly, "although that isn't what I meant." He drew a deep breath, seeming to gather his strength. "Aelanni understood the risks involved, Colonel. She was not . . . *is* not a soldier, in your sense—we have had none for a long, long time, as I have explained. But she has always had a comparable sense of duty." He paused. Was there the slightest hint of malice in his eyes? "And, if memory serves, she showed no great hesitation about leaving, Colonel!"

A cold anger flared in DiFalco, banishing everything he had started to feel for an old man who had reason to believe both his children were dead. "Yes, there is something soldierly about her, isn't there? She'll follow orders . . . no matter what she thinks of them! No matter how cynical and unworthy she knows their motivations are!"

For a long moment they glared at each other in dead silence. It was a subject they had both shied away from—this was the closest either had ever come to an open acusation. It was Varien who blinked first, and lowered his eyes with a sigh.

"Whatever I did was done for the good of everyone concerned. You can have no conception of the cultural gulf! And Aelanni has led a life that perhaps leaves her unprepared for some things . . . unable to see beyond the glamor of novelty." He stopped with an annoyed look. "But I have permitted myself to be distracted from my original purpose, Colonel! A ship has, in fact, arrived under continuous-displacement drive . . . but from Alpha Centauri!"

DiFalco at once forgot everything but the implications of Varien's news. It went without saying that the Raehaniv had known about the ship's arrival first; their gravitic technology included grav scanners, capable of realtime detection over interplanetary distances due to gravity's instantaneous propagation. They could detect a ship's emergence from a displacement point—although the scanner, being directional, had to be trained on the displacement point at precisely the right time. And the continuous-displacement drive, with its ongoing series of intense grav pulses, showed up like the proverbial sore thumb. Both were, of course, undetectable by any instrument known to Earth's science. (He recalled, with a flash of amusement, the we-are-alone types in the last century who had made much of the absence of visible Bussard ramjet exhausts in the skies between the stars.)

"Alpha Centauri," he repeated. "So it can only be . . ."

" . . . the remaining picket ship from Tareil," Varien finished for him. "Which was under orders to abandon its station and come here under one and only one set of circumstances. I fear, Colonel, that that ship brings news that transcends our personal concerns—even our concern for Aelanni."

* * *

Naeriy zho'Troilaen was young for a ship captain, but she had aged quickly of late. That was clear as she told her story in the briefing room of Varien's ship. (It still bothered DiFalco that the Raehaniv ships lacked names; the custom had never arisen among them. Wasn't it supposed to be bad luck?)

"The Korvaasha began routine surveying almost as soon as they had settled into their occupation of Raehan. It seems they didn't trust the official records, taking for granted that our government must have been keeping secrets. At any rate, it was sheer chance that one of their ships blundered onto the fourth displacement point. We stepped our power output down to miminal life-support levels and waited them out. After they departed, we powered up and transited—they had no reason to have a grav scanner trained on the displacement point by then. We then," she finished anticlimactically, "proceeded here."

Varien slowly rose and faced the Terrans—most of the original members of the cabal. The Raehaniv in the room already knew, and their expressions made clear their understanding of the implications.

"We are undone," he said in a voice of ash. "The Korvaasha now know of the Lirauva Chain—we must assume that they have already begun to explore it. Our base at Alpha Centauri has been obliterated"— Naeriy nodded in confirmation—"so even when they reach it they will have no certain knowledge that we have been there. But they will, at a minimum, mount a heavy guard on Tareil's fourth warp point, and garrison the systems between Tareil and Alpha Centauri as quickly as they can survey them, merely as a matter of routine procedure." His dark eyes held all of theirs as he spoke the doom of all their hopes. "We can no longer enter the Tareil system from an unsuspected displacement point, which has been the basis of our plans from the beginning. We would have to assault a defended displacement point—hopeless in itself without overwhelming numerical superiority—after fighting our way through several intervening systems." His concentration seemed to waver, and when he resumed it was with a vague bewilderment that, in him, was shocking. "I never dreamed that the Korvaasha would discover the fourth displacement point so soon . . . their instrumentation is so unsophisticated . . . well, they *have* had centuries of experience in surveying. . . ."

"Wait a minute, Varien," George Traylor interrupted, brow furrowed with thought. "Okay, so we can't follow the, uh, Lirauva Chain to Tareil. But even if we can't do it the easy way, via displacement points, can't we still do it the hard way?"

"What do you mean?" Varien barely sounded interested.

"Well, why can't we take your continuous-displacement drive all the way back to Tareil? I know it's a long way. But we could enter the Tareil system from nowhere near *any* displacement point!"

"*That'd* shake 'em up!" Levinson leaned forward, dark eyes snapping.

"Don't be absurd!" All at once, Varien was his old, fortunately inimitable self, and once again DiFalco was surprised at his own relief. " 'A long way' indeed! It is, in point of fact, a thousand of your light-years! At the maximum speed of which most of our ships are capable, that means a journey of . . ."

" . . . almost twenty years. And since we're not talking about real velocity, there's no time dilation effect. Yeah, yeah, yeah." Traylor did not take well to being patronized, which made for problems in dealing with Varien. "But you Raehaniv are way ahead of us in cryogenic suspension; you can actually freeze the metabolism altogether, not just slow it down. Maybe we could spend most of the trip frozen, and man the ships in shifts!"

Varien took a deep breath. "Permit me to elucidate certain facts. First, the suspended-animation techniques to which you refer involve substantial risks. If the subject is to have an acceptable chance of safe revival, an extensive array of equipment is needed. We have very little of such equipment, never having needed it except in rare medical emergencies. Even if it is practical for us to build more of it—as to which I would have to consult with medical experts—such a project would make our departure deadline even more unrealistic than it is already proving to be.

"Secondly, as a practical matter the journey would take far, far more than twenty years. You must understand that the continuous-displacement drive, involving millions of intense gravitic pulses per second, requires *enormous* amounts of power, even on the standards of our technology. To make the concept workable, I had to develop a special type of fusion reactor, which attains an unprecedented output-to-volume ratio at the expense of fuel efficiency. It consumes hydrogen at a rate which necessitates frequent refueling—most of our ships can only sustain continuous-displacement drive for thirty or forty light years. Fortunately, the refueling requires no special facilities; we can skim hydrogen from the atmospheres of gas-giant planets and process it into useable form, using the same techniques with which we obtain reaction mass for our fusion drives. But it takes time! And we could not proceed in a straight line; we would have to . . . 'leapfrog' is the expression, I believe, from one hopefully planet-bearing star to another."

They were silent. They had all known, in the abstract, what an energy hog the continuous-displacement drive was, but they hadn't thought through the implications. There had been no need to—the drive merely had to get them to Alpha Centauri!

No one even suggested collecting hydrogen from the interstellar medium en route with the electromagnetic ramscoops so beloved of twentieth-century science fiction writers; such a thing was still beyond Earth's engineering capabilities, and the Raehaniv had never developed it. Besides, as Varien was overly given to pointing out, the continuous-displacement drive, with its ongoing series of quantum jumps, imparted no actual velocity beyond what the ship already possessed at the time it engaged the drive. A ramscoop would require near-relativistic velocities.

"Thirdly, we would not even know what star to set our course for." Varien saw the surprise on his Terran listeners' faces. "Oh, you didn't know that? Well, we've never *had* to locate Tareil in the sky—it's just one of the countless millions of small main-sequence stars roughly a thousand light-years from this one. In fact, that realspace distance, like its approximate bearing, is only an estimate we arrived at using the positions of certain identifiable supergiant stars as seen from here and from Tareil—an intellectual game of no practical value, since we travel between here and there using displacement transitions.

"Finally," Varien continued in a voice whose despair could no longer be masked by annoyance, "the whole idea is fundamentally impractical. It is beyond belief that ships—especially improvised ships using hybrid technology—could endure over twenty years of continuous-displacement flight, stopping and starting thirty or more times, without suffering breakdowns. No engineer would take such a notion seriously." Traylor's expression confirmed it. "No, I fear we must relinquish our hopes and begin to consider what other alternatives are open to us."

DiFalco and the other Terrans sat, stunned. However irritating Varien could be, he had become more and more their oracle, with his knowledge of things far beyond Earth's horizons. If he had indeed abandoned hope, then what hope was there? And none of his "other alternatives" could be pleasant ones for them, who had effectively burned whatever bridges were not being burned for them on Earth.

Varien seemed to sense it, for when he spoke it was with an odd gentleness. "You of Earth—no, of RAMP—have committed yourselves to this enterprise on the strength of my promises, my schemes, and my hopes. I fully recognize my responsibility to you, and you may rest assured that whatever plans we Raehaniv make will take that responsibility into account. . . ."

All at once, a computer that had never been taught manners cut in with a stream of Raehaniv that seemed to come from the middle of the air. The effect was electrifying; Varien, suddenly agitated, snapped out a series of queries to which the computer responded in its precise way, while the other Raehaniv sprang to their feet in an incomprehensible babble of excitement. DiFalco cursed himself for not having learned more Raehaniv—there had never been a pressing need, as all the Raehaniv knew English. He had picked up some, of course, but even people like Rosen who were approaching fluency in it were baffled by this rapid-fire exchange.

Varien finished with what was clearly a command to the computer and then turned to the Terrans, switching to English. "Your pardon. The ship's computer, which has had standing orders to maintain gravitic scanner coverage of the appropriate region of space, reports a ship's arrival, under continuous-displacement drive, from the direction of Altair!"

A storm of exclamations and questions followed, but DiFalco heard nothing after Varien's final word.

* * *

"We detected Altair's two displacement points almost immediately after our arrival. So I decided to test out the experimental devices for predicting the realspace direction of a displacement point's terminus."

Aelanni was addressing a briefing room that was full to capacity—predominantly with Raehaniv, but also as many Terrans as could manage to be there for the tale of her adventures. All of them knew, or had been told, that heretofore the only way to find out where you would arrive after transiting an unfamiliar displacement point was to actually do it. Now it was possible to infer the bearing of your destination in advance, and the more experienced Raehaniv space captains were already being heard to mutter that the younger generation had it soft.

"The results for one of the displacement points were inconclusive," she continued. "But the second one provided unambiguous readings: the displacement chain clearly led in the direction of Raehaniv-explored space!

"I therefore decided to take *Pathfinder* through and confirm these findings." She gave Varien the kind of apologetic/embarrassed/defiant look with which a teenage daughter presents her father with the *fait accompli* of an unconventional hairstyle that she *knows* he doesn't like. And, for a fact, Varien didn't like the way the younger Raehaniv were starting to bestow names on their ships in the Terran fashion. His expression showed it as he sat in the front row beside DiFalco, two men united in their mixed emotions.

"Why the hell didn't you come back and report this instead of charging through on your own?" Difalco blurted out. "I . . . we were worried sick! Of all the . . . !" He could not continue. He could only look at her, lovely and strong, a living dark-red flame, eyes gleaming as if with the reflected light of suns they alone had seen. He was absolutely furious with her. And he loved her as he had never loved her before, as he had never imagined it was possible to love anyone.

She smiled at him, but answered in precisely the tone one would use to address a senior officer of an allied power. "I judged that to be an impractical course of action, Colonel. Even if I had returned immediately, and even if another ship could have been dispatched without delay on my arrival, simple arithmetic shows that that ship would barely have been able to go to Altair and return here in time for our scheduled departure date. It would have had no time for any extensive displacement-point exploration. The fact that *Pathfinder* was already on the scene gave us a priceless opportunity to investigate a highly relevant new datum."

DiFalco had no answer. He and Varien subsided as one, exchanging a rueful glance of shared futility.

"We transited the displacement point," Aelanni resumed, "and emerged in the vicinity of a young type Fliv subgiant"—she used Terran stellar classifications for the benefit of her American and Russian listeners as she indicated a light in the holographic display generated by the ship's computer from data downloaded from *Pathfinder*—"which proved to be almost three hundred light-years closer to Raehaniv space, and which possessed three displacement points. Using the new instrumentation, we chose the most likely of them, and transited to a red giant/white dwarf binary which seemd no closer to Tareil than the previous star, though at a significantly different bearing from it. This, and the fact that the binary possessed no planetary bodies suitable for refueling caused us to seriously consider turning back. However, we still had enough reaction mass to cross the binary system to its other displacement point."

Varien could no longer contain himself. "And what if the next system had had no gas giant planet from which to obtain more reaction mass? How, pray tell, would you have gotten back?"

"That," she admitted thoughtfully, "might have presented a problem. But," she hurried on before her father could have a stroke, "inasmuch as the vast majority of stars seem to be accompanied by gas giants, the commonest type of planet by far, I deemed the risk to be an acceptable one. At any rate, we transited"—a white light obligingly flashed along the string of pale-blue luminescence indicating the final displacement connection of what was already being called the Altair Chain—"to find ourselves in a G0v system with only the one displacement point. We were able to determine that this system is only ten light-years from Seivra in realspace." As the Raehaniv all began to talk at once, she explained to the Terrans. "Seivra is a system without habitable planets. It has been known to us for some time because it is only one displacement connection from Tareil. In fact, it is separated from Tareil in realspace by little more than one hundred light-years." As they sat absorbing the implications, she continued to the room at large. "What is more, the star has a life-bearing planet. The ecosystem is a rather young one, and the planet is less than comfortable for us . . . but we can live there!"

The hubbub rose in volume, then began to subside as DiFalco stood up and turned to face the crowd. He waited until he had silence.

"I think, people, that what we've just heard knocks our earlier gloom and doom into a cocked hat." Most of the Raehaniv had never heard the expression, but they caught his meaning. "The front door to Tareil may be closed to us now, but Aelanni has given us a way of entering through the back door!"

Varien also rose, and faced the American. "If I understand what you are suggesting, Colonel . . ." He shook his head uncertainly. "Remember, we've already come to the conclusion that we can't be fully ready by our departure date, and that we will therefore need the help of the Raehaniv resistance fleet in the Tareil system. There would be no such help awaiting us in an uninhabited system."

"No, there wouldn't. We'd have to make our own help." DiFalco swung around as he spoke, facing everyone in turn, and his voice gradually rose in volume. "When Moving Day for Phoenix arrives—less than three months from now—that's the end of the Project. We'll *have* to depart this system. That's the inflexible deadline we've been up against from the beginning. We can depart under continuous-displacement drive then, taking as much of our industrial plant as possible . . . depart for Altair, not for Alpha Centauri! Once we've transited the Altair Chain and established ourselves on this new planet, we'll be able to complete our preparations. Oh, yes, we'll have to do it on our own; we'll be isolated like no other group of human beings, Terran or Raehaniv, has ever been isolated before. But we won't have a rigid deadline to work against! We can take however long the job requires. I say we can do it!" Traylor nodded slowly, and some of his Raehaniv counterparts began to do likewise.

DiFalco turned back to Varien. "Can you suggest any viable alternative?" The question could have been belligerent, but it wasn't; it was asked in a tone that was oddly deferential.

The old Raehaniv gazed at him for a long moment. Then he smiled, and spoke almost inaudibly. "No, I cannot." He sat down, and a few in the room dimly sensed that a change of command had occured, as surely as the one that had accompanied Kurganov's departure, for all that it had required no honor guards or music.

*   *   *

"I *still* wish you'd come straight back! The risk . . . !"

Aelanni gave him her impish smile. "And if I had, where would we all be now?"

"Don't confuse the issue with facts!" DiFalco grinned at her like an idiot—he suspected he had been doing that a lot, of late—as she stood in the starlight of the wide viewport outside *Liberator*'s engineering spaces, which had become a special place for them. (Varien had, with much grumbling, granted his crew's petition to name the ship. The name was really *Arhaelieth*, but English translations were more and more widely used.) On an impulse, he reached out and brushed a lock of hair away from her forehead, emphasizing her hairline—it came to the sharp widow's peak that characterized far more Raehaniv than Terrans, one of the little differences of degree that kept popping up whenever one began to forget that the two races had spent at least thirty-two thousand years a light-millennium apart. She flinched slightly at the physical contact that was still less than entirely natural to her, then relaxed, her smile softening.

"I missed you," he said, silently cursing himself for banality.

"And I you." She paused, then continued hesitantly but irrevocably. "I knew what father was up to when he sent me to Altair. And I could understand his reasons, and even share them to some degree, for I was frightened of what was happening. So part of me kept hoping that his plan would work. But it didn't. And that part of me, that frightened part . . . it isn't here anymore. I left it somewhere out beyond Altair."

With utmost gentleness, they came into each other's arms. Through the armorplast, the stars continued to gleam, unnoticed.

CHAPTER EIGHT

Moving Day arrived.

Phoenix was, despite everything, ready to move out of its immemorial orbit and swing into the sunward course that would bring it into collision with Mars. Ballistic calculations of incredible sophistication and complexity had been required to assure that the two bodies would arrive at the same place at the same time. Planning of nearly equal subtlety had assured that the relatively few remaining personnel to whom the conspiracy had not been revealed, and they alone, were at the small observation station near Phoenix—as near as would be reasonably safe when the mammoth fusion drive was ignited. They, of course, *knew* that everyone else was aboard the various ships to observe the event from other vantage points while they handled the ongoing transmission to Earth.

There were, of course, a few exceptions. . . .

* * *

Major Levinson and Sergeant Thompson walked briskly along the curving corridor in Phoenix Prime. On their approach, Corporal Ramirez came to attention at his post outside Computer Central.

"As you were, Corporal," Levinson acknowledged. "Sergeant Thompson and I need access."

"Certainly, sir." Ramirez indicated the retinal scanner beside the hatch.

"You go first, Sergeant," the Space Force major said offhandedly. "I just remembered something I need to check." He set his briefcase on a ledge projecting from the bulkhead and unlocked it with a snap.

"Aye aye, sir." Thompson moved to the scanlock, Ramirez turning to watch him and therefore missing the object that Levinson drew from the briefcase. It consisted of a small box with a pistollike grip and, extending from what seemed to be the front end, a translucent probe surrounded by metallic rings that tapered to smaller and smaller diameters toward the tip. Holding it like the pistol that it resembled in size and overall shape, Levinson aimed it at the corporal's back.

Suddenly, Thompson's face lost all expression, and he crumpled silently to the deck. Ramirez, momentarily paralyzed by the sheer unexpectedness of the sergeant's collapse, began to open his mouth just as Levinson pressed a firing stud, producing no visible effect and only a faint whining sound. But Ramirez fell unconscious, in the odd way things fall under the Coriolis force of a spin habitat.

"Bravo, Sergeant," Levinson said, smiling, as Thompson got to his feet. "An amazing performance—I hope everybody put on as good a show for the people we're leaving behind. The world lost a great actor when you joined the Big Green Machine."

Thompson grunted skeptically. "What's amazing is *that*." He indicated the major's Raehaniv stunner. "When I was in covert ops, there were times when I would have given my left nut for one!"

Levinson couldn't argue. The thing projected ultra-high-frequency focused sound that attacked the target's nervous system, resulting in unconsciousness (lasting for hours if the zapping was done at this range) but producing no ill effects beyond a splitting headache on awakening and leaving absolutely no physical trace. He imagined there were crowd-control types who would echo the sergeant's sentiments.

Without further conversation, they carried Ramirez to the airlock where he would join the other non-cleared individuals still in Phoenix Prime. They would awake to find themselves aboard a shuttle, non-functioning save for life support and the emergency transponder that would bring quick rescue from the ships now raptly observing Phoenix. And each of them would have the same memory of passing out in company with whoever was in his or her field of vision. And a mystery would be born, to dwarf that of the *Mary Celeste*.

* * *

DiFalco listened to the last of the reports and, nodding in satisfaction, signed off. (Communications security was not a problem; all their ships had Raehaniv neutrino-pulse communicators now.) He swiveled his chair around to face Varien and Aelanni.

"Everything appears to be in readiness. I'd better get back to *Andy J.*"

"And I should return to *Pathfinder*," Aelanni added. DiFalco had hoped they could be side by side at the moment of departure, her clean features and darkly burnished hair silhouetted against the blazing star-fields that seemed her natural and proper backdrop. But they each had their own responsibilities. The Raehaniv lacked, or had forgotten, many of the unwritten laws that enshrined the intangible mystery of command; but they were relearning them, and *Pathfinder* was Aelanni's ship now, beyond all possibility of argument or evasion.

Varien looked at one of them, and then the other, and smiled faintly. He had long since resigned himself to the inevitable, but DiFalco could never be absolutely sure how much was resignation and how much was secret satisfaction. The old Raehaniv was, after all this time, still awfully hard to figure out. *I*

*suppose I'll never really know where I stand, Varien.
So I suppose I should stop worrying about it.*

Spontaneously, they all turned to the holo tank at
the center of *Liberator*'s control room, in which was
displayed their fleet—such as it was. Four *Washington* class cruisers—*Andrew Jackson, Theodore
Roosevelt, Ronald Reagan,* and *Judith Kramer*—and
three of their Russian *Aleksandr Nevsky* class counterparts, led by *Boris Yeltsin.* A gaggle of
interplanetary personnel transports and cargo carriers
which, like the military cruisers, had been equipped
with Raehaniv fusion drives and continuous-displacement generators. Varien's twelve survey/factory ships
(variations on the same basic class as *Liberator* and
Pathfinder) and five fast courier ships. A few thousand Terrans and a few hundred Raehaniv. The bolt
they were preparing to hurl at an interstellar empire
of unknowable extent and limitless resources.

Aelanni shook her head slowly. "We must be
crazy!"

DiFalco smiled crookedly. " 'If we weren't crazy
we'd all go insane.' " They both recognized a quote—
Varien from his in-depth knowledge of English and
Aelanni from her in-depth knowledge of him—and
two left eyebrows rose in unison. He smiled more
gently and explained. "Jimmy Buffett. A poet of my
people. Last century. Seems every generation since
his death has rediscovered him." His eyes strayed to
the viewscreen, from which the barely visible blue
planet of his birth was absent—mercifully so. For his
mind had, unwillingly, free-associated from tropical
beaches across ocean and steppe to a colder land
and a man who would remain there despite a promise DiFalco had meant to keep.

*I tried, Seryozha. I even thought I had something
worked out, a couple of times. But you were right all
along. There was no way. There never was.*

Forgive me.

*   *   *

A small sun flamed into life, seeming to erupt from the asteroid Phoenix—an asteroid which began to move ponderously into a new orbit, which was to be its final one.

The enormous outpouring of gamma radiation from that artificial sun (or, strictly speaking, ongoing series of suns) would have been fatal to any organic observer at close range. But remote cameras transmitted the spectacle to the people of Earth, who watched transfixed, not noticing the departure of an unsuspected fleet of vessels from another region of the asteroid belt.

DiFalco stood on *Andy J.*'s control room deck, to which he was attached by the serene one gee of Raehaniv artificial gravity, and marvelled at the inventiveness inspired by humankind's quest for comfort.

The Raehaniv vessels were designed with an "aft-equals-down" orientation. The bogus weight supplied by their drives served when they were accelerating— sometimes too much so, when powerful accelerations were called for and the waste plasma of their fusion-powered photon drives was dumped into the exhaust, causing the flames that twentieth-century science fiction illustrators had considered essential to belch forth; the crews simply took it. In free fall, the artificial gravity fields operated in the same direction.

But Terran spacecraft were arranged otherwise. In their control rooms and spin habitats, aft meant toward the rear bulkhead—not a great problem for vessels that were usually in free fall. The ships couldn't be rebuilt from scratch, so a way had to be found to make them liveable under conditions of long-term acceleration. The application of fresh Terran perspectives to Raehaniv technology had produced the solution. Now the spin habitats no longer spun; some gravitic generators provided a "down-equals-inboard" orientation for them, while others compensated for whatever acceleration the ship was undergoing. It was a cumbersome, Rube Goldbergish arrangement, which the Raehaniv would never have thought of if they hadn't been faced with the problem of adapting quaint, pre-gravitic designs. But it had started Varien thinking, and now he was working hard on the software for a genuine inertial compensator—the "acceleration damper" that had always eluded him. DiFalco wondered how many more unthought-of possibilities would emerge from the cross-fertilization of Raehaniv and Terran viewpoints.

For now he was content to take advantage of this one, although he and the others who passed for old-timers in the Space Force still found the absence of the familiar sensations of free fall and acceleration unsettling. It was almost comforting when the artificial gravity wavered queasily—not all the bugs were out of the system—as the drive cut off and it shifted to free-fall mode. They had reached the cold outer regions beyond the orbit of Uranus, where the continuous-displacement drive could be engaged without interference from Sol's gravity well.

"Colonel," Loreann zho'Trafviu said quietly from her communications console, "Varien reports that all Raehaniv ships are ready to commence continuous-displacement drive." Every Terran ship had a Raehaniv gravitics technician to intercede in technological realms where Americans and Russians were still newcomers, and Loreann would implement DiFalco's commands. A glance at a status board showed him that the Terran ships were likewise prepared.

"Acknowledged," he spoke formally. "Tell him that we will be ready as soon as the purging of our data bases is complete." Loreann spoke a liquid Raehaniv sentence, and the fleet was effectively tied into *Andy J.*'s command net for the departure.

"Major Levinson," he continued, "please execute." Levinson's fingers flew over the keyboard that was still used for operations above a certain level of complexity, and blocks of data—indeed, the fact that the data had ever existed—began to vanish from the memory of *Andy J.*'s computers. The same was happening on all the Terran ships, as it already had aboard the Raehaniv ones.

DiFalco gave a further series of terse commands, setting in motion phase after phase of the long-planned procedure. When it was over, nothing remained in the fleet's data bases that could be any use in identifying, or finding, Sol. The coordinates of the displacement points in the Altair Chain remained, but they would be wiped in succession as each transit was made. All printed matter had already been sanitized.

Earth's people were, unknowingly, secure in what amounted to an informational black hole. And the fleet had cast off from its last moorings, with nothing but a star to steer by: the blue-white flame of Altair, dead ahead.

But every Terran eye in the control room was on the shrunken sun in the view-aft screen, and every imagination pictured a now-invisible blue planet orbiting close to its warmth. A long moment passed before DiFalco turned to Loreann and spoke the command that sundered them from that world.

There was no sensation of motion. Indeed, there was no *motion*, in the true sense. But the little yellow sun in the screen began to shrink with soul-shaking rapidity.

That he could see it (and Altair, far too distant to be visibly growing in the forward viewport) was, DiFalco knew, no mystery. The ship still possessed only the velocity it had attained in its journey to the outer system—considerable, but far from relativistic. And now, making several score thousand instantaneous displacements per second, its occupants saw the outside universe as if it were a video film with that many thousands of exposures per second. And so the sun, impossibly, receded in the screen at an apparent rate of over fifty times lightspeed without any visual distortion. The more theoretically minded among the scientists were still muttering darkly about things like "causality violation."

(No, of course the displacements weren't *really* instantaneous. As Varien never tired of pointing out, that would have required an object to be in two places at the same time. He'd just never succeeded in measuring the time elapsed. At some point, he was sure, the drive's pseudo-velocity would run up against an upper limit imposed by quantum indeterminacy; but as yet there was no indication of what that limit was.)

DiFalco thought of none of these things. He looked around the control room at his fellow Americans, from whom America was receeding more swiftly than light, and knew he must say something.

"We're not leaving our country," he began hesitantly. "We're taking it with us! We're not leaving *this*!" He slapped the stars and stripes on the left shoulder of his space service grays. "It meant something once, and we're taking with us the memory of what it meant. All we're leaving behind is the bullshit!" He took out his brown Ethnic Entitlements Card.

"Our country made a mistake, long ago, in drawing distinctions between groups of people. Then, in the last century, we froze those distinctions into law so that we could try to atone for them by *reversing* them instead of simply abolishing them. Well, that's all over. From now on, among us, men and women will be judged as individuals—the way they should have been judged in the first place—and not as symbols of some historic grievance that political careerists can cash in on!" He strode to the waste disposal chute and thrust in the card. It flamed for an instant as it was reduced to its components. He turned and swept the control room with his eyes.

Levinson gave DiFalco a smile that spoke volumes, and flicked his card into the chute.

Sergeant Thompson stepped slowly forward, looked DiFalco in the eye, and said, "Now people will know for *sure* how good I am!" His ebon card followed Levinson's white one into the chute.

One by one, everyone in the control room followed suit. Loreann looked away . . . this was not her rite. When it was over, they all looked at each other with a self-consciousness that might have seemed strange, given that they had all committed, or been accessories to, offenses under American law that were far worse than the minor felony of destroying an Ethnic Entitlements Card. But this act was a symbolic one; it was their final rejection of what America had become and, by the same token, their reaffirmation of what it had once been. Everyone was silent for a moment, and then looked to the view-aft screen.

Sol had dwindled to a mere star, lost among the star-fields. They could no longer find it.

                    *   *   *

Snow had fallen for two days, and tonight it blanketed Smolenskaya Street. Sergei Kurganov, looking skyward from the window of his third-storey apartment, could see that the clouds were finally breaking up. It must, he reflected, be a relief to the guards out there keeping watch on this window.

Like everyone else connected with the Project, he had been placed under house arrest by a government which was feeling the primordial tingle of fear in the face of unfathomable mystery. He couldn't deny that he had been treated well, under the circumstances. But now superstitious terror was beginning to shade over into vindictiveness. Some, he knew, had been tortured. He was too high-ranking for that. But soon would come the drugs from which truth could not be withheld. *How sad, that courage, loyalty and friendship count for nothing in the face of mere chemistry!*

Yes . . . I have waited too long.

He turned and took a quick look around the apartment, eyes lingering on the photo of Irina as she had been, a decade and a half ago, before she had died with the child she was carrying. He squared his shoulders, strode to the display case, and took out the Nagant Model 1895G officer's revolver that his great-grandfather had carried in the Great Patriotic War.

All the arrestees had, naturally, been denied weapons. But this wasn't a weapon. Of course not. It was an antique. He took out the brass cartridges which had also seemed self-evident antiques to men who were searching for caseless ammunition cassettes, and loaded the pistol. It was good to know that some things were forever unchanging . . . like the stupidity of *chekists*, or whatever they were currently calling themselves.

He next took out the equally-antique silencer. As a rule—and contrary to the belief of twentieth-century television producers—revolvers could not be effectively silenced. The gas-sealing Nagant was the exception. And the guards in the corridor need not be alerted any sooner than necessary. With any luck they wouldn't know until breakfast was delivered.

Preparations completed, he returned to the window. Yes . . . rifts were appearing in the clouds.

I shouldn't have waited so long, he thought again. *It was an unwarranted risk to take. But I had to wait until the snowstorm ended and I could see the stars.*

He gazed at the twinkling, ice-rimmed lights between the clouds. Altair wasn't visible, of course. That would have been too much to hope for. These paltry few stars would have to do.

*   *   *

For what Varien insisted were perfectly logical reasons, displacement points occurred at great distances from giant stars. So the blue-hot inferno of Altair appeared small in viewports that were polarized to shield human eyes from a light at which they had never been meant to gaze. And the fleet had been able to approach reasonably close on continuous-displacement drive before commencing the maneuvers that would bring the ships into correct alignment for transition.

Now DiFalco stood in *Andy J.*'s control room and reflected that the universe needed a good special-effects man. Nothing showed ahead but stars, with Altair flaming off to the side. The displacement point itself was perceptible only to Raehaniv instrumentation—and even for that instrumentation it was more a matter of inference than of detection.

Aelanni, and *Pathfinder*, had led the way, vanishing eerily. Others had followed, and now it was *Andy J.*'s turn. DiFalco had done his part, directing the ship into the volume of space that defined the displacement point. Now he could only turn to Loreann and give the command: "Execute!"

The stars wavered in the viewport as the space-distorting gravitic pulse built up. Then, too quickly to fully register on human optic nerves, they seemed to crowd together and then explode outward before settling into a serene new pattern. Simultaneously, every human felt a sensation, over almost too quickly to be felt, that something had *happened*—something outside the ordinary range of human experience in that homely subset of reality described by Newton.

DiFalco and Levinson looked at each other, shaken. "Did you feel that, XO?"

Levinson nodded. "Yeah. It wasn't painful. It was just . . . *wrong*."

"One grows used to it," Loreann put in. "We haven't been able to account for it; the displacement has absolutely no detectable physiological effect. But everyone feels it. Evidently the ongoing small transpositions of the continuous-displacement drive are individually too slight to trigger it. And we have learned that the Korvaasha do not experience it. Varien has speculated that it may operate on the same level as psionic phenomena, a subject which is still as much an uncharted swamp to us as it is to you."

"In short, he doesn't know squat about it," DiFalco grunted, obscurely pleased. He gazed out the viewport, studying the sky.

Constellations are invented by people who live at the bottom of a dense atmosphere that filters out all but the brighter stars; in deep space, they are lost among the unwinking stellar multitude in which only trained eyes can discern patterns.

DiFalco had such eyes, and even without the white sun that shone off the port bow it would have been clear to him that *Andy J.* lay in a new sky, rendered unrecognizeable by a transposition of three hundred light-years. Not only Sol but even Altair was invisible. And, all at once, he knew what he had only thought he had known four months earlier, when they had departed Sol: absolute severance from his home and the home of all his ancestors, the setting of all his memories.

So be it.

"X.O.," he said in a voice of iron, "wipe the data on that displacement point from the computer. Mr. Farrell," he continued, turning to the helm, "proceed in formation with *Pathfinder*, to this star's other displacement point."

They drove on into the void.

CHAPTER NINE

One by one, the ships flickered into existence in yet another new sky. After the last one, with its mismatched stellar pair (an intense little white dwarf whipping in a high-velocity orbit around a bloated red giant that somehow seemed bored with its antics), this one made them homesick. The distant G0v sun was very nearly the yellow-white of Sol—a half-shade whiter, just as it was fractionally hotter, more massive, and therefore more luminous.

And, DiFalco reflected, there was an even better reason why this system should seem like home. It *was* home now, at least for the immediate future, and they might as well get used to it.

Not only the sun but also its family of planets had a homelike aspect. He had studied the data from Aelanni's initial survey; the planetary orbits more or less conformed to the old Titius-Bode Relation (as did those of almost all the systems on which the Raehaniv had data, which had given the Terran astrophysicists furiously to think) but were slightly more closely spaced than those of the Solar System. The fourth planet, their destination, was only 1.28 astronomical unit from its sun, putting it just beyond the outer edge of what would once have been thought to be the liquid-water zone, before the discovery of what had once been river beds on Mars had caused a rethinking of such things.

One difference was the lack of a well-defined asteroidal belt. Here, no Jupiter-sized bully of a gas giant had precluded a planet's coalescence by its brutally disruptive gravity. The largest gas giant was little more massive than Saturn. It was for this planet—the seventh outward from the sun—that their course was now set.

Using a giant planet's gravity well as an interplanetary "slingshot" was not a new concept; Terrans had used it to speed their earliest unmanned probes into the outer Solar System. Computer projections of the relative positions of this system's planets at the time of their emergence fron the one local displacement point had suggested the possibility of using the technique to shorten their travel time to the fourth planet. That this system was being so obliging to its new residents seemed to DiFalco an excellent omen.

Of course, he had never heard of doing it with a fleet before. Varien and Aelanni had assured him, via communicator, that there was no theoretical difficulty involved . . . but, to be on the cautious side, the ships would proceed one by one rather than attempting the manuever simultaneously, in formation.

*   *   *

The gas giant grew rapidly until it seemed to fill the universe, banded in shades of orange and yellow, with swirling storms that could have sucked all Earth down into the deep hydrogen atmosphere under those methane/ammonia clouds. It lacked the ring system that graced many such planets, but it possessed the usual extensive family of satellites.

With its occasional, unpredicatble course corrections, this would have been a rough ride indeed without artificial gravity. As it was, *Andy J.*'s control room crew kept to their acceleration couches as the ship began to swing around the "rim" of the gravity well, down which it otherwise would have fallen without hope of escape. That awesome pull would now be used, in a kind of cosmic judo, to fling them onward . . . as it had already flung *Pathfinder* and *Liberator*.

DiFalco was thinking about the first of those ships, and its captain, when Aelanni's voice come over the communicator, taut with more strain than could be accounted for by the bumpiness of the ride.

"Urgent," she snapped. "All ships in position to do so should train every available sensor on the third satellite!"

He looked at the situation board. Yes, that satellite was in view, just "above" the limb of the planet. No one had thought of looking at it before; it was so ordinary, doubtless an asteroid captured from this system's relatively sparse supply of such bodies.

"Why?" he asked.

"Just do it!" Her voice was even harsher. "There's no time to explain. But I think you'll understand if you look at a blowup of the imagery you're getting."

He gave the necessary orders, and Levinson entered the commands to *Andy J.*'s computer. The ship's main telescope was now slaved to the little satellite, and its image appeared, after a moment of wavering snow, on DiFalco's command screen. He gazed at it critically—a very typical specimen of such bodies, irregular in shape (unlike the larger moons, which were massive enough to have been rounded into spherical form by their own gravity), a mere flying mountain. What had gotten Aelanni so upset?

"Anything unusual about that rock, X.O. ?"

"Not really," Levinson replied. "Pretty low density. And maybe its albedo is a little higher than predicted—and getting more so as our relative motion takes us into view of its other side. Maybe something odd about its composition . . . we'll have to wait a while for the spectroscopic readings. But otherwise . . . Hey!" He sat bolt upright in his acceleration couch. "The albedo *can't* be that much higher on this side! I mean, this is almost what you'd expect for worked metal. . . ." His voice trailed a halt. DiFalco knew why; he had also seen that which stood revealed as the satellite rotated relative to *Andy J.*

Worked metal indeed . . . and patterns that incorporated straight lines. Expanses of artificiality amid the rough surface, like the visible surface components of an installation that must occupy much of the interior. *What was that again about low density, Jeff?*

No lights, though. No activity. Just an impression, as overwhelming as it was without logical foundation, of deadness.

He finally opened his mouth to say something . . . and the maneuver was completed. *Andy J.* sped on toward the fourth planet, leaving enigma behind.

*   *   *

"No." Aelanni shook her darkly burnished head. "There was absolutely no indication of life on—or *in*—that moon. Of course we tried to communicate, but all we got was silence. And we had our full battery of sensors trained on it for as long as we were within range. If there's any power supply there, for life support or anything else, it doesn't involve fusion reactors or anything else that produces neutrinos. And passive IR confirms the impression that we all had: the entire satellite is uniformly cold. No," she repeated, "that base, or whatever, is dead."

She was addressing a hastily convened meeting in *Liberator's* lounge. It had been their first order of business after taking up orbit around Planet Four. But, by common consent, they had met not in the usual briefing room but somewhere with a viewport. DiFalco's wasn't the only gaze that kept straying to the planet which curved so majestically and invitingly below.

Mass 1.57 times Earth's. Surface gravity 1.18 G. Axial inclination 37.21 degrees, augering a lively climate. And so on . . . none of which seemed to relate in any way to the heart-stopping blue loveliness, swirling with clouds and crowned with blindingly-white polar caps, beyond the viewport. Not exactly the same blue as Earth, of course—this planet had a somewhat denser atmosphere, and its oceans covered nearly nine tenths of its surface. But still . . .

I last saw such a sight from Earth orbit, about to depart for Mars and then the asteroids . . . how long ago? Not even my final memory from Earth—Erica crying that she didn't want me to leave, and Nicole's glare of cold resentment while pulling her away—could spoil that sight! I thought surely I'd see Earth, and Erica, again. Eventually, as the letters got fewer and more dutiful, I gave up on the second. But never the first.

And now . . .

He turned back to the holographic image of that rocky little satellite that had suddenly disrupted all their calculations. The ships following *Andy J.* had had advance warning before they swept around the gas giant, and had been able to obtain far better imagery than Levinson's hurried efforts had produced; the computers had produced a detailed composite. Rosen was studying it dourly, while referring to a table of figures on his perscomp.

"The excavations must be extensive," he said at last. "In fact, the installation must take up most of the satellite's interior. The average density is *much* lower than it should be for a body like that." Planetology was his specialty, and nobody argued with him.

"The real puzzle," George Traylor rumbled, "is what the hell it's doing here. Who built it?"

"Could it be the Korvaasha?" Rosen sounded skeptical even as he posed the question.

Varien, who had seemed lost in thought, looked

up. "Hardly. This system has only one displacement point, at the end of a displacement chain entirely unknown to them. And even if they could have gotten here, why would they have built an outpost on a gas-giant moonlet and ignored *this*?" He waved a theatrical hand in the direction of the life-bearing planet they orbited, on which absolutely no trace of past occupancy had been observed. "And finally, the mind boggles at the thought of them abandoning a system they've occupied; it runs counter to their entire mentality."

"Are we, in fact, absolutely certain that the base is abandoned?" Arkady Kuropatkin sounded glum. The mind-set of the professional security officer is not an optimistic one.

"Come, Arkady Semyonovich," Colonel Aleksandr Ilyich Golovko chided. He was the senior Russian officer, and thereby DiFalco's second in command. "You've heard Aelanni's reasons for supposing it is. And ever since we arrived here we've had every available scanner activated at full power, and we've detected no activity of any kind in this system."

"Still," Aelanni said thoughtfully, "there's only one way to be absolutely sure." She looked at her father and DiFalco in turn. "I want to take *Pathfinder* back to that gas giant and investigate the satellite in depth. This needn't delay the disembarkation here; the preliminary landings and tests can proceed while we're outbound, and of course we'll transmit confirmation that the base is deserted as soon as possible."

"Agreed," DiFalco said. "With one proviso: I'm coming." He turned to Golovko. "Sasha, you're in charge in my absence. We'll be in continuous contact." The exiles' "government" was still an ad hoc affair. The old Management Council of RAMP had been expanded to include Raehaniv members, while the military CO continued to wield what amounted to ongoing emergency powers.

Varien wasn't a member of the Council. His position

was a curious one: an advisor whose advice was always followed.

The whole thing would have to be regularized eventually, of course. But for now it seemed to work.

Varien was nodding emphatically. "Yes. It is essential that we learn all we can about that base without delay. I don't take seriously the notion that it could still be occupied, or that it was ever connected with the Korvaasha. But the fact remains that it is a high-technology artifact in a system with no connection that we know of to any high-technology civilization. We can never be secure here with such a mystery in our skies!"

DiFalco and Aelanni looked at each other and then at the blue planet that would have to wait a little longer.

*   *   *

Rosen had been right; the satellite's surface was little more than a shell around the installation through whose endless passageways they now floated, speaking in hushed voices as though in the presence of ghosts.

They had been prepared to use Raehaniv weaponry to gain access to the silent base, but that had been unnecessary. A vast spacecraft hangar deck had stood open to vacuum, and *Pathfinder* had maneuvered gingerly into the satellite's airless interior. By then there had been no further room for doubt that the base was abandoned.

"Abandoned" was, in fact, precisely the right word. There was no indication of violence or destruction, from battle or any other cause. The occupiers had simply packed up and left, stripping the base of everything moveable with single-minded tidiness and leaving it infuriatingly bare of any clues to their identity.

Some things could be inferred, though. One look at the dimensions of rooms, doors and so forth had satisfied Aelanni that the builders had not been

Korvaasha; everything was too small. They must have been on the same order of size and shape as humans. And they had possessed the technology of artificial gravity—that much was clear from the installation's layout. As to their other capabilities there was little evidence, save for one fact. There was no sign that there had ever been any way to close the hangar deck's cavernous opening, and yet various indications led the Raehaniv specialists to conclude that the deck had not been designed for airless operations. The builders must have used some kind of nonmaterial barrier that allowed space vehicles to come and go but kept air in—a thing beyond Raehaniv capabilities.

And that, DiFalco thought sourly, was about all they had: inferences from negatives. They were even having to scrounge for radioactives with which to determine the installation's age.

His train of thought was suddenly derailed as Aelanni, floating beside him through this wider-than-average corridor, suddenly stopped short with a burst of compressed gas from her EVA stick. "Wait, Eric. The grav scanner indicates a very large empty compartment beyond this." She indicated a wall.

"That the door to it, maybe?" He pointed at a portal, a little further down the corridor. Like others in this sector, it evidenced attempts at ornamentation—stylized fluted columns flanking it, and a kind of pediment overhead—which were entirely lacking in the rest of the base, with its stark utilitarianism.

"Let's find out." They drifted through the opening into a space so large that the helmet-lamps of their heavy-duty vac suits could not make out the walls. A short Raehaniv sentence, spoken to Aelanni's implanted communicator, brought the team that had been following them with heavy lighting equipment.

Light flooded the space, large enough to have been a ballroom and clearly designed for some ceremonial function. Here was more architectural elaboration than they had yet seen, notably a series of decorative bas-relief carvings around all four walls. At first DiFalco thought they looked like infinity symbols, or figure-eights lying on their sides. Then he pushed himself forward for a closer look, and saw them for what they were.

Planets. Each was a world depicted as two hemispheres joined side-by-side, as if they had swung open at some equatorial hinge. There were no alien map-making conventions to confuse him, just obvious continental outlines.

"Well, they couldn't take *these* with them," he observed dryly. "They're an architectural feature. Of course . . ."

"Eric," Aelanni interrupted in a voice that brought him up short. She pointed at one of the maps. His eyes followed her finger . . . and, all at once, he saw nothing else.

After a moment, he grew aware that Aelanni was speaking quietly in Raehaniv, and he was sure that a map of Earth was being projected directly onto her vision. "It doesn't seem quite right," she spoke hesitantly. "Peninsulas seem . . . fatter. Of course, it's obviously a work of decorative art, and isn't necessarily intended to be a precise representation. But *this* . . ." She indicated the Mediterranean—or, rather, where the Mediterranean ought to be.

He had already noticed. When he spoke, it was like an automaton.

"Oh, it's precise enough—but not for the present era. This is what Earth looked like during the last ice age, when a lot of water was locked up in glaciers. The ocean level was lower than the strait—we call it Gibraltar—at the mouth of that sea. So there were just those two big connected lakes. There were a lot of land bridges where there are straits now. Like there"—he indicated the connection between Britain and the European continent—"and there." He pointed to a dry Bering Sea that the remote ancestors of the Cherokee had yet to cross—and his skin prickled.

"Eric," Aelanni spoke as if against her will, "how long ago was this ice age?"

He turned to face her squarely. "I'd say this map represents the situation around thirty thousand years ago, Aelanni."

For a long moment they looked unseeingly at each other as the implications sank home. Then, without a word, Aelanni began darting grimly—almost desperately, it seemed—from one of the carvings to another.

It didn't take long to find the map of Raehan.

* * *

"So that's the story?"

DiFalco and Aelanni nodded in unison to Levinson's question. "Yes," the woman amplified. "We just finished giving the Council our full report. We have nothing to fear from that satellite. Nothing, that is, but a new set of enigmas."

"Well," Levinson began hesitantly, "doesn't this at least settle the paradox of two unconnected human races? Whoever built that base must have taken Palaeolithic humans, and other animals, from Earth to Raehan."

DiFalco laughed harshly. "Yeah. Somebody—identity unknown—may have done it, for some unknown and unimaginable motive. And afterwards . . . *where the hell did they go?* As far as I'm concerned, we're just as much in the dark as before; we're just more tantalized!"

"Anyway," he continued, "for now we can table the problem. We're alone in this system, and the transfer of our population from orbit is almost complete. The Council got a lot accomplished while we were gone." He smiled. "I was glad they went along with my suggestion for a name for this planet."

"Right!" Levinson snorted. " 'Terranova.' Very appropriate choice!"

"Well, it is," DiFalco insisted. "it means 'New Earth,' which this certainly is . . ."

" . . . and it's a word that comes easily to Rae-
haniv-speakers. I know, I know. And of *course* you
being Italian"—"One-quarter Italian," DiFalco muttered, unheard—"couldn't possibly have anything to
do with it!"

"Of course not," DiFalco replied blandly. Aelanni
smiled dutifully; child of a culture whose local languages and national identities were centuries in their
graves, she was still getting used to this kind of
byplay. That the Russians used not just a different
language but even a different alphabet was still
beyond her comprehension.

"Oh well!" Levinson gave a resigned sigh which
turned into a yawn. "It's been a long day. I'm going
to crash. See you two tomorrow." He walked down
the hillside toward the cluster of new buildings, leaving the night to the other two.

They still hadn't adjusted to the beauty of Terranova's nights. The planet—unique anong known
life-bearing worlds, according to Varien—possessed a
ring. It wasn't as spectacular as that of Sol's Saturn,
of course; just the fragments of a moonlet whose
orbital decay had brought it within the planet's
Roche Limit. In fact, it was invisible in daylight. But
on a clear night in these latitudes, it was a sparkling
faery-bridge arching overhead. Both moons—neither
as massive as Luna, but both closer and with higher
albedos—were visible tonight, revealing a landscape
of mountainous grandeur. (More massive than Earth,
Terranova had a hotter interior, hence a more active
geology.)

On a more prosaic level, the planet's biochemistry
presented few dangers to humans. They could eat the
local life forms without ill effect, though several
vitamins were missing; Terran and Raehaniv food crops
would always be necessary as dietary supplements.

DiFalco looked at Aelanni's profile in the double
moonlight. She was holding up well, but like all the
Raehaniv she would take longer than the Terrans to

think of this world as home, if she ever could. The higher gravity, colder climate and whiter sun were little more than novelties to Terrans; to Raehaniv, bred of a warm world of deep-yellow sunlight and 0.87 G gravity, they were burdensome.

He wanted very much to speak of her high fine courage in words that would convey all that he felt—but, as always, he achieved nothing but a renewed realization that he was not, and would never be, a poet. She spoke first, and it was of other things—of the mystery that lived in the outer reaches of this system.

"Do you think we'll ever know the answer?"

"I can't say," he spoke almost gruffly. "All I know is that we can't worry about it now. We have too much to do, and too much depends on it."

They walked, arm in arm, toward the infant town.

CHAPTER TEN

Even in these times it was good to be home. And Tarlann, while as cosmopolitan in background as most Raehaniv, had for most of his life thought of Sarnath as home.

He had left Norellarn that morning by suborbital shuttle—Norellarn, where only a tropical village had stood before the coming of the orbital tower and where today's megalopolis had no roots in the soil from which it thrust its gleaming modernity skyward. Of course, the centers of all Raehaniv metropoli were like that. And many of the older cities had fed the flames of the Fourth Global War. But Sarnath had stood for almost six thousand of Raehan's years, wearing the clothes of one civilization after another (and having those clothes ripped from it by one conqueror after another); in its older districts the works of those civilizations were visible like geological strata. An apartment building that had been a luxury hotel in the last innocently manic days before the First Global War might rise from a foundation that had been the base of a temple when the Khaemiriv Empire had ruled half this continent with iron swords and built on the foundations of its own bronze-age predecessors. In the shadow of soaring towers of crystalline metal and transparent plastic, crooked old streets opened unpredictably onto plazas laid out by forgotten princelings, and eccentric bridges spanned the Lural River while aircars flitted overhead. A kind of historic erosion had worn a dozen architectures down to a curiously harmonious unity that was uniquely and recognizably Sarnathiv, giving the city the kind of character that can only come from millennia of civilized occupancy.

Sarnath's peculiar ambiance of sophisticated urban continuity, together with its economic importance, had made it the natural capital city for Raehan's world government. Inevitably, it had become the focus of much of the Tareil system's financial activity. Varien, born in Trelallieu (though of mixed ancestry like nearly everyone else), had moved the headquarters of his enterprises to Sarnath when Tarlann was still a boy. It was among the narrow streets and picturesque taverns of the Old Town's university district that he had undergone the adolescent discovery (unique in all history, as it always is) that the world was not precisely as he had been led to believe as a child.

Now he was back in Old Town, walking incognito—he had always managed to keep out of the public eye—along a street which ended at a seawall overlooking the estuary of the Lural, on whose opposite shore the modern towers blocked out half the sky like a wall of faceted light. It was a fine spring night—the seasons had returned to normal, as the planetary weather had cleansed itself of the atmospheric detritus of the Korvaash nuclear strikes—and he could almost imagine himself a young man again. Almost.

Even Old Town had changed. It had not escaped the creeping squalor that seemed to be growing over all of urban Raehan like a fungus as more and more resources were diverted to feed the conquerors' forced-draft heavy industries. The social fissures that were opening as real want began to encroach on Raehan's lower income levels were a matter of indifference to the Korvaasha. Indeed, Tarlann often wondered if they secretly welcomed any source of divisiveness among their subjects. Even if they had never thought of it on their own, it might well have been suggested to them by those who now swaggered past in the orange coveralls of the Implementers of the Unity.

The first Raehaniv collaborationists, Tarlann reflected as he stepped aside as was required, had been motivated by classic Raehaniv rationalism—or, at least, able to frame their motivations in rationalistic terms. After all, were the Korvaasha not utterly indifferent to human life? Had they not shown that the continuity of human society concerned them only insofar as that society supported the industry which now served them? And so, the argument ran, would humans not be better off under a puppet government of their own kind than under the direct rule of aliens whose language contained no such concept as "mercy"?

And yet, Tarlann thought as he stepped off the curb into the stinking runoff of a sewage system whose new energy allocation was more and more overloaded, the well-meaning intellectuals of the early days had been elbowed aside and pushed out by thugs like these two who strode past in such a way as to take up the entire sidewalk. The human type that had supplied the totalitarian regimes of the Global Wars era with secret policemen and concentration-camp guards had never disappeared, as people had fondly imagined after the Unification. It had merely bided its time, awaiting better days; and now it had returned to Raehan, wearing an orange coverall and restrained only by its alien masters' requirement that productivity not be impaired.

He stepped back onto the sidewalk after the two Implementers had moved on, dourly contemplated the filth on his expensive shoes, and proceeded along the street toward Dormael's wineshop.

*   *   *

The taproom was narrow but extended far back from the street entrance. Only a few furtive customers clustered around the small tables under the low ceiling with its age-darkened beams.

Dormael approached, smiling. He had the look of the original Khaemiriv-speaking people of this city: short and stocky on Raehaniv standards, getting fat in middle age.

"Ah, Tarlann! Welcome! It's been a long time."

"Yes," Tarlann drawled. "I've been in Norellarn. Ghastly place. What a relief to be back in civilization! Speaking of which . . . I trust you have, ah, entertainment tonight?" His left eyebrow rose with his inflection.

Dormael's expression grew even more unctuous. "But of course! Please come this way." As he turned to usher Tarlann through an inconspicuous door in the rear wall, he signalled almost imperceptibly to one of the drinkers and received an equally subtle acknowledgment.

They proceeded along a narrow, crooked corridor, Tarlann's assumed personna slipping from him as he walked. (He sometimes wondered if he overdid the languid foppishness. Not *all* the Implementers were stupid brutes, after all. A few of them were clever brutes.) The final doorway on the right gave access to a small, functionally furnished room. Dormael let him in, then departed without a word. As he entered, a lean middle-aged man rose from a table.

"Greetings, Tarlann! You can talk; I've been able to use my equipment freely in here, and I guarantee this room is secure."

"Then it's secure." Tarlann gave the forty-five-degree bow that was the equivalent of a firm and enthusiastic handclasp. "I was worried, Tharuv. After your last escape . . . well, never mind. How is Arduin?"

"Older and tougher. Also crazier. Everybody in the asteroids is by now." For an instant his eyes saw far

beyond old Sarnath to the asteroid belt where the
Free Raehaniv fleet continued to disrupt the flow of
raw materials and harass the Korvaasha.

Tarlann seated himself and stared at the tabletop.
"You know, I've often daydreamed about joining you
out there."

Tharuv looked at him sharply. "Don't talk
nonsense, Tarlann! What you're doing here—what
you're in a unique position to do—is far more
important than playing space pirates! We couldn't
function without you as our planetside contact. . . ."

"Yes, yes, I know. But have you ever thought of how
bloodless that all is, Tharuv?" His eyes held a look that
would have shocked anyone who had known him in the
prewar era that seemed to be receeding beyond
memory, leaving people wondering if they had merely
dreamed such a world. "I have to sit around, playing
the fool and watching them ruin Raehan, and I've
never once been able to do anything direct—I've never
been able to strike back at them!"

Tarlann stopped abruptly. He couldn't even voice
his real source of frustration: the utter lack of news
from his father, as the years had passed and they
had learned of the Korvaasha's discovery of the
fourth displacement point and subsequent exploration
of the Lirauva Chain. So he hadn't even been able
to bury his hopes—they lingered on, undead.

But he knew that he was only fantasizing about
seeking oblivion in space combat. If nothing else,
there was his family to consider. And this Tharuv
also knew.

"Well," the Free Raehaniv officer finally said,
"here's something you can do to help *us* strike back
at them: get Luraen hle'Nizhom offworld for us!"

Tarlann looked up sharply at the name of the emi-
nent gravitic engineer. "You're in contact with him?"

Tharuv nodded, which meant the same thing to
the Raehaniv that it did to most Terrans. "He wants
to join us. We can arrange the contact with your

people. If you can provide him with a new identity and get him into space, we'll take it from there."

"Of course," Tarlann nodded. "I was just in Norellarn, greasing the people we need so that the company's passenger manifests for the orbital tower aren't looked at too closely. I'll . . ."

An ear-bruising explosion shook the building, followed by a chaos of screams and shouts. Their eyes locked for an instant, before Tarlann spoke with a steadiness which pleased and surprised him.

"Come on; Dormael has an emergency exit in the hallway."

Without a word, Tharuv rose to his feet and they moved toward the door—just before it was flung open and Dormael staggered in, clutching a bleeding abdomen. Tharuv ran to him, weapon already out—a laser pistol, characteristic arm of a spaceman, for whom its lack of recoil more than made up for its susceptibility to the defensive aerosols that nobody wanted to fill a closed-cycle artificial environment with anyway. The taverner had just collapsed in his arms when the Implementers appeared in the doorway, orange coveralls largely hidden by the combat dress they wore.

Tharuv dropped Dormael and got off one shot, stopped by the reflective material that made up one layer of his target's combat dress. The Implementer staggered backwards from the kinetic energy transfer, but two others' railgun carbines opened up on full automatic with a horrible crackling sound as the steel needles went supersonic. Rows of tiny holes appeared in Tharuv's back, and the wall behind him was sprayed with blood. The little hypervelocity flechettes didn't knock a man over backwards; Tharuv just stood still for a fraction of a second, then blood gushed from his mouth and he collapsed. Tarlann, not even in shock yet, managed to raise his hands, palms outward.

The Implementers crowded into the room, two of them grasping Tarlann by both arms while a third searched him. An assault leader swaggered in, idly swinging a truncheon. He surveyed the room supercilliously, finally running his eyes over Tarlann's expensive clothes. He started to turn away . . . and then, without any warning, raised his truncheon and brought it down on Tarlann's right kneecap with all his strength.

Beyond a certain level, pain overloads the nervous system's capacity to perceive it as pain. Tarlann, passing this point as he collapsed, heard as if from a great distance his own screams and the assault leader's rasping voice.

"Kill the others but bring this rich piece of shit along. The Director wants to question him."

*   *   *

They had given him something to dull the sickening pain, and he was able to appreciate—if that was the word—the headquarters from which Gromorgh, Director of Implementation, oversaw the subjugation of Raehan.

Whole city blocks had been demolished to make room for the fortresslike structure, so typical of Korvaash construction (you could not call it "architecture") in its massive, crude, utilitarian hideousness. The inside, he decided, was even worse. No attempt had been made to ameliorate any noise, stench, inconvenience, filth, or ugliness in a structure whose perpetrators had stopped at minimum functionality.

The Korvaasha, he thought through his haze of drug-masked pain, must have been civilized once. Surely civilization was a precondition to the development of high technology. Which led him to the depressing conclusion that technology could survive the death of the civilization that had created it. Or—even more depressing—perhaps this was what civilization looked like in its Korvaash manifestation.

He had little but these dreary thoughts to occupy him as he waited in a cold, dimly lit chamber—brutally massive, grimy, with bunches of power cables hanging

fron the overhead against unfinished walls—with three
Implementers (the assault leader and two underlings)
who shuffled their feet and darted furtive glances
around the home of their owners. The Implementers'
attitude was not doglike; they were as incapable of
loyalty as they were of any other decent impulse. They
felt nothing for their Korvaash masters but fear.

Suddenly, the huge door slid open with a grinding
crash, and two Korvaash guards stalked in.

It was difficult to make sense of the Korvaasha at
first glance—alienness posed a barrier to coherent
impressions. It was hard to say why; the overall
design—bilaterally symmetric two-armed biped, aver-
aging a third again the height of a man—wasn't
fundamentally weird. Of course, part of that height
was accounted for by a long thick neck, and the
blocky torso itself was broad even in proportion. And
the skin was thick, tough and wrinkled, in shades of
gray, with no apparent hair. But it was an indescrib-
able wrongness about every angle and proportion,
and about the mechanics of movement, that gave
humans the flesh-crawling sensation that the Korvaasha did not belong in the universe . . . that, and
the head. The head was the worst.

Four slits on each side of the neck performed
the functions of respiration and speech. The head
itself—armored with serrated ridges of bone under
skin that was unpleasantly thin on top—held a wide
gash of a mouth that served only for the ingesting
of food (a process that no normal human, and few
abnormal ones, could watch without nausea),
pulsating tympanums that served for ears on the
sides, and the single eye that, while perhaps not
overtly repellant, was the most deeply disturbing
feature of all. It was a darkly glowing amber, with a
faceting pattern that allowed for depth perception.
A human was ill-advised to gaze into it for long.

But what was most instantly noticeable about the
guards was not their alien physiology but the extent to

which that physiology had been replaced by machinery. The Raehaniv had made a fine art of lifelike bionic replacements; the Korvaasha had never bothered. Artificial arms with built-in weapons, sense-enhancing implants, and the rest were attached obscenely to the flesh that had been chopped away to make room for them. But at least these two were only ordinary warriors, not the totally cyborgian elite of whom little that was natural remained other than the brain.

The two enhanced Korvaasha took up positions on either side of the door, and Gromorgh himself entered. The stench of fear exuded by the Implementers grew truly disgusting.

The Director of Implementation was short for a Korvaasha, and lacked any visible enhancements. But he wore around his neck the pendant that produced realtime Raehaniv translation of the wearer's speech, in frequencies humans could hear rather than the inaudibly low Korvaash speech. (The Raehaniv had once thought the aliens communicated by telepathy, especially given the distance the subsonic speech carried.) Likewise, a device attached by suction to the head beside the ear-membrane enabled him to understand human speech. It was a kind of technology that had been successfully discouraged on Raehan, on the grounds that it would remove all incentive for linguistic unity.

At a gesture from the assault leader, his two subordinates grabbed Tarlann by the arms, hauled him up from the floor and slammed him to his feet. No drugs could suppress the pain that shot from his knee through his entire being; only nausea prevented him from fainting.

The assault leader stepped forward, demonstrating that it is possible to crawl in an erect posture. "Director, we have brought our fellow inferior being Tarlann hle'Morna as you commanded. He is . . ."

"Silence." Gromorgh's pendant emitted the flat, tinny "speech" that made him seem even more machinelike than his enhanced soldiers. His eye contemplated Tarlann. "Your contacts with the feral inferior beings of the asteroid belt have long been known to us. But your death would result in more disruption and loss of productivity than we wish. Instead, you will remain in your present position, heading the enterprises you inherited when your father died."

Again Tarlann almost fainted, this time from relief. The Korvaasha still believed Varien was dead; all this had nothing to do with the Lirauva Chain, and suicide would not be necessary.

"But," Gromorgh continued, "in the future you will report to us on the plans of the feral inferior beings. Thus you will buy your life . . . and theirs." He gestured with a hand whose four fingers were all mutually opposable, and two more Korvaasha entered the chamber, shoving Tarlann's wife and children in front of them.

Nissali's eyes were glazed with terror, but she clutched her son and daughter convulsively. Iael's fear warred with his early-adolescent boy's pride. But Tiraena, for whom puberty still lay a couple of years in the future, was too young to understand what was happening to her; her uncomprehending fear was still tempered by wide-eyed wonder at the novel surroundings.

"Daddy!" she cried out, great dark eyes widening even more, and tried to run to Tarlann. Nissali, darting a terrified glance at the nearest Korvaash guard, restrained the child with desperate strength and locked eyes with her husband.

"Director," Tarlann stammered, thinking furiously, "the Free Rae . . . the feral inferior beings may not trust me after seeing me emerge from this building. They will assume I am working for you. . . ."

"It will be your task to make them trust you," the mechanical voice cut in. "I see that you need more incentive. You have not yet learned that we are to be taken seriously." He looked down at the woman and the two children. Irresistably, their gazes were drawn to that enormous eye. Tiraena looked upward and actually gave Gromorgh a tremulous little smile.

The Director made an abrupt gesture and one of the guards, moving with the speed of the bionically enhanced, grasped Tiraena's small head in his massive hands. Her scream died aborning as he wrenched her head around almost almost a full circle and her neck snapped. He dropped the small, weakly twitching corpse to the floor and, too quickly to fully register, it was over.

Tarlann, existing in a universe of horror in which time did not exist, heard Nissali's gasping sobs as she tried to form a scream that would not come, and saw Iael's eyes glaze over with shock. But mostly he heard the empty expressionlessness of Gromorgh's voder, addressing the assault leader. "Laerav, you may have the remains. I believe your perversions include a preference for immature females of your species . . . and that you are not averse to the recently deceased."

The assault leader stepped forward, anticipation momentarily overcoming cravenness on his face. Little flecks of spittle appeared at the corners of his mouth.

Tarlann, moving like an automaton, tried to break away and reach toward Laerav. One of the Implementers, grinning, smashed the butt of his weapon into Tarlann's fractured knee. Tarlann crumpled to the floor and vomited, over and over.

When he was finally aware of his surroundings again, that which had been Tiraena was gone, as was Laerav. A part of what Tarlann had been was gone too. He tried to make eye contact with his wife, but there was nothing there to make contact with. Nissali was no longer there; she had taken refuge in a place where her baby was with her and the Korvaasha could not follow.

"I have illustrated," came the voice from Gromorgh's pendant, "what should already be obvious: since the lives of individual members of our own species mean nothing to us, the lives of individual inferior beings mean less than nothing. If you do not cooperate to the full, or if you attempt any treachery, the female and the immature male will be made available to the Implementers before being butchered, and you will watch both processes."

Tarlann looked up into the face that held no more expression than the uninflected mechanical voice. When he spoke, it was with a strange calmness that came of having passed beyond all feeling except a certain curiosity.

"You don't even enjoy it, do you?"

"Your question is without meaning. I simply do whatever is necessary to further the expansion of the Unity. It must incorporate the entire accessible physical universe into itself. This is the only imperative. Nothing else matters."

"But . . . why?"

"This question, too, is meaningless. When our race attained the Unity we reached the end of all such philosophical problems. The Unity settles the question of means and ends, for it is both means and end. It settles the question of good and evil, for it is neither good nor evil. It simply is. The Unity is the goal toward which all sentient life strives, however unknowingly, for through it sentience will eventually be transcended—in the absence of choice, thought itself will become unnecessary. But its guiding control can only be entrusted to our race, which brought it into existence. Your species, and all other inferior beings, can aspire to no higher destiny than to serve it in subordinate capacities.

"The fundamental fallacy of your values is revealed by the fact that you allow yourselves to be intimidated and dominated by the specimens of your race that are, by the terms of those very values, the lowest: these vermin that we employ." Gromorgh gestured at the Implementers, whose cringes intensified lest they inadvertently display any resentment. "This is why we use them. They will continue to keep your race terrified and submissive, so that it can better serve the Unity under our direction. Thus it will be . . . forever.

"Remove him."

* * *

Arduin stared at the tabletop as he listened to the report, oblivious to the occasional exclamations from the others. Tharuv dead. The entire operation centering on Dormael's establishment exploded. And Tarlann . . . ?

No one could be sure. He had been taken to Gromorgh's headquarters, as had his family. Later, he had emerged—alone. And there were no apparent obstacles to resuming contact with him, which was in itself suspicious.

"Of course," Daeliuv was arguing, "we can take advantage of the fact that we *know* they're using him. We can pretend we don't know it, and feed them false information through him." Since becoming the Free Raehaniv intelligence chief, the former professor had displayed a surprising aptitude for the more devious aspects of espionage. Maybe it wasn't all that different from academic politics.

"*Rhylieu* shit!" Yarvann's outburst was characteristic, and not nearly as startling as it would have been in the old days. They had all changed; Yarvann had merely changed a little more than most. He was one of the rare Raehaniv who had actually taken to military life. The wiry little man had been the space fleet's most aggressive combat officer before the fall, and one of the few officers in Arduin's experience who actually managed to look right in the uniforms that had been inflicted on them. In fact, alone among them all, he still wore them—or, at least, his own flamboyant versions, complete with a brace of custom-made laser pistols. In a historical drama, or a space-pirates fantasy, nobody would have believed him. But as a combat commander he was still in a class by himself.

"I know Tarlann," he was saying, "and he'll never betray us! What we need to be thinking about now is reprisals! If we don't keep the initiative, the *mneis-afv*-fuckers will think they've shocked us into immobility. It's time to activate our plan for hitting one of the big mining stations here in the asteroids."

Daeliuv ignored all of Yarvann's speech except the first part. "He would not *willingly* betray us, granted. But . . ."

"You're all forgetting something." Arduin's flat voice came abruptly from the head of the table. "You're forgetting what Tarlann knows."

There was a shocked silence. All of these people knew the truth about Varien—Arduin had had to reveal it, to give them a gleam of hope. And they *had* forgotten it. It had become easier and easier to forget as the years had passed with no sign of the old man and the allies he had gone to seek. But now they remembered that Tarlann knew it too— which meant that the Korvaasha might now know it.

But their silence also said that it probably didn't matter very much. None of them really expected Varien to ever return, whatever had happened to him and the others at Landaen. They hadn't expected it since the day they had learned of the Korvaash discovery of the Lirauva Chain, for they knew full well what that meant for Varien's schemes. There would be no relieving fleet for them to aid. They fought on simply because, knowing what was happening to their homeworld, they could not do otherwise. They could continue the struggle for a long time, but not forever. Sooner or later, the Korvaasha would wear them down and starve them out. And eventually the Korvaasha would stumble onto the secret of the continuous-displacement drive, whether or not Tarlann had already revealed to them its basic principle.

Arduin was silent, his face like stone. But inwardly he wept—for Raehan, for the Landaeniv (or whatever they called themselves), for all humanity.

CHAPTER ELEVEN

Liberator floated in high Terranova orbit, the picture of lordly serenity—or so it seemed to DiFalco, viewing it from the safe remoteness of Kurganov Station. Any time now . . .

There! A series of flashes awoke against the blackness of space off to one side of the Raehaniv ship, without apparent cause. Squinting, DiFalco thought he could make out a certain wavering of the starlight behind the area where the lights were blossoming, as if something odd were being done to space there— as, indeed, it was.

He became aware of Aelanni stepping up beside him and gazing intently at the viewscreen. "Well," she breathed, "so far so good. Now for Phase Two." Very little of her Raehaniv accent remained.

DiFalco had barely nodded when a different sort of light show erupted off *Liberator*'s other flank. Rippling flame like sheet lightning seemed to corruscate in space, the same distance from the ship's skin as the flashes had been. Then, abruptly, the fun was over.

Aelanni made inquiries of the station's main computer, then seemed to focus on a point in midair as she consulted her neural data display. Then she turned to DiFalco with the smile that still excited him after . . . how long? Nearly seven Earth-years since he had first set eyes on her while picking himself up from a deck equipped with the manmade gravity that had turned out to be only the first of many miracles.

"It's definite," she announced. "The deflectors performed almost up to theoretical predictions, against both railguns and particle accelerators. We can tell father and the others that they haven't been wasting their time after all."

It had started with the mysterious abandoned base that continued to haunt their thoughts from the darkness of the outer system. Varien hadn't been able to get those wide-open hangar spaces out of his mind—how could such a thing ever have been workable? Others had wondered as well, including Terrans who were too new to gravitics to be aware of all the things the Raehaniv *knew* were impossible. Their speculations had caused Varien to exceed even his usual capacity for condescension . . . and then to think even harder. He had brought the Terrans into contact with Raehaniv specialists, who had begun by ridiculing and ended by refining.

The end result was the series of generators aboard *Liberator*, which projected (to a very short range) a disc-shaped zone of force that deflected incoming objects with a force proportional to their own kinetic energy. Very fast-moving ones were generally incinerated by the heat of their own shedded energy. Lasers, made up of photons which lacked mass but possessed momentum and energy (the Raehaniv had confirmed the Terrans' current tendency to abandon the notion that they had "relativistic mass" though no "rest mass"; zero times infinity is still zero) were made to red-shift, becoming less destructive.

Varien believed the ancient builders had been able to fine-tune the effect to prevent the passage of air molecules while allowing large solid objects like vehicles and personnel to come and go as long as they did it slowly, and had used this capability to fashion the perfect airlock. This still eluded him—but even the admittedly crude applications that he had achieved held potential for fending off attacks that were only now being appreciated.

"Of course," Aelanni cautioned, "we have to bear in mind that this isn't a realistic test. The technicians aboard *Liberator* knew exactly when, and from what bearing, those attacks were coming, so they could put out their deflectors in advance."

"Yeah. It would be nice to be able to travel around inside a permanent bubble-shaped deflection field. But the effect doesn't work that way—and even if it did, the generators use too much power to just leave 'em switched on all the time. In actual combat, it'll be a guessing game. Still . . ."

Thoughtfully, they turned away from the screen and walked across the control center to the wide viewport. Kurganov Station had grown from the nucleus of one of Varien's factory ships, and now it sat like a spider at the center of a vast web of construction and refitting work that drifted in silent majesty in low Terranova orbit. The panorama beyond the curving wall of transparent plastic had never lost its power to raise DiFalco's spirits.

It might have seemed incredible that their small band could have wrought so much in so short a time. But Varien had brought with him the capacity to produce all the essentials of Raehaniv industry. Once established, that industry had grown by geometric progression, with machines making machines. Their only real limiting factor had been the shortage of raw materials outside planetary gravity wells, in this system that lacked a resource-laden asteroid belt like Sol's. But Terranova's active geology had left its many mountainous regions rich in accessible heavy elements. Those riches had to be lifted into orbit—but with Raehaniv shuttles whose atmospheric drives manipulated the planet's gravity into a force that pushed them to a significant altitude and speed before their fusion drives had to take over, this became workable.

After a few moments they spontaneously turned and faced each other, losing themselves for the moment in common memories. Soon after landing on Terranova they had been married according to the forms of the austere Raehaniv tradition, to the music of Varien's muttering. And they had shortly settled for all time the question of whether the humanity of Earth and Raehan belonged to the same species. Jason hle'Morna DiFalco (a name to which Varien was still far from reconciled, although he doted on his grandson whenever he thought no one was looking) was now in his fourth Earth year, an age at which he had other things on his mind than the distinction of being the first Terran-Raehaniv child. He had not been the last.

Rememberance caused them to notice, as they usually did not, the changes wrought by the years. DiFalco's hair was as thick as ever, but it was now iron-gray, shading to nearly white at the temples. Terranova's ultraviolet-rich sun had darkened his skin to a mahogany tone that was different from Aelanni's dark reddish copper, and drawn squint-lines at the outer corners of his eyes. Aelanni showed fewer visible signs of ageing—provided from birth with the best that Raehaniv medical science could offer, she had a life expectancy of over a hundred twenty-five Earth years. (Her prospect of lengthy widowhood had been a source of soul-searching for them, and of grumbling for Varien. Both had been overcome, partly by the argument that they couldn't count on living to peaceful old age anyway.)

The moment passed, and Aelanni spoke briskly. "Well, let's return planetside. I want to tell father personally. We can start retrofitting the ships with deflectors, after which. . . . Eric, it may be that we're ready!"

*   *   *

Their drop shuttle had only just landed when a second one swept in from the south and settled down onto its yielding landing jacks. It was different from theirs, armed and armored, and a squad of heavily-equipped infantry emerged from its wide hatches, just back from the latest of the gruelling exercises laid on by Sergeant Thompson (now Major Thompson, by grace of one of what Difalco continued to insist to everyone—including himself—were temporary field promotions under extraordinary emergency circumstances).

It was clear to everyone that their attempt to liberate Raehan would not necessarily be resolved in the clean, remote abstractness of space war—the only kind of war the Raehaniv had experienced in fighting the Korvaasha. A ground-combat capability would probably be needed. So Thompson had set himself grimly to the task of creating one from his own U. S. Marine detachments, their Russian counterparts, and whatever promising recruits he had been able to harvest from the Raehaniv and the upcoming generation of Terrans. He had welded them all into a single organization and trained them exhaustively. But to arm them with weapons fit to face the Korvaasha he had had to turn to Miralann and his beloved historical databases.

Stepping from their shuttle, DiFalco and Aelanni waved to the Raehaniv linguist, who was watching the return of the assault shuttle from the edge of the landing area. Miralann waved back and approached through a cloud of dust stirred up by the odd things the shuttles' grav repulsors did to molecular motion. He wasn't as plump as he had been—years under Terranova's high gravity had seen to that. Like all the Raehaniv, he had a toughened, pared-down-to-essentials look. But his air of absent-minded geniality remained.

"Hi, Miralann," DiFalco greeted him. "From the

smile on your face, I assume all the bugs are out of the infantry equipment."

"Most of them," Miralann allowed. His exhaustive library—portable, given the density at which the Raehaniv could store data—had yielded the specs from which the infantry weaponry of the Fourth Global War had been resurrected. Thompson had been reluctant to give up his tried-and-true M22, with its solidly reassuring old 2030's technology. Then he had seen a demonstration of what the Raehaniv had been using on each other five hundred years before.

"It still amazes me," DiFalco admitted, "that you people had all this stuff that far back."

"Remember," Miralann said, "at the time of the Fourth Global War we were almost as advanced as we are now, with the exception of artificial gravity; technological change was frozen after that."

"If our history is any indication," DiFalco mused, "all those total wars must have been a stimulus to technological advancement, with governments subsidizing R&D."

"Oh, yes. In fact, now that I've had time to study your history in depth, I can see clear parallels with ours." Miralann warmed to his subject as he watched a second assault shuttle approach. "The First Global War was fought on a technological level somewhere between your two World Wars; it was as though World War I had been postponed until around your year 1925. The explosion, when it came, was correspondingly more destructive.

"By the time it was over, the scientific groundwork had been laid for a whole new order of weaponry—including fission and fission-triggered fusion bombs. The Second Global War was rather like the war that was expected to break out in the nineteen fifties between your people and the Russians *would* have been. We could have destroyed our civilization then, but mutual fear prevented widespread strategic use of nuclear weapons. Still, it was devastating. By the time the Third Global War began, we were at a somewhat more advanced level than that of your 'Operation Desert Storm'—but we were also at the end of an arms race without parallel in your history. Very extensive orbital anti-ballistic-missile defenses were in place, and they probably saved our world. But by the end of the war, clean laser-detonated fusion devices were available, and they were employed tactically under the terms of a strict though unacknowledged code."

Miralann paused to watch the new assault shuttle land. It was a design variant on the first one, and the hatches in its flanks were a different configuration.

"It was a long time before we had recovered sufficiently to fight the Fourth Global War," he resumed. "It started in space, but before it was over a quarter of our planetary population was dead. Hardly surprising; by then we had all the weaponry you've seen—including those." He gestured at the grounded shuttle, from whose open hatches the first of the armored titans had just emerged.

"I remember reading," Miralann went on somberly, "that in the aftershock of World War I your people were haunted by the image of thousands of men advancing across open fields of mud to be mowed down by autoloading machine guns. Since the Fourth Global War, our culture has had a comparable nightmare image: infantry in powered combat armor smashing its way through devastated cityscapes."

DiFalco could believe it. He had checked out in the three-meter exoskeletal suits (if something you had to climb into as opposed to putting it on could be called a "suit") and found that he had an aptitude for their operation. The myoelectric "muscles" reproduced the wearer/operator's movements with a strength far beyond his own, and the armor gave a sense of invulnerability which wasn't entirely illusion as far as infantry weapons were concerned. And as for the integral weaponry, and that which could be carried . . . !

DiFalco saw the twinkle in Aelanni's eye, and spoke wryly. "Yeah, I know: these high jinks aren't my job. Whenever I'm in danger of forgetting that, Thompson just loves to remind me!"

As if to prove the old adage about the consequences of talking of the Devil, one of the powered suits walked over with the gait that seemed so ponderous (though DiFalco had run in one). The viewplate rose with a quiet hum, revealing Thompson's face. He flipped his plasma gun up to a casual salute; his unaided strength couldn't have lifted it from the ground.

"Welcome back, Skipper! Good news from the orbital tests?"

"Yes, you might say that. Why don't you get cleaned up and come on over to the HQ building? I'll tell you all about it, and I want to hear about today's exercises. We may be getting close to the real thing at last."

* * *

"I'm the first to admit it," George Traylor was saying earnestly. "Some of my attempts haven't exactly panned out. But try *this*!"

They had gotten agriculture started early on Terranova, with the stocks they had previously used for Terraforming research plus those that Varien had brought, resulting in an introduced ecology that was a melange of Earth and Raehan. After it was established, Traylor had been able to resume his hobby with fanatical dedication.

So it was that DiFalco now sat sipping homebrew ale—*not* the same thing as the beer, and entirely different from the mead, as George insisted at mind-numbing length. The Raehaniv, wine snobs all, had by now achieved something quite drinkable from their world's analogue of grapes. Of course *they* didn't think it was drinkable, and could explain why with a profusion of oenological arcana that would have reduced the French to a state of cowed submission. But they drank it anyway, and DiFalco wished he could join them instead of fulfilling his social obligations by drinking George's latest effort and *not* telling him that it tasted like fermented cat piss.

Jeff Levinson—he should only fry in Hell!— approached with a wineglass and a satisfied expression. Traylor screwed up his face. "How can you stand to drink that stuff, Jeff?"

"Well," Levinson drawled complacently, "admittedly it's not kosher. But, then, neither am I." He looked around at the small gathering. Everyone had agreed that a get-together to celebrate the successful testing of the deflector was in order. And as it was a fine early-fall afternoon, with none of the biting cold that winter would soon bring, what better place than here on the hillslope outside the HQ building, overlooking the town of New Phoenix and the mountain range beyond it? Of course, they wouldn't have much time—the afternoon of Terranova's 18.9 hour day never lasted long, and the days were getting shorter. But for now the westering sun warmed them and the view was unbeatable.

Levinson sat down, took a sip, and leaned forward to face DiFalco, eagerness awakening. "Well, what's the word? If, like Varien says, getting deflector generators installed in all our ships should only take four months"—they still thought in the Terran units— "then can we maybe set a date to take Seivra?"

Nearby conversations quieted as people listened for DiFalco's reply.

He sighed, and made no attempt to lower his voice. "I think we'll have to. By then we'll be as ready as we're ever going to be; and while we have no knowledge of what's happening on Raehan, we sure as hell don't want it to go on happening any longer than absolutely necessary. But . . . our basic problem is unchanged. Hopefully the deflectors will help us overcome it."

The sky remained crystal-clear, but it was a though a cloud had passed over the gathering. They all knew what the "basic problem" was—indeed, they were too familiar with it to need holographic star-displays to visualize it.

Two and a half months away by continuous-displacement drive at the best speed most of their ships could make was Seivra, a red dwarf system with no life-bearing planets and only a small Korvaash garrison. Even before the deflector had proved out, they had been confident they could take it, attacking from nowhere near either of the system's two displacement points. But after that . . . ?

One of Seivra's displacement points gave instantaneous access to one of Tareil's. But the first rule of interstellar war was that you didn't even try to attack through a defended displacement point without overwhelming numerical superiority and a willingness to take hideous casualties. They had neither . . . and in the Tareil system the Korvaasha would be the defenders. Of course, they could proceed directly to Tareil by continuous-displacement drive—a hundred of Earth's light-years from Terranova, nearly as far from Seivra, either way a journey for their fighting ships of over two years plus whatever time at least three enroute refuelings would take.

There seemed only one alternative: smash the Korvaasha at Seivra as quickly as possible and, without even pausing to repair their battle damage, roar across the system to the Tareil displacement point and transit it at once, praying all the while that the Korvaash occupiers of Raehan hadn't had time to prepare a defense. But they all knew how unlikely that was.

It was standard Korvaash procedure to keep at least one small picket ship on station at every displacement point in their empire, for the rapid transmission of urgent messages. One of the little craft would transit to the next system along the displacement chain, immediately broadcast its tidings, and another messenger would depart through another displacement point. The Seivra pickets, seeing the system being overrun by unknown attackers from out of nowhere, would surely depart for Tareil at once with tidings of impending attack.

They had gone over it a thousand times, always coming back to the same dilemma. A moment's silence was all it now took for them to come back around to it once again. Levinson, knowing they had, spoke without preamble.

"Well, we could detail a small detachment of ships to proceed by continuous-displacement drive to the vicinity of the Tareil displacement point and hit the pickets at the same time the rest of us are taking on the main Korvaash base, before they know what's going on. . . ." He trailed to a halt. They had been over this, too. Sasha Golovko spoke the conclusions they had already reached.

"Yes, but can we be sure of getting the picket, or pickets, before one of them can transit? I doubt it. And even if we do sail unmolested out of an undefended displacement point into the Tareil system, we'll have to face a vastly superior Korvaash fleet in open battle there, too deep in Tareil's gravity well to use continuous-displacement drive, and with our reaction mass depleted by the dash across the Seivra system."

The silence returned. The air began to take on a chill.

"We have no choice," DiFalco finally said. "We'll always be able to think of reasons—no, excuses—for delaying. But the longer we wait, the more firmly established the Korvaasha are going to get on Raehan, and the harder it'll be to get them off it. We'll just have to shoot the displacement transit as fast as possible, or a little more so, and hope that the deflectors plus the overall Raehaniv technological superiority give us the edge we need. We'll . . ."

"One moment."

The quiet voice from off to one side stopped DiFalco in mid-sentence, and caused every head to turn to where Varien sat under one of the trees that were the evolutionary equivalent of Earthly conifers but looked altogether different. At the precise moment when he had their maximum attention, he rose and walked slowly to the center of the gathering. Spontaneously, they all formed a ragged circle around him. When he spoke, it was in the same mild tone.

"You are quite correct, Colonel." (It was still the only title DiFalco allowed himself.) "We have delayed far longer than I had originally contemplated, and the those in the Tareil system who anticipated my return must have despaired of ever seeing me again. Without the hope of outside deliverance to sustain it, the resistance I worked to prepare will inevitably wither and die. We must move on Tareil soon, or we will not be able to count on finding help there. I only hope we still can." He paused, thoughts momentarily wandering a hundred light-years to the son who might still live. Then he blinked, and resumed more briskly.

"Now, as to our immediate problem. I've been keeping this to myself because I wasn't entirely certain about it; but I see the time has come when we cannot wait for certainty. As a few of you know, I have been exploring the possibility of increasing fusion powerplant efficiency by supplementing the electromagnetic containment fields with a gravitic component. Our recent work in developing the deflector shield has resulted in a . . . spinoff? Yes, that's it. At any rate, I now believe we can, in a matter of a few months, modify the powerplants of our major Raehaniv combattant ships, enabling them to attain a continuous-displacement performance comparable to the present capabilities of our courier ships."

For a moment, everyone was silent, eyes riveted on the old man at the center of the circle. DiFalco realized anew that, however much of the time Varien seemed to fit comfortably into the world of human ordinariness, there would always be moments like this one, when the old Raehaniv's true home seemed either the far future or some old, enchanted country, with none of the present in him at all.

Aelanni broke the spell. "So we could reach Tareil from here in less than five months?"

"Closer to six," Varien admitted. "I calculate that one enroute refuelling would be required. But there is a system almost on the direct straight-line route where . . ."

"Wait a minute, Varien," Traylor broke in. "Did I understand you to say you could do this with the *Raehaniv* ships?"

"Yes, yes," Varien replied, nodding. "I wouldn't dream of trying this modification on the scratch-built fusion plants of the American and Russian ships, with their lower-technology components. Also, there's the matter of resource allocation; we haven't the industrial plant to perform this enhancement *and* install deflector generators on all our ships simultaneously. It would double our preparation time.

"So," he hurried on, "I propose that we equip the Terran ships with deflectors and reconfigure the Raehaniv ships' powerplants, which we *can* do at the same time."

"But, Varien," DiFalco began hesitantly, "then the Terran ships won't be able to make it to Tareil in any useful length of time, any more than they can now."

"No, but they can proceed to Seivra as per our original plan, timing the attack so that by the time they secure Seivra the Raehaniv ships will have reached Tareil! Then," Varien continued with the enthusiasm of a civilian who thinks he has had a brilliant military insight, "at a prearranged moment which allows the Korvaasha time to concentrate defenses at the displacement point connecting the two systems, we can attack through that displacement point while, simultaneously, the Raehaniv ships take them in the rear!"

"Wait a minute, Varien . . ."

"Think of it! We can trap the defending fleet and wipe it out at a single crushing blow! We can . . ."

"Wait! *Wait!* WAIT!" With Varien's excited flow finally stemmed, DiFalco took a deep breath. "Look, Varien, haven't you ever heard of . . . but no, of course you haven't. But *you* have!" He turned rather desperately to Miralann. "Remember the Battle of Leyte Gulf from our history? Tell him!"

Miralann nodded slowly. "Yes. Varien, what Colonel DiFalco is trying to say is that military history teaches us to beware of complex battle plans that require precise coordination of widely separated elements. In particular, the folly of attempting a rendezvous in the presence of the enemy is a cardinal principle. Our own distant past is replete with similar instances."

Varien looked uncharacteristically crestfallen. "Perhaps I underestimated the difficulties involved. I am more than willing to leave the details of implementation to the military professionals. But, Colonel," he continued, holding DiFalco's eyes with his own, "I must ask you a question you once put to me: can you suggest a viable alternative?"

DiFalco thought hard. Could he? No. Half-baked as Varien's plan might be, at least he had offered them a way out of the dilemma they had been trapped in, a way to change the equation. It would be risky as hell, however much they fine-tuned it— but at least it made them a little more the masters of their own fate than the plans they had come up with so far, all of which had violated an even more basic military maxim by depending on good luck.

"Something else you haven't mentioned, father," Aelanni said, frowning. "The Raehaniv ships will enter the Tareil system without deflectors."

"Well, yes," Varien admitted. "They will have to do

without that advantage. They will have to rely on the element of surprise, on the overall superiority of Raehaniv technology . . . and on the fact that it is their own home they are fighting to free."

Aelanni nodded slowly, and her eyes met Varien's in a moment of understanding from which all who were not Raehaniv—even her husband and his son-in-law—were excluded. And DiFalco, looking at her, suddenly knew who would lead those Raehaniv ships into battle with the greatest military machine known to exist in the universe.

The sun began to dip below the mountains, and it grew cold.

CHAPTER TWELVE

The sullen red sun his people had named Seivra rose over the edge of the gas-giant planet. Aelador hle'Terull, gazing at it through the faceplate of his heavy-duty vac suit, hated the sight, for it was visible evidence of the passage of time as this station swung in another of its sterile orbits around the gas giant. So it was like the face that gazed back at him from the mirror in all its haggardness as he aged at a rate the Raehaniv hadn't experienced since primitive times. It was incontrovertible proof that time truly was passing and that his life was draining away, however much it might sometimes seem that he was suspended in a timeless bubble of misery in which even the periodic punishments had begun to dull.

The Korvaasha had brought him and the others from Raehan to replace their own crude and inefficient grav scanners with state-of-the-art Raehaniv ones. They had all been highly-paid specialists before the war, and it had taken some of them a long time to adjust to slavery—the gruelling labor, the squalid quarters, the tasteless food paste eaten from a common trough. It had taken some of them too long; the human mind and body could only absorb so much of the torment of discipline by direct neural stimulation, and some had found the refuge of death or madness. The Korvaasha didn't care—they had factored in a certain rate of attrition. They had much experience in such things, although more experience with the human species would doubtless allow them to refine their parameters.

Aelador was one of the unlucky ones . . . the survivors. And so he now labored on the outer skin of the station, performing repairs to one of the exterior components. He was not under guard; there was no need. His suit had internal contact points through which the Korvaasha could invade his body with agony if he deviated from his instructions in the least. And they all knew the consequences of any attempt at sabotage; the Korvaasha had demonstrated them early on, using a human chosen at random.

He was almost finished when the tinny pseudo-voice of Uftscha, Seventh Level Embodiment of the Unity and commander of the station, sounded in his helmet.

"Attention! All personnel and inferior beings on outside duty return inboard at once. An anamoly has appeared in the scanner readings."

Aelador knew what awaited him if the anamoly involved any of the equipment for which he was responsible. He discovered that even terror had lost its power to impart the sensation of being alive.

*   *   *

"Coming up on the mass limit, Colonel," Terry Farrell reported. It was the label they had assigned—despite Varien's complaints that it was meaningless—to the distance from any given star within which continuous-displacement drive was unuseable due to a kind of harmonics it set up with the star's gravity. It varied depending on the strength of that gravity, and for a M3v red star like Seivra it was close in. DiFalco had no desire to go to reaction drive until he had to, and since they were approaching Seivra from a region of space nowhere near either of the system's two displacement points there was no reason why they should be picked up on grav scanners. The Korvaasha would have scanners trained on this stretch of nothingness only by sheer chance—for example, as part of a test of new scanners. And how likely was that?

They had cautiously scouted this system several times during the years of preparation at Terranova, and they knew in general what to expect. The Korvaasha had put a fortress/fuel refinery into orbit around the gas-giant second planet, and Varien had assured them that it was a standard design, built around a core which had come through the displacement points behind the conquering Korvaash fleets and whose minimal fusion drives had since been cannibalized to provide station-keeping capability—it could not maneuver. The mobile force-level varied, but a squadron of five small combatants was permanently stationed here. And, of course, there were the virtually-unarmed pickets at the two displacement points. It should, DiFalco thought, be a cakewalk. The real test would come at Tareil.

Belatedly, he realized that thinking of Tareil was a mistake. As he watched the ruddy ember of Seivra grow in the view-forward, his mind went back almost four months to his last night on Terranova with Aelanni. . . .

Jason had gone to sleep, and they had bundled up and braved the cold to walk under the stars and the ring and one frost-rimmed moon. It hadn't been too bad; the dead of winter was past, and this hemisphere would soon enter into a spring which, if somewhat lacking in color on a planet where evolution hadn't yet put forth flowering plants, at least held the promise of relief from the cold.

Wordlessly, they had gazed upward at the little cluster of lights that drifted in orbit: Kurganov Station and the ships of their fleet, including those which Aelanni would, on the morrow, lead out of this system.

She had finally broken the silence, smiling bravely, her breath frosting in the moonlight. "Haven't we had a farewell like this before?"

"Yes," he had lied, "when you left for Altair." It wasn't really the same at all. She hadn't been going into battle then, and they hadn't yet belonged to each other and to Jason. But the two departures had had one thing in common: her buried, unwilling eagerness. Before, she had quested for new horizons; now she sought the homeworld she had not seen in almost ten of the years of distant Earth. And, even more, she sought the deaths of that world's rapists.

He had taken her in his arms. "Aelanni, whatever happens, I want this to be our last farewell. I'm no damned good at it! And besides . . . we'll have given enough."

She had looked at him gravely. "You're right, Eric. We'll meet on Raehan, where"—a flash of the sudden impishness he knew so well—"I'll show you some great beaches! *Warm* beaches! And you can show me your Earth. And after that, we'll have to begin forging an alliance between Raehan and your people to face the Korvaasha . . . but whatever we have to face we'll face together. No more farewells!"

They had held each other until the cold had begun to seep through to their flesh, and then gone inside.

The next day she had departed for the outer system where the mass limit lay, and then vanished into the strange state of continuous-displacement travel, outrunning any possible attempt to communicate with her. For the next month DiFalco had lost himself in the hectic toil of final preparations for the American and Russian ships' departure for Seivra. At last the day had arrived and they had left Terranova behind, with the noncombatants left there to care for the children (he had sternly ordered himself not to think of Jason) and maintain a colony of which, win or lose, the Korvaasha would not learn.

They had set out in two waves. First were the seven heavily armed and extensively modified cruisers, and three personnel transports which had been converted into carriers for Thompson's ground-assault force. Behind had come the cargo carriers which had been fitted out to serve as a fleet train (the goddamned ex-Navy types again!) with supplies and mobile repair facilities whose personnel travelled aboard other transports—transports which also carried one other . . .

Varien had been adamant: he would not wait on Terranova. Aelanni had been equally unyielding about taking him along to share the extraordinary risks involved in the Raehaniv ships' part of the plan. So he had resigned himself with no good grace to the primitivism of the transport *Irkutsk*, for DiFalco wasn't about to let him expose himself to the hazards of space combat aboard one of the cruisers of the first wave. At least he had spent more than his share of the two-and-a-half-month journey in the cryogenic hibernation in which they had all taken turns. Officially, this was a concession to his advanced years; in fact, DiFalco had wanted to minimize the old coot's opportunities to exercise his talent—verging on genius—for exasperating people.

And so they had proceeded to Seivra, occupying themselves with the operational readiness exercises that DiFalco had laid on for the purpose of keeping them busy and which almost succeeded in keeping nerves from stretching to nearly the snapping point.

And now they neared journey's end and the first of their tests.

"Two minutes to Seivra mass limit, Colonel." Farrell's crisp voice broke into DiFalco's reverie.

He looked at the Raehaniv-installed holo tank, in which the positions of his ships were displayed in accordance with their instantaneously propagated gravitic signatures. Most of the first wave were in

what passed for a tight formation in space, flanked at
a great distance by the cruisers *Therdore Roosevelt*
and *Aleksandr Nevsky*.

"Mr. Farrell," he spoke levelly, "signal the rest of
the main body to secure from continuous-displacement drive at . . ." He glanced at the chronometer
and gave a time less than a minute away. No need
to push the mass limit.

"Aye aye, sir." Farrell spoke into the communicator. Ships in continuous-displacement drive could see
and communicate with each other normally as long
as they were popping in an out of normal space at
exactly the same rate, a synchronicity into which they
could only be tied by Raehaniv computers; they
were, as DiFalco found helpful to think of it, existing
at the same frequency. Should one such ship "switch
frequencies," it would simply vanish from the ken of
the others. It was just one of the effects that placed
continuous-displacement travel outside the range of
possibilities defined by normal human experience,
and DiFalco had long ago stopped worrying about it.
On a more practical level, it made ship-to-ship combat under the drive so easily avoidable that such
combat almost certainly could never take place,
except possibly by mutual consent in accordance with
some fantastic code of high-tech *bushido*.

Farrell received acknowledgments, the moment
arrived, and the ruddy light of Seivra suddenly stopped
growing in the viewport. The holographic blips wavered
in the tank before steadying as the display began
reflecting input from more conventional sensors—all
but *Roosevelt* and *Nevsky*, which remained under the
drive and proceeded to veer off in opposite directions
toward Seivra's two displacement points.

DiFalco released a pent-up breath. So far, so
good. Levinson and Golovko had responded as
planned to the realtime signal provided by the
cessation of the others' gravitic pulses and departed
to fulfill their roles—a tricky role in the case of

Levinson and *Roosevelt*. DiFalco's part was, by comparison, simplicity itself: the brute simplicity of combat with the Korvaash station toward which the main body now proceeded in free fall.

*   *   *

"Seventh Level Embodiment!" The Korvaash scanner officer's exclamation was meant for Uftscha alone but his translator/voder made it audible and comprehensible to the humans . . . at least to the extent that it could be heard over Aelador's screams. "The gravitational anamoly—or, rather, cluster of anamolies—has suddenly ceased to register on the scanners."

Uftscha gestured, and the Korvaash guard withdrew his neurolash from contact with Aelador's flesh. The human's spine relaxed from its convulsive curve and he collapsed, shuddering, to the deck. With a soft hum the neurolash retracted into the guard's artificial forearm. Uftscha ignored the scene as he considered the scanner readouts.

"Perhaps the malfunction was a temporary one, in which case it could recur," he mused. "Clearly, it *was* a malfunction; the readings made no sense, being of an unprecedented nature and coming from a region of space remote from either of the two displacement points. Disengage the new gravitic scanners." He turned ponderously and directed his eye to where Aelador lay gasping on the deck in front of a clump of other humans. "You will form a work crew and track down the source of the problem." He turned to go, then paused and addressed the scanner officer. "Order two frigates to proceed outward on that bearing and locate any possible external source of these readings. And place the pickets on low-level alert."

He departed, and Aelador led the humans to the antechamber that gave access to the scanner system's power leads and connections with the actual hardware on the station's outer skin. As the tide of molten pain ebbed from his nervous system, he wondered what the scanner readings portended. Uft-scha had been right:, there was no reasonable possibility other than a malfunction. But Aelador knew these systems, and he could imagine no malfunction that could have produced these particular readings.

He was thinking about it as they removed the detachable panels along the base of the chamber's walls and gazed down into the system's glowing guts.

*   *   *

Aleksander Nevsky disengaged its continuous-displacement drive and resumed the intrinsic vector it had possessed back in the outer system of Terranova. (Strictly speaking, it had never lost it, but this was a minor problem of interstellar navigation.) Golovko noted with satisfaction that the Korvaash picket lay almost dead ahead, so only minor course corrections would be needed.

He spoke an order, the attitude jets performed their aligning function, and the fusion drive roared to life. After the few seconds it took lightspeed phenomena to cross the distance that still separated the two vessels, the picket's reaction appeared on *Nevsky's* sensors.

"Yes," Golovko muttered to his executive officer, "they picked us up as as soon as the burn commenced. And they're following their standard procedures as Varien described them." He indicated the readouts that told of the picket's broad-band shout of warning to all Korvaash units in the system, and of its simultaneous powering-up as it prepared for the emergency acceleration that would take it through the nearby displacement point to the star that lay on the far side of Seivra (in terms of the displacement connections) from Tareil.

But Golovko knew it would never make that transit, to alert the remainder of Korvaash space. They hadn't been able to drop out of continuous-displacement drive right on top of the picket, of course—Varien had explained that displacement points always occurred inside a star's mass limit. But they were never very far inside it, and *Nevsky* was already coming into range, approaching on a heading less than twenty degrees from the displacement point. The picket (already burning its fusion drive, by dint of who knew what frantic efforts) was heading almost directly into its doom.

He spoke another order, and a salvo of four missiles leaped forth. The picket exerted its limited defensive capabilities, and point-defense lasers actually stopped one of the missiles while ECM caused a second to detonate too soon. The other two sped home, and the picket died in glare whose magnified image left spots in Golovko's eyes.

The Russian settled back in his acceleration couch and released a long-held breath before ordering the ship turned around to commence the retrofiring that would bring him into position to cover the displacement point in case any chance Korvaash traffic should pass through. It had gone so smoothly as to almost worry him. But, then, the operation had been meticulously planned so as to assure that he would succeed . . . and that Levinson would not.

Similar thoughts were going through Levinson's mind at substantially the same instant, as he watched the Korvaash picket that was *Teddy R.*'s ostensible target accelerate toward the Tareil displacement point.

He had disengaged his continuous-displacement drive sooner than necessary, outside Seivra's mass limit, and approached from almost dead astern of the picket. Now he ordered two missiles launched—no need to be too wasteful of expensive munitions, as long as realism wasn't compromised.

The missiles did their robotic best, but a stern chase is a long chase. The picket reached the displacement point and seemed to flicker out of existence. The missiles swept on through the volume of space where their target was no longer located, and receded swiftly into the void.

"And so much for *that*," *Teddy R.*'s executive officer muttered. "Now the goddamned Russkies will be insufferable! We could have gotten that bastard if we'd intended to!"

"But we didn't, XO," Levinson reminded her. "Just remember that. Our job was to let him get away to Tareil while *seeming* to try our damnedest to stop him. And as far as I'm concerned, we succeeded in that. I don't care how stolid the Korvaasha are supposed to be; you can't tell me that wasn't one badly scared crew!

"And now," he continued, "let's take up station at that displacement point. Cheer up—if they send anything back through to take another look at what's going on here in Seivra, you can blast it to your heart's content! Otherwise, we wait."

He couldn't let the XO or anyone else know how hard that waiting would be for him, while DiFalco and the rest proceeded into a battle that was not a charade.

*   *   *

The two Korvaasha frigates that Uftscha had dispatched outward from the station had approached at a relative velocity that had allowed for nothing but an exchange of fire *en passant* that could have but one conclusion. *Andy J.* had rung with cheers as they had hit one of the bogies dead-on with the spinal-mounted particle accelerator, only to grow silent as a Korvaash missile had gotten through and inflicted more damage on *Ronnie R.* than DiFalco allowed himself to think about. But the storm of missiles from the Terran cruisers had saturated the Korvaash defenses, and they had flashed on past a thinning cloud of debris.

Now they had turned end-for-end and commenced retrofire, braking themselves with blinding violet-white plasma jets into an orbit that would intersect that of the station. (*Ronnie R.* was able to keep up, to DiFalco's relief.) The fusion drives themselves were formidable if clumsy weapons of destruction, but DiFalco didn't intend to turn them on the station. Nor would he use missiles. He wanted to leave as much of that station in existence as possible, to glean as much as they could of the intelligence information that was the rarest and most precious commodity in interstellar, interspecies war.

Of course, that meant they just had to take it on the way in. . . .

DiFalco, like everyone else, was confined to his acceleration couch, even though the deceleration could not be felt—the G forces they were pulling were such that a momentary failure of the compensating artificial gravity fields could have been catastrophic for anyone caught standing around. So he couldn't even pace as the first of the Korvaash missiles began to arrive.

*   *   *

Aelador and the other humans knew nothing of the signals that had arrived from the frigates and—shortly thereafter, travelling at lightspeed from the outer system—from the pickets. All they knew was that something had unleashed pandemonium among the Korvaasha, and that Uftscha made an announcement whose disjointedness not even the voder/translator could entirely smooth over, ordering the new grav scanners to be reactivated.

But Aelador could draw inferences, and as they worked frantically under the eyes of unwontedly nervous-seeming Korvaash guards to reconnect all the circuitry they had disconnected in their search for a malfunction that evidently didn't exist after all, a suspicion grew in him. When they were finished, and the rumble of missile launches began to vibrate through the station, the suspicion became certainty.

Seivra was under attack. Someone had, impossibly, gotten into the system by some means unconnected with either of the displacement points. He couldn't imagine how, and he couldn't conceive of who the intruders might be. But he knew one thing, and as he was hauled up through the hatches by the other humans he was sure they all knew it, even though they didn't dare talk among themselves. Someone was attacking the Korvaasha. Someone was *hurting* the Korvaasha!

The astonishing thought immobilized him for an instant at the edge of the hatch, and one of the low-ranking Korvaash guards rounded on him. "Move, inferior being! We must close up the hatch!" Without waiting for a response, he jabbed Aelador with his implanted neurolash.

Aelador gasped as the jag of unendurable pain shot through his nervous system and fell forward into the arms of one of the other humans—it was Turiel—and suddenly something seemed to lift from him, leaving nothing except the certain knowledge of what he must do, a certitude marred only by what he knew would happen to Turiel and the others after he did it. Their eyes met and Turiel nodded his head very slightly. All the understanding and forgiveness that the universe could hold flowed between them, wordlessly.

Aelador stood up on the lip of the hatch—the guards were too startled to react—and met the eyes of the other humans for an instant, with an odd little smile. Then, slowly, he toppled over backwards and fell toward the glowing mass of wiring below.

With a crackling roar and a blinding, spark-showering flash, he vanished, and the chamber filled with the stench of burned meat. And electrical systems began to die.

*   *   *

"Colonel!" Farrell sounded puzzled. "Something's happened to the incoming missiles. There are just as many of them, but it's as if their fire control has suddenly become a lot less effective."

DiFalco could see it himself from the readouts. Their point-defense lasers no longer had precisely coordinated time-on-target salvos to deal with, just straggling individual missiles they could easily handle.

"Yes," he said slowly. "They must have had some kind of major systems failure on that station—a big short-out or something. God knows why; we're not even hitting them yet." He turned his attention to other matters. "Guess we'll never know."

* * *

Retrofiring steadily, the cruisers matched orbits with the station. The three remaining Korvaash frigates, after the tactical datanet they had shared with the station had become useless, had been sent outward on an intercept course which had ended in their deaths in a storm of fusion warheads.

And now the Terrans drew close enough to the station for energy weapons to come into play. First lasers—they were the longest-ranged, but their effectiveness was downgraded by ablative and reflective armor materials, as well as by various countermeasures. Then, as the range closed still further, the plasma guns opened up, bringing deuterium bullets to near-fusion heat with enfilading lasers and electromagnetically expelling the resulting bolts of plasma. The plasma's unavoidable dissipation limited the weapon to short ranges—but within those ranges it was devastating. And, DiFalco thought, it produced a properly-cinematic blinding flash, unlike the laser beams which were invisible in vacuum and only faintly visible in the clouds of vaporizing ablative armor that they themselves created.

The station, of course, had similar weapons—relatively inefficient, clumsily massive as was typical of Korvaash engineering, but a lot of them and a hellacious powerplant for them to draw on. And the Korvaasha were veterans in their use.

But the deflector operators, overseeing computers with reaction times no human could match, artfully interposed their nonmaterial shields between the ships and the stabbing energy swords while the cruisers' weapons ripped and tore at every area of the station's surface where a weapon revealed itself by firing.

After a time, DiFalco was satisfied that the enemy's volume of fire had dropped to the level deemed acceptable for the next phase of the attack. He contacted Major Thompson on the assault carrier *Guadalcanal* and spoke a brief order. Then he watched as the assault shuttles dropped away from *Guadalcanal* and her two sisters. (No, damn it; *Sevastopol* was, he supposed, a brother. Why couldn't the Russians ever get it through their thick heads that ships were female?) Under covering fire from the cruisers, the stubby little craft accelerated toward the station, then began burning their forward-facing retrorockets to reduce their velocity and allow ramming without self-immolation.

DiFalco couldn't imagine what that impact was going to be like for Thompson and his men. It would, he imagined, be a foretaste of hell. And he could only watch and wait.

*   *   *

With a grinding, screaming roar of tearing metal, the specially reinforced snub nose of the still-retrofiring assault shuttle penetrated the outer skin of the station. The small craft's rudimentary artificial gravity could not begin to cope; Thompson and his men were thrown about in the webbing which, with their powered combat armor's shock absorbers, would hopefully limit their injuries to bruises.

The shuttle, like a slow-motion bullet, ground its way as far into the station as it was going. Thompson slapped the switch that disengaged the webbing, and the shuttle's blunt clamshell nose opened to reveal a vista of wreckage.

"Alright people, move it or lose it!" The armor suits were sealed against vacuum lest the Korvaasha, deciding they had nothing to lose, played cute tricks like letting the air out of the station. But the helmet communicators carried Thompson's voice to the entire squad as he leaped out into the ruined, dimly-lit passageway. Scanning for hostiles and finding none, he consulted the heads-up display that seemed to float a couple of inches from his left eye. Yeah . . . according to what Varien's people knew of the layout of this kind of installation, the command center should be *that* way.

"To the right," he called out. "Follow me." He had just turned into the branching passageway when an electronic scream awoke in his ear to inform him that a laser target designator had touched his armor. His reflexes were very nearly as instantaneous as the sensing system; he twisted aside just as a burst of hypervelocity, hyperdense slugs crashed into the bulkhead. Only one connected, and it caromed off his armor. Swinging in the direction of the hostile fire, he brought his plasma gun up into the socket that allowed it to tap into the armor's own powerpack. By the time he had completed the movement, he was facing his first Korvaasha. Without pausing to let weirdness register, he blasted the alien into flaming, nondescript ruin.

His squad, most of them armed with heavy-duty mass-driver weapons not unlike the one the Korvaasha had tried to use on him (although a human needed a strength-enhancing powered exoskeleton to carry one) came around the corner and proceeded to mow down the Korvaasha that had followed the first one out of the twisted ruins. The remains, he noted with relief, were more flesh than machinery. These were ordinary security guards. They weren't the fully-cyborgian warrior elite he had studied—those might well give even power-armored troops trouble.

Plenty of time for that later.

Motioning to the squad to follow him, he proceeded along the passageway.

*   *   *

The second wave had arrived, and the scientific and intelligence specialists were combing over what was left of the station. It was, on the whole, a disappointment. In particular, Kuropatkin and Tartakova would have liked prisoners to interrogate. But there were only corpses . . . not all of them Korvaash.

DiFalco stood with Varien in the chamber near the scanner controls, gazing at the abattoir that Thompson's men had found. Not even the butchery that had occured here could conceal the species of the victims.

I will not *be sick*, DiFalco commanded himself. He looked at Varien, who *had* been sick at his first sight of this room. But now he was gazing at the remains of his fellow Raehaniv with an expression neither of nausea nor of shock but rather of infinite sadness.

The old man finally turned to him and spoke with a strange gentleness. "Your weapons didn't do this, you know. They were obviously slaughtered by the Korvaasha—slaughtered with a ferocity I cannot understand. But *you* didn't kill them."

"No," the American said harshly. "But we both know that we *are* going to have to kill humans— probably a lot of them—when we reach Raehan. Unless the Korvaasha magically go away in a puff of smoke, there's no way we're going to be able to avoid it." His eyes met the Raehaniv's, and there was almost a challenge in them. Varien looked away.

"I know," he finally said, almost inaudibly. "I suppose I've known it all along. I've simply avoided thinking about it. Like all Raehaniv, I've found that easy to do where the realities of war are concerned—it's all seemed so abstract, so . . . historical." He straightened, and his voice firmed. "No more. Do what you have to do at Raehan, Colonel. You cannot let yourself be deterred by blood, any more than any other surgeon."

They departed, leaving the room to the dead.

CHAPTER THIRTEEN

"Quiet, everyone! Order!" Arduin's bellow finally silenced them. He ran a threatening look around the table, then spoke in a normal tone of voice. "We may be pirates by Korvaash definition, but that's no excuse for *behaving* like pirates. Now, Daeliuv, please continue."

The intelligence chief gave a professorial harrumph, and his eyes focused on his neural display. "To repeat," he began frostily, "our routine monitoring of the Seivra displacement point detected realtime gravitational emanations that indicated the arrival of what appeared to be a Korvaash picket ship, or other vessel of comparable mass and power. Afterwards we, like everyone else in the system with the proper receiver, picked up a signal which, while naturally in Korvaash code, gave every indication of being a system-wide emergency alert.

"The result," he continued in the same pedantic tones, "was dramatic. Korvaash operations against us here in the asteroids have come to a standstill—they have assumed a defensive posture as their mobile forces have departed for the Seivra displacement point. Likewise, their combatant ships at Raehan itself have been dispatched to the same destination.

To it . . . but not *through* it. We have detected no departures for Seivra. Courier vessels have, however, transitted this system's other displacement points.

"Information from our sources on Raehan is, of course, still too sparse to allow meaningful evaluation. . . ."

"Come on, Daeliuv," Yarvann broke in, risking Arduin's wrath. "You must have *some* feedback from your dirtside sources by now! Give us your first-sense impression."

Daeliuv's voice dropped a few more degrees in temperature. "Subject to later verification," he said heavily, "the early indications we have received suggest that the Korvaasha on Raehan are in an uproar, as if they are responding to some emergency. Security has been tightened still further, and the Implementers"—a kind of subliminal growl ran around the table—"are behaving with a nervous bluster that suggests that they are feeling pressure from above.

"Any conclusions must, at this time, be tentative. . . ."

" 'Tentative' nothing!" Yarvann swung around to face the head of the table, eyes glowing with a fire that had not been seen among the Raehaniv for a long, long time. "Arduin, there's only one possibility, only one thing that could account for all this. Somebody, from somewhere, has taken Seivra! And," he continued, grinning savagely, "whoever that is has got the Korvaasha here in the Tareil system by whatever they use for balls!" He spoke a command that awakened a holo display above the center of the table. "The only displacement chain that connects this system with the Korvaash empire runs through Seivra! Of course, those departing couriers have warned the Korvaasha in the other chains that converge here at Tareil—but those are just light forces, mopping up our research stations and such. The Korvaasha in this system are on their own, cut off from their own higher echelons!"

"And just where could these mysterious Unknowns have come from?" Daeliuv's sarcastic tone didn't quite make it to the end of the sentence.

Yarvann shrugged. "Who's to say? Seivra has only the two displacement points, and the Unknowns obviously didn't come from this system, so they must have come through the other one, from somewhere beyond Seivra."

"But," Daeliuv argued, "that leads to Korvaash space."

"True, but between Seivra and the old Korvaash frontier lie all these displacement connections"—he indicated the holo display—"that we explored before we blundered onto the Korvaasha, and all these displacement chains that branch off from them. We never explored very far along the branching chains; maybe, since occupying Raehan, the Korvaasha have ventured farther along them than we did, and stirred up a *zorat's* nest! Or maybe the Unknowns have been expanding along one of those chains and encountered the Korvaasha and decided something had to be done about them. Either way, we can't say how much they've conquered beyond Seivra. All we know for sure is that any enemy of the Korvaasha is a potential ally of ours!"

Arduin held himself aloof from the desperately-hopeful excitement that visibly awoke among the others. "Let's consider all the possibilities, Yarvann. For one thing we don't know that these hypothetical conquerors of Seivra reached it via displacement points. They might have the continuous-displacement drive."

That brought them all up short. He had told them about Varien's invention, of course, but it still wasn't altogether real for them—they hadn't grown up with it. They had discussed the possibility of equipping some of their ships with the drive and leaving the Tareil system to search for a new home among the stars. But nothing had come of it. Too much of the vital technical information had departed with Varien, and the task of recreating the drive from theoretical generalities was beyond their capabilities, or at least beyond any capabilities they could spare from the day-to-day desperation of their struggle against the Korvaasha. Arduin suspected there was a deeper reason: such a project would have represented an admission of their cause's long-term hopelessness, and this was precisely the admission they could not afford to make to themselves.

"Well," Yarvann began after a moment's hesitation, "I hadn't thought of that. But if the Unknowns have the continuous-displacement drive and can go where they please without regard to displacement points, why should they have gone to a miserable little red dwarf like Seivra?"

Miranni zho'Traellann spoke up hesitantly. "Unless . . . could it be Varien? Or somone somehow connected with Varien?" She spoke the questions with an eagerness that reminded Arduin of her prewar friendship—and, some said, more than that—with the long-time widower Varien. When he spoke, it was with a careful gentleness.

"I don't see how it can be, Miranni. In straight-line distance, Seivra is even further from Lirauva or Landaen than this system is. At the top pseudo-velocity most of Varien's ships can manage, a nonstop continuous-displacement flight from either of those stars to Seivra—as if such a thing were possible—would take more than three times as long as he's been gone! No," he continued, meeting one pair of eyes after another around the circuit of the table, "I want to believe in Varien's return as much as any of you. But we can't let our hopes run away with us.

"Yarvann, you may be right: *something* has caused the Korvaasha to take the pressure off us. So perhaps it's time to put some pressure on them! I want a detailed operational plan for an attack on the mining station at Raesau. In the meantime, we'll continue our surveillance of the Seivra displacement point and stand ready to respond to whatever happens in that direction."

Yarvann slapped the edge of the table and sank back into his chair with an exclamation that a Terran of the American persuasion, had any such been present, would have instantly recognized as Raehaniv for "Hot damn!" Then he leaned forward as if energized by a new thought. "Something else, Arduin. If we're going to put pressure on them, we should do it *everywhere*. Maybe it's time to signal our people on Raehan to commence some serious guerrilla action."

Daeliuv looked on the verge of a stroke as he tried to form words. "Are you insane?" he finally blurted out. He turned to Arduin beseechingly. "We can't commit our planetside organization to overt action now! Even if they succeeded, the result would be massive, bloody reprisals—we learned that early in the occupation. And the consequences of failure would be catastrophic: the destruction of our hidden munitions caches and the severing of our contacts. We can't jeopardize our intelligence sources!"

Arduin nodded. "You're right, Daeliuv. Yarvann, an armed uprising on Raehan would be premature at this time. Rmember, we've discussed this before." They did remember—none of them could forget the sickening butchery of the massacres that had followed the first attempts at resistance. "We decided then that our groundside combat capability can only be used once, so we have to hold it in reserve for a final, all-out effort to liberate Raehan. The logic of that decision still holds." Even Yarvann's mutter of disappointment was pro forma, as if he knew it was expected of him. "No, for now we'll continue to keep the full extent of our organization on Raehan secret. That . . . and the Turanau find."

An uneasy silence descended, for Arduin had reminded them of an irrelevance that was too massive to ignore. Probing further and further into unfrequented regions of the asteroid belt in search of potential fall-back bases, their scouts had stumbled onto the asteroid he had named, with its enigmatic works that some unknown intelligence had wrought and then abandoned in the unguessable past. Before the war it would have been a discovery of epoch-making importance. In their present pass, it represented only a hope that novel alien weapons technology might be discovered—a hope that had been completely disappointed, for the mysterious builders had left their chambers and corridors stripped clean of everything except the relief sculpture that had identified them.

Humans. The ancient builders of Turanau had been humans. Viewing the hologram that the scout ship had brought back, they had all stared across the ages into the vacant eyes of that serene and entirely human face.

First the Korvaasha, then enigma in the form of the Landaeniv, and now this. The universe isn't a comfortable and secure place, like it it was when I was young. Arduin smiled inwardly at himself. *That's been the lament of every old fool since time began. It's just that in my case it happens to be true.*

He spoke quickly, banishing with his voice the silence in which each of them had to confront the unknowable alone, just as humans had always strengthened their common defenses against the great darkness outside their campfires with the cement of words. "We can't let ourselves think about it now. We must leave it for later." *If there is a later*, he did not add. "All we can do is try to take advantage of whatever it is that's got the Korvaasha stirred up, and hope that it portends a miracle. We need one."

* * *

The crudely massive chamber held the chill air and dim orange light of the Korvaash homeworld that was little more than hearsay to most of the figures who sat around the long table conversing in what would have been, to human ears, dead silence.

Only the gravity was that of this world of Raehan, sybaritically low. Sugvaaz, as Conservator of Correctness, had grumbled about that, but he had been overruled. A continuously maintained artificial gravity field set at the homeworld's force (two-thirds again Raehan's) would have been costly in energy that could otherwise be powering the furtherance of the Unity. It was the type of argument Gromorgh and the other pragmatists had found most effective with Sugvaaz.

At any rate, they had Lugnaath's voice to remind them of the homeworld. The Third Level Embodiment of the Unity spoke with its pure accent, having been born there, and his every word seemed to evoke the massive, incredibly distant world that represented the ultimate (so far) triumph of the Unity, with its biosphere consisting of several score billion Korvaasha, a lot of food yeast, and a few million inferior beings of assorted species who had been imported to perform specialized tasks for which their physiologies made them particularly suited. To listen to him was to visualize the cities, domed against polluted air, rising above plains that had long ago been cleansed of their inefficient and redundant species of animals and plants. Lugnaath hadn't come directly from it, of course; if he had departed on the day Raehan had fallen he would still be enroute, such was the vastness of the Unity. He had left the homeworld behind in his youth, progressing through one post after another, most recently on the regional headquarters world of Izgnad from which the incorporation of the Raehaniv into the Unity had been directed.

And now, as highest authority in the Tareil system, he presided over this emergency meeting. He sat wordlessly, listening to the report of Zagthuud, Obtainer of Foreknowledge, and watching the reactions of the other males present. (Korvaash females had no function beyond procreation and, after they were no longer suitable for that, food. In the Unity, nothing went to waste.)

"We conclude," the intelligence chief was saying, "that the unknown inferior beings who have temporarily"—he stressed the word and glanced involuntarily at Sugvaaz—"occupied Seivra must have entered that system through an undiscovered displacement point."

"But," Lugnaath inquired in the voice that made the others so acutely conscious of their birth on the outer fringes of the Unity, far from its near-legendary center, "how can such a displacement point have been missed? Were our standard survey procedures not carried out at Seivra? And did the inferior beings of this world not survey the system before that?"

"Indeed, Third Level Embodiment. It does seem unlikely. But perhaps the displacement point is freakishly far from the system's primary. At any rate, there seems no other explanation."

"In the early days of the Unity," Lugnaath mused, "before the discovery of displacement points, our ancestors considered an attempt to cross normal space to the nearer stars. Could the attackers have come to Seivra in this manner?"

"My staff considered that possibility, Third Level Embodiment, and we studied historical records of the period of which you speak. Those interstellar ships were to have been enormous vessels designed to obtain reaction mass from the interstellar hydrogen; the designs were nothing like the ships that attacked Seivra, judging from the imagery our picket was able to obtain before transiting. Of course, this unknown race of inferior beings could, perhaps, have developed propulsion technologies that we have not. . . ." Belatedly, Zagthuud realized what he was saying and his voice trailed to a stop.

"It is a prime tenet of Acceptable Knowledge," Sugvaaz spoke coldly, eye darkening, "that the inception of the Unity was shortly followed by the attainment of the ultimate possibilities of technology. Further refinements such as those achieved by the inferior beings of this system are, of course, possible; but fundamental breakthroughs are not, for the Acceptable Knowledge is, by definition, complete. Any other view is . . . incorrect."

"Of course, Conservator," Zagthuud murmured. "I spoke without thinking. The scientific plateau reached by the Unity with the discovery of displacement points of course represents . . ." He went on miserably. Lugnaath said nothing. He was, in theory, the ultimate authority in this system, but for purposes of maintaining the integrity of the Acceptable Knowledge the Conservator of Correctness held transcendent powers.

After a while, when Zagthuud showed signs of running out of self-abasement, Gromorgh broke in. "At any rate," he said smoothly, "it seems unlikely. The fact that the attackers made special efforts to destroy the pickets at the displacement points—fortunately unsuccessful in the case of the one that escaped here to warn us—suggests that they are aware of the existence of displacement points." Sugvaaz glared at him but couldn't very well say anything since the Director of Implementation was, after all, agreeing with his conclusions. He had never liked or trusted Gromorgh, and in any Korvaash administration the Conservator of Correctness was chronically suspicious of the Director of Implementation; anyone who worked so closely with, and through, inferior beings *must* be unreliable.

"I agree," said Kulnakh, the Effectuator of Expansion, with a combat officer's bluntness. "But the question now is what to do about it."

"Do about it?" Lugnaath gazed curiously at the military CO. "I would have thought, Effectuator, that we were already doing everything possible to strengthen our defenses against any attack from Seivra."

"Of course, Third Level Embodiment. That is

elementary prudence. But consider: the fall of Seivra represents the first military setback, even of a temporary nature, that the Unity has ever suffered in its entire history. It is essential that we crush these attackers without delay! Furthermore, the longer they are left undisturbed in Seivra the longer they will have to strengthen their own defenses. We should counterattack through the Seivra displacement point as soon as possible!"

There was a long, uncomprehending silence. Finally, Lugnaath spoke in puzzled tones. "We have received no orders to mount a counterattack, Effectuator."

"Of course not, Third Level Embodiment. It is impossible for us to receive such orders; the fall of Seivra has cut off our communications with the rest of the Unity. We must therefore act on our own initiative!"

Sugvaaz spoke quietly. Too quietly. "The Administrative Directives state quite clearly, Effectuator, that offensive military action must be approved at the regional level, by none less than a Second Level Embodiment of the Unity. So authorization for the action you are proposing must come from Izgnad."

"But, Conservator," Kulnakh said patiently, "to repeat, we are cut off from Izgnad! Besides, it can be argued that a counterattack is a defensive measure, such as can be initiated at the system level, rather than an 'offensive operation' within the meaning of the Directives."

"Questions of interpretation concerning the Administrative Directives must also be resolved at the regional level, Effectuator. The Directives themselves state as much."

Kulnakh's voice began to take on a note of desperation. "Conservator, we find ourselves in an unprecedented situation!" He turned to Lugnaath. "Third Level Embodiment, you are empowered to take all measures for the defense of this system. I urge you to act under this authority and give the order now!"

Before Lugnaath could reply, Sugvaaz continued in the same horribly quiet voice. "The Administrative Directives state . . ."

"I tell you, the Directives simply don't cover this situation!" Kulnakh was actually shouting. "It was never foreseen when the Directives were formulated!"

Without any warning, Sugvaaz snapped up his left arm—the one that had been fitted with an implanted weapons-grade laser. The characteristic crack of air rushing back into the tunnel of vacuum made by the beam came simultaneously with a hissing sound as Kulnakh's eye was boiled away. He was dead before he could make a sound, before his corpse even began to collapse.

"The Administrative Directives," Sugvaaz stated in exactly the same quiet voice, "are an integral part of the Acceptable Knowledge. To deny that they anticipate all possible contingencies within their purview is to call the Acceptable Knowledge itself into question."

Lugnaath kept his face expressionless—easier for a Korvaasha than for a human. Too bad; Kulnakh had been an excellent Effectuator of Expansion, bringing a certain youthful energy to the position. But there was no help for it, of course. Any Conservator of Correctness had absolute power of life and death over all Korvaasha under his jurisdiction except Embodiments of the Unity. That was axiomatic—one of the pillars of the Unity.

He gave the faint whistling sound that was the Korvaash equivalent of a sigh, and spoke the code that activated his implanted communicator. "Inform Grashkul that he is now Effectuator of Expansion," he ordered the computer. "And now," he continued, addressing the meeting, "let us consider ways to enhance the defenses of the Seivra displacement point."

They continued, doing their best to ignore that which lay among them. Fortunately, the Korvaash sense of smell is almost vestigial.

*   *   *

The defenders of a displacement point enjoy the advantage of knowing where and on what heading their attackers will appear. On the other hand, they have absolutely no warning of *when* the attack will take place, and no military unit can stay permanently at a high state of alert.

So universal tactical doctrine calls for stationing the defending fleet fairly far back from the displacement point while strewing the region of space along the emergence bearing with millions of small, dense objects—scrap metal if nothing better is available. This puts the attacker in a dilemma: if he shoots the displacement point fast, to take advantage of the defender's lag in reaction time, he encounters swarms of artificial meteorites at a relative velocity that turns them into devastating kinetic-energy weapons; but if he transits slowly to avoid this, he gives the defenders time to initiate the response for which they are ideally positioned.

Thus it was that lumbering Korvaash freighters dumped the contents of their cavernous holds into the space near the Seivra displacement point over and over, to replenish an astronomical junkyard whose contents tended to drift away. Meanwhile, warships waited at a position prescribed by immemorial tactical doctrine. It took frequent burns of their fusion drives to do so, for a displacement point, being a nonmaterial function of the relative positions of stars, does not in any sense orbit the star with which it is associated. But the Korvaash ships kept station with the professionalism of long tradition, waiting in precise formation to reduce to component atoms those unknown inferior beings who had dared to challenge the Unity.

CHAPTER FOURTEEN

It had been longer than she wished to remember since she had seen a sun of that particular shade of deep gold, and now Aelanni gazed at the distant gleam of Tareil through a blurring mist. For a moment, she could only turn away from everyone else in *Liberator*'s control room and swallow hard. Then, in command of herself, she swung around and managed to face Yakov Rosen with a smile.

"Do you suppose," the middle-aged (on *their* standards) Terran asked rhetorically, "that we'll ever be able to scientifically pinpoint the moment at which a star one is approaching ceases to be a star and becomes a sun?" He spoke in English. He liked to practice his already-fluent Raehaniv with her, but to do so at this moment would have been somehow wrong—almost patronizing. He had had more than five months (minus his turns in cryogenic hibernation) to sharpen his sense of what was fitting in dealing with the Raehaniv.

Aelanni's glance showed her gratitude to the Terran. (But he wasn't simply a Terran, she reminded herself; none of them were. He also thought of himself as a Russian and, in other contexts, as a Jew. It was so confusing!) Before their departure from

Terranova, it had been decided that one Terran should accompany Aelanni's fleet; when she made contact with the Raehaniv resistance in the Tareil system, such an emissary would carry more impact than any amount of holographic imagery. Rosen, a noncombatant with a good working knowledge of Raehaniv, had been the logical choice. And so he had shared the strain of their voyage, the longest by far ever attempted under continuous-displacement drive and the first ever undertaken with powerplants overhauled in accordance with Varien's new theory.

It had, all in all, gone better than they had had any right to expect. Only one ship's drive had failed, and they had stopped to take its personnel aboard the others. This had not caused serious overcrowding—but then had come their midway refueling stop, and the accident that had damaged *Vindicator* beyond their ability to make repairs in that desolate system. That was when things had become seriously uncomfortable, and Rosen had shared the discomfort uncomplainingly for the remainder of the voyage that was now coming to an end only a little behind schedule.

"No," she answered him gravely. "The concepts of 'sun' and 'star' are too subjective. But everyone knows when the moment has arrived—especially for one's native sun." Her eyes wandered again to that golden flame. Then she shook herself and turned to the holo display, currently set for large-scale representation. Tareil appeared as a dot in its own deep-gold color, and the orbits of the inner planets were traced out in ellipses of light (a trick which never ceased to fascinate Rosen), with a kind of necklace-like effect for the asteroid belt. Off to one side was the purple circle that denoted the Seivra displacement point. From far above the plane of the ecliptic the white arrowhead marking their own position moved inward at the impossible rate of their pseudo-velocity.

The tricky part of their manuevering was already over. While still too far from Tareil for any kind of detection, they had burned their fusion drives while jumping in and out of reality, building up the 'real' vector they would need when they reached Tareil's mass limit and disengaged their continuous-displacement drives. This was perfectly possible, but created navigational problems beyond the capacity of organic minds, reducing them to little more than an audience for a computer-choreographed performance. But now the fusion drives were cold, and the mass limit was approaching.

A digital countdown seemed to hover in midair just in front of Aelanni's eyes, invisible to anyone else. "Naeriy," she said to her flag captain (a Terran concept which, like so many in the military sphere, had proven to hold the practiality so often embedded in tradition), "on my command, cut the continuous-displacement drive and implement the prearranged emission-control guidelines."

"Aye aye," Naeriy acknowledged in English. Her voice, and profile, held a fierceness that Aelanni noted, not for the first time. Naeriy's persistent belief that she was under a cloud was irrational, of course; the Korvaash discovery of the Lirauva Chain had not been in any way her fault, and she had acted properly in all respects. But the role of bearer of ill tidings was not a congenial one for the young Raehaniv, whom DiFalco had long ago diagnosed as a classic "hot dog." Irrational or not, Naeriy's need to erase a nonexistent stain was like an elemental force that Aelanni had learned to direct. And, like every other destructive agent at her command, she would have need of it shortly.

She turned to Rosen. "Yakov, you realize that when we disengage the continuous-displacement drive we will be irrevocably committed to battle?"

"Our plan isn't entirely unfamiliar to me," he replied drily.

Aelanni made the vague wiping gesture with which the Raehaniv indicated a desire to correct a misunderstanding. "Of course not. But you are, after all, a civilian. . . ."

"So is everybody here." Rosen grinned. "That's one reason I was so willing to come along: no professional military people! There are, however"—he glanced at Naeriy, then gazed up into Aelanni's eyes for a long moment—"warriors. You Raehaniv have changed since I've known you. You'll go on changing. Even if we win, your people will never be the same again. We may defeat the Korvaasha, but we can't defeat time. The old days you've told me so much about are gone forever, Aelanni." He grimaced with the wry self-mockery she had come to know. "Remind me never to try to give the troops a rousing speech before battle!"

Aelanni's tension broke in a laugh that caused heads to turn. "I will, Yakov, I will. You just don't have it in you!"

Then she sobered. "But you're right. The most we can hope for is to win back Raehan's freedom. We can't win back the way it was. The Korvaasha have irrevocably destroyed that. Eric likes to say 'There ain't no justice.' He's right; there isn't. In a very real sense, aggressors *can't* be defeated, because the harm they do is irreparable. The very act of doing what is necessary to stop them changes their victims' world forever." Her eyes took on a look that caused his to drop. "What about it, Yakov? What does your religion, that you've tried to explain to me, have to say about this imbalance? Why does your God allow evil to do undying hurt without even having to be victorious?"

Rosen tried to meet her eyes again and could not. "I do not know. No one can answer that question."

Aelanni took a deep breath and let it out. "Well," she finally said, "we may not be able to undo the damage the Korvaasha have done . . . but we can damned well do our best to prevent them from doing any more!"

Rosen could not respond. The seconds slid by in silence as Aelanni watched the countdown. Just before they entered Tareil's mass limit, it reached zero and the woman of dark-red flame spoke in a voice like a clarion. "Execute!"

Abruptly, Tareil stopped growing in the screens, just as the marker of their fleet stopped dead in the holo tank. But of course it hadn't really stopped—after a moment, its crawling motion became visible. For they had merely ceased to outpace light, proceeding onward in free fall along the vector that they had established outside the borderlands of Tareil and kept while under the strange not-velocity of continuous-displacement travel.

All right, Rosen thought, unconsciously gazing slightly upward. *We're obeying Your laws again. Happy?*

Power stepped down to life-support requirements, effectively indetectible, they fell along a hyperbola that would bring them to the region where tactical analysis—and their hopes—told them the Korvaash fleet should be crouching, ready to pounce at the Seivra displacement point.

* * *

There was really no need for DiFalco to be in *Andy J.*'s control room just now, and he knew that Farrell and the others would be inexpressibly relieved to have him out of their hair. But the control room had one advantage over his cabin, now that it was equipped with artificial gravity: it was—almost—big enough for satisfactory pacing.

For a time, the tension had let up fractionally as their worst nightmare had begun to recede. They had all known, too well, that they could not possibly stop a determined counterattack in force from Tareil. But weeks had passed and no Korvaash warships had emerged from the displacement point, and their minds had downgraded the threat from unbearable suspense to mere background worry. DiFalco still wondered why the Korvaasha had missed their chance.

Their other waking-nightmare had been that a Korvaash convoy or reinforcing battlefleet would come blundering through the other displacement point from the Korvaash-held systems beyond that had, as yet, no way of knowing what had happened at Seivra. But none had—only one nondescript courier that they had blasted out of existence. Eventually, of course, that courier would be missed. But not yet.

So they had repaired their battle damage and taken up their planned position . . . and begun sweating again, for they had entered into the time-frame within which they could realistically hope for word from Aelanni. An open-ended time frame, of course; no one could know what delays she might have encountered on her long, risk-fraught voyage to Tareil. They could only settle grimly into a state of readiness that was exhausting over the long haul but which they would maintain until the word to move arrived—or until the Korvaasha finally got over whatever it was that was keeping them sitting passively in Tareil.

Gazing at viewscreens, DiFalco could see the other cruisers that lay off *Andy J.*'s flanks. And he could almost hear the thrumming of overstretched nerves from across space, for they had entered into the real nightmare: the protracted time-scale of helpless anticipation.

A rustling sound of movement behind him brought his head snapping around. It was Varien.

"Goddamn it, don't *ever* sneak into the control room!" He was instantly sorry, but a shift to mere grumbling was the closest he would let himself come to an apology. "You shouldn't even be in the control room at all, you know. Hell, you shouldn't even be aboard this ship! When we go through that

displacement point blind, with God knows what
waiting on the other side . . ."

"We've been over this before, Colonel," Varien
said mildly.

"Yeah, but I still don't understand why you insist
on going in with the first wave. When we attacked
Seivra you were willing to follow along in a transport
and wait until we'd secured the system."

"The situation is quite different now, as you must
realize. When we transit this displacement point, we
will be . . . 'going for broke'? Yes, that's it. This will be
our first, last, and only opportunity to liberate Raehan,
and if we fail there will be no *point* to my further
survival, Colonel. To use another of your idioms, I have
nothing to lose. And I have no desire to sit in this
system waiting for word of the outcome at Tareil.
Patience is not my strong point; I have been told that
by so many people that I must reluctantly admit it is
probably true."

DiFalco was silent. He had thought he knew the
full spectrum of Varien's moods, but he had never
seen this fatalism. And yet the old Raehaniv was
right. This one was for all the marbles.

"You could wait with the transports, you know. The
whole point to stationing them in the outermost
outskirts of this system was to enable the
noncombatants to get away to Terranova on
continuous-displacement drive if we blow it. The
settlement there could use you."

Varien smiled. "I know you mean well, Colonel.
But over these last years the freeing of Raehan has
become the only meaning my life has, other than my
son and daughter—and they, too, are on the other
side of this displacement point. You see," he continued, as if carefully explaining something that *must* be
made clear, "I can no more *not* be on the first ship
through than you could . . . Eric."

For a long moment there was no sound but the
low hums and beeps of the control room, and no

motion in the two shadowed faces that regarded each other in the dim light. When DiFalco broke the silence, his voice was very matter-of-fact. "When we start to accelerate, I want you in an acceleration couch, and I want you to *stay* there. I still don't trust this artificial gravity of yours. . . ."

*   *   *

Aelanni did trust artificial gravity, which to her was old technology, and she stood with arms folded in *Liberator*'s control room, gazing unblinkingly at the Korvaash warships in the screen.

Huge, as if designed in proportion to the creatures that built and crewed them. Ungainly seeming, although like all Raehaniv she knew too well their basic functionality. Crudely ugly, with none of the aesthetic flourishes that Raehaniv engineers had always found a way to work into spacecraft designs. And numerous—appallingly numerous. Scores of them, arranged in the precise alignments of what was clearly a standard formation.

Rosen, too, could not take his eyes from the screen, for on it he saw the nightmare that had haunted his world for generations: technology as Leviathan, soulless and hideous and deadly to all that was human. *How pathetically mild our imaginings turn out to have been*, he thought, and wondered what nightmares from Raehan's Global Wars the sight awoke in Aelanni.

She gave no sign, but continued to stare fixedly at the magnified images in a silence that Naeriy finally broke. "We have now entered our extreme missile range," the flag captain said quietly. "Shall I . . . ?"

"No." Aelanni spoke the flat monosyllable without moving her eyes a micron from the screen. "Is there anything to indicate that we have been detected?"

"There is not," Naeriy replied emphatically. There was no reason why there should have been. As soon as they had detected the Korvaash fleet they had made the course correction—minor, as it had turned out—needed to assure that their hyperbolic orbit would bring them sweeping past that fleet's sterns. The short burn, far out in the darkness of the outer system and far above the ecliptic, had elicited no response, and they had continued to coast in silence toward a consummation of thunder.

Time ticked by and Rosen began to fidget. "Aelanni . . ."

She waved him peremptorily to silence. "I want to get closer. The shorter the range at which we launch, the less time their countermeasures will have to respond."

Rosen composed himself to wait.

Chagluk gazed critically at the sensor readouts and recalled his earlier pride that a mere courier ship like the one he commanded should have received the new, upgraded instrumentation. Now he wasn't so sure. The sensor suite had been endless trouble, and he suspected subtle sabotage by the humans who had labored on the refitting. But now they seemed to be on the way to getting the bugs out, and he felt sure that by the time they rendezvoused with the still-distant battlefleet all would be in order.

"Do another grav scan of the battlefleet," he ordered the engineer (no separate sensor billet on a craft this size), "and compare the readings with the known masses of the ships."

"Acknowledged," Gozthag replied, then stiffened with annoyance. "The directional controls are *still* off. I must search for the correct region. . . ." Suddenly, he stiffened again, in a very different way. "What . . . ? Look—approaching the battlefleet at interplanetary velocities . . ."

Chuglak looked over Gozthag's head at the readouts. His paralysis lasted only an instant, and while Gozthag was still blithering he roared at the communications officer.

Rosen could keep quiet no longer. "Aelanni, you

must give the order! We're close enough! They're bound to detect us any time."

"But they haven't yet," Aelanni replied calmly, without taking her eyes from the magnified images in the screen. "I want to close the range a little more."

Rosen started to open his mouth, then clamped it shut. He didn't trust his voice to keep steady, any more steady then his hands. He clenched his fists, despising himself for his jitters, and looked again at the range readout. Then, irrationally but irresistably, he darted a glance out the wide-sweeping armorplast viewport.

Good God! Does the crazy woman mean to get within visual *range?!* Rosen wondered wildly if, in spite of everything, maybe the Raehaniv weren't really human after all. But then he swept his eyes over Naeriy and the others in the control room. They all looked as nervous as he felt.

Grashkul, Effectuator of Expansion, surveyed the expanse of the flagship's commamnd center with satisfaction. He had only recently arrived to take personal command of the system battlefleet, although he had departed from Raehan as soon as possible after taking over from the late Kulnakh.

The thought of the former Effectuator of Expansion soured his mood. Kulnakh had been right, of course. They should have launched probing attacks through the displacement point to gauge the strength of the opposition in Seivra. And if that opposition had proved to be no stronger than he thought it was (having exhaustively studied the picket's report, including the imagery of the oddly old-fashioned-looking ship that had attacked it) then they should have gone through in full force, accepting whatever losses it took to recapture Seivra. Yes, Kulnakh had been right . . . but Grashkul wasn't about to say so aloud.

At least the unknown inferior beings had displayed equal caution, allowing time for the entire battlefleet to be concentrated here. Brobdingnagian battleships like this one, armed primarily with long-range missiles, made up the rear echelons, behind the somewhat smaller, faster battlecruisers with their batteries of energy weapons, including plasma artillery powered by fusion plants of the scale on which the Korvaasha built ships. Nothing could come through from Seivra and live—of that he was certain.

A harsh series of sounds suddenly awoke at the communications console. After a moment, the operator turned and spoke across the command center in the far-reaching low frequencies of Korvaash speech.

"Effectuator, I have received a somewhat incoherent message from the commander of a courier vessel enroute from Raehan. He urgently advises us to scan a certain region of space which I have taken the liberty of downloading to the sensor controls. Of course," he continued, doing a rapid calculation, "the message was sent over twenty *rizhula* ago."

Grashkul understood. Neutrino-pulse communication over a sufficiently long range ouside a gravity well could effectively exceed lightspeed—the carrier beam itself did not, of course, for neutrinos were not really massless as had once been thought; but the information-carrying pulses could be propagated along it faster, as much as five times as fast in fact. But it took *real* distance to take full advantage of the effect. So this courier commander's alert held a slight time lag.

"Instruct the computer to compensate, and scan the area," he ordered. A few moments ticked by while his command was carried out. He motioned a subordinate aside and seated himself at the scanner console. Then he gazed at the readout and froze.

"Now, Aelanni?"
Aelanni shook her head in a preoccupied way,

oblivious to the pleading note in Rosen's voice. The Terran drew a shaken breath and glanced out the viewport again.

There was no possible doubt. He could distinctly make out the serried ranks of tiny objects far ahead, their visible separation gradually growing as he watched.

They really *were* coming into visual range!

Grashkul surged erect from the scanner console. "General fleet alert!" he bellowed. "All ships are to come up to full power and . . ."

"*Aelanni, you crazy* shiksa!"

Simultaneously with Rosen's yelp came Aelanni's command. "Launch all missiles!"

Naeriy's hand swept over an array of lights and the fleet's linked computers implemented the targeting solution they had already worked out during the long approach. Full salvos of missiles leaped from all the ships simultaneously and sprang ahead. Piling their acceleration atop the ships' velocity, they swept into the Korvaash formation too swiftly for any thought of defense by ships in the process of receiving new orders.

The first hit awoke like a small but very intense sun. Others followed in such rapid succession as to seem a chain reaction, a spreading contagion of flame as one Korvaash ship after another expanded and split apart in a horrible, unnatural birth of hellfire.

The armorplast of the viewport automatically polarized, saving the eyesight of all in the control room of the still-approaching *Liberator*. Aelanni, eyes riveted on the spectacle, gave a second order. "Launch message drones!"

A second series of salvos dropped from the ships, but these sped toward the Seivra displacement point, past the savaged Korvaash defenders who grew in the screens at an ever-accelerating rate.

And then they were past, flashing by with the velocity to which they had been pulled by Tareil's gravity over the past weeks. And as they passed the holocaust, insanely close, the shock wave reached them. The expanding, superheated gas of vaporized metal, plastic and Korvaasha formed a wave front through which they passed, still in free fall.

Artificial gravity could not begin to compensate, and *Liberator* bucked and plunged madly. Rosen was flung to the deck but Aelanni hung onto a stanchion and remained grimly erect. Rosen gazed up, half-stunned, and saw her standing steady amid chaos, illuminated by the lightninglike flashes of continuing explosions from the screens. There was no wind for her hair to blow in, but there should have been, for she was like an elemental spirit of vengeance and destruction riding the storm that she herself had loosed on the world.

And then the moment was over. The still-exploding Korvaash ships were receding astern, the deck steadied, people picked themselves up, and Aelanni calmly gave the order for the prearranged course change. Then she extended a hand and hauled Rosen to his feet.

"What's a *shiksa*?" she inquired.

* * *

"Quiet!" Grashkul thundered, momentarily stemming the flood tide of panic-stricken reports and queries. By sheer presence, he quelled the incipient hysteria (which would have looked like mild agitation to human eyes, but which was without precedent among the Korvaasha) in the command center of the undamaged flagship.

"No more reports! We can assess the damage later." He turned to his chief of staff. "Get all ships with undamaged drives turned around and go to maximum boost in pursuit of those ships. The damaged ships that still have weapons capability can keep watch on the displacement point."

"But Effectuator," the chief of staff replied with a slight quaver in his voice which meant what open hand-wringing would have in a human, "we'll never catch them! A stern chase . . ."

"Effectuator!" The impropriety of the interruption from the scanner chief would have been shocking at any other time. "The inferior beings have altered course! They have ceased retrofiring and are now proceeding on a course of . . ." A series of figures followed, delivered with the machinelike precision of old, to Grashkul's relief. Conditioning was reasserting itself.

"Then it *won't* be a stern chase," he declared with vicious satisfaction. "We can intercept them on that course—it will take time, but we can do it. And"—he glanced at the command readouts, noted the estimated tonnage of those ships, and made a mental adjustment for the efficiency of Raehaniv engineering—"we still have what must be ten times their firepower." He turned back to the chief of staff. "Get with Navigation and carry out your orders, Kaathgor!"

"At once, Effectuator!" But Kaathgor hesitated momentarily. "Ah, Effectuator . . . what of that second salvo of missiles the inferior beings launched?"

"What of it? They all missed and proceeded outward. Something must have gone wrong with their targeting." Grashkul was as close as any Korvaasha ever comes to fidgeting with impatience. He *had* to overhaul and obliterate these intruders, whoever they were, thereby salvaging something from this debacle.

Kaathgor's voice broke into his thoughts. "That is the point, Effectuator. You see, they are proceeding directly toward the . . ."

Grashkul's pent-up rage erupted. "Enough!" he roared with a volume that hurt Korvaash auditory apparatus. "Stop wasting time and carry out your orders, you . . . female!"

At the deadliest insult in the Korvaash language, Kaathgor's face and voice went totally expressionless.

"Of course, Effectuator," he said smoothly. "It will be as you command."

*   *   *

The Korvaash warships that could still do so lumbered into correct alignment, and fusion fire speared blindingly from their drives, sending them on the optimum intercept course. No one except Kaathgor—who had no intention of bringing it up—noticed that that course happened to take them away from the Seivra displacement point on its emergence bearing.

Meanwhile, unnoticed, the missiles that were not missiles reached that displacement point.

*   *   *

DiFalco tumbled into *Andy J.*'s control room, cursing the fate that had—of course!—brought the long-awaited alarm in the middle of his first sound sleep in far too long. Varien, he noted, was already there, strapping himself into his assigned acceleration couch.

"Report!" he rapped, midway into the command couch.

"It's confirmed, sir," Farrell stated, excitement barely under control. "That first emergence was one of the message drones—it's broadcasting like mad now. The other one should start any time . . . there! They're both ours!"

DiFalco and Varien exchanged looks. The weak link in their plans had, from the beginning, been the problem of coordinating two fleets on opposite sides of a defended displacement point. No non-material signal could be sent through, so they had devised material ones: missiles whose warheads had been replaced by very simple transponders and very complex nav computers that might attempt the displacement transit that had heretofore been the exclusive province of manned vessels. Of course, they knew better than to rely on such new and chancy devices; the odds against one of them making a successful transit were overwhelming. So Aelanni's ships had foregone a second missile salvo, instead devoting their entire launching capacity to a swarm of the new drones that would—they hoped—beat the odds by sheer numbers.

DiFalco expected exultation on Varien's face and saw annoyance. "Only two, out of all those drones . . . !"

"That's exactly two hundred percent of what we need," DiFalco snapped. "Aelanni's there! Mister Farrell, execute Plan Omega, Phase One!"

Fusion drives roared and, at an acceleration that only their counteracting artificial gravity fields made endurable, they began their run at the displacement point. By the time they reached it, they had built up such a velocity that precise computer control was required to activate the gravitic pulse that would hurl them through it at precisely the right moment. But the programming did its work, and they burst into the Tareil system at a pace that would normally have been sheer insanity for attackers of a defended displacement point.

At least, DiFalco thought as the stars rearranged themselves into the sky of Raehan (*the sky Aelanni grew up with*, flashed through his mind), the speed of their transition didn't seem to intensify its discomfort. Then the instrumentation stabilized, and scanners began to detect the drifting wreckage from which they could deduce the full dimensions of what Aelanni had wrought.

"Holy shit," DiFalco breathed, looking up from the readout. Varien muttered something in Raehaniv.

Then they were in among the fields of ball bearings the Korvaasha had strewn along the emergence heading. The millions of dense little objects would normally have reduced ships moving at their velocity to collanders. But each cruiser put out its forward deflector shield and, like a man advancing into driving rain with an umbrella held in front of him, drove grimly through the metal storm.

"Colonel," Farrell called out, "we've pinpointed Aelanni's force, and their pursuers." The tactical holo tank activated, revealing a small cluster of friendlies and a larger mass of bogies on converging courses only a few degrees apart.

It was, DiFalco thought dourly, going suspiciously well. Aelanni had led the Korvaasha on almost precisely the chase they had planned on. Now they'd have to start playing it by ear.

"Mr. Farrell, resume acceleration on optimum pursuit course. And give me a projection on when we can expect to catch up to the Korvaash force."

Fusion drives that had been cut off for the transit—no need to unnecessarily complicate an already tricky maneuver—reawoke, and again there was a slight surge before the compensating fields could take hold. Ahead of them, the pyrotechnics intensified as ball bearings impacted the deflector shield at an even higher relative velocity and were burned out of existence by lost kinetic energy that had to go somewhere.

"Ready with that computer projection, Colonel," Farrell reported. DiFalco nodded, and the holo tank awoke into new activity as glowing lines curved ahead along projected courses at accelerated time. Aelanni's green line and the red Korvaash one slid together while his own green track was still some little distance away. Then it, too, intersected the others, and all three continued on together in what would be an embrace of death.

Aelanni would just have to take it for a while.

Varien was also looking at the tank, face expressionless. DiFalco recalled his own attempts to convey the difficulty of coordinating simultaneous force deployments over vast separations of space and time, but he did not remind Varien of it. *My character must be improving*, he thought gloomily.

"Continue on course, Mr. Farrell," he ordered. "And pass the word to stand by for combat with those immobile Korvaash units ahead. It looks like we're going to pass them within missile range."

*   *   *

Grashkul kept outwardly impassive as he received the report—delivered without inflection by Kaathgor—of the seven newly arrived hostiles from Seivra. They had flashed past the damaged ships he had left to watch a displacement point that had seemed no longer so important, exchanging missiles in a brief spasm of violence, but had not paused. Instead, they had continued accelerating, adding onto a velocity that should have brought them to grief in the obstructed zone. And now they were on a course which would bring them into the battle that was about to begin with the nine mysterious intruders that had savaged his fleet and now approached this system's asteroid belt on their sunward course.

Inwardly, his guts seethed. Kaathgor could, of course, not remind him that his own impatience had prevented the chief of staff from reporting the heading of those missiles of the second salvo, which would have mandated the incredible conclusion that these raiders, already here in the Tareil system, were somehow connected with the conquerors of Seivra. No, Kaathgor couldn't *openly* bring it up—but his entire attitude fairly screamed it.

"It appears," the chief of staff was concluding, "that our cripples were unable to inflict appreciable damage on the newcomers in the brief time available to them."

"Of course not," Grashkul replied testily. "They were unprepared, and most of them have damaged targeting systems. . . ." He let the futile line of thought die a natural death. "It is clear that these two groups of inferior beings are acting in concert," he resumed, watching Kaathgor closely for anything that even resembled smugness. "So we must defeat them in detail. We will overwhelm the ones who attacked us before those from Seivra can overhaul us."

"There is another possibility, Effectuator," Kaathgor said diffidently. "We could break off the engagement. The dynamics of our present astronomical situation would permit us to retire on Raehan if we commence the course change within . . ."

"Preposterous!" Grashkul's eye bulged with astonished fury. "What are you suggesting? We could still defeat *both* these pathetic forces together in a straightforward battle, if we had to! Open fire on the ships we are pursuing as soon as we enter missile range!"

"As you command, Effectuator."

Grashkul turned away without even formally dismissing Kaathgor and studied the tactical display. Of course they would win. Of course. If he had still had his full strength of battleships, there would have been no doubt; he would have smothered those ships ahead of him in an avalanche of long-range missiles. But unfortunately, his losses had been heaviest in the missile-armed behemoths—the raiders must have specifically targeted them. So the brunt of the first battle would fall on the battlecruisers, which had been pulling steadily ahead and would come into energy-weapon range of the enemy only minutes after the missile engagement began. Of course, it would take them longer to close to the short ranges where energy weaponry was really effective.

His eye glowered at those nine blips. Who *were* they? Their design was pure Raehaniv, and he had been going on the working assumption that they belonged to the *Free* (of necessity, he used the Raehaniv word for the untranslatable concept) Raehaniv Fleet. But their order of battle for that fleet included no such ships. And how could they have gotten away from the carefully monitored asteroid region to launch an attack that had clearly originated in the outer reaches of the system, far from the ecliptic? (He would have words for the Obtainer of Foreknowledge after this was over!) And how could they be coordinating their actions with the mysterious occupiers of Seivra?

If Grashkul had been human he would have shaken his head ruefully. This newly incorporated region had yielded one surprise after another of late. Through all the centuries in which the Unity had expanded in precisely the manner predicted by the Acceptable Knowledge, nothing had ever surprised the Korvaasha.

Then the deck vibrated under him and he heard the rumble of the first missile salvo. Soon it would all be academic.

*   *   *

Liberator's control room seemed to lurch as they absorbed another hit. Aelanni rapped out a series of orders, then studied the status readout.

They had given far better than they had gotten. Their defensive lasers had been able to cope with the big missiles from the depleted ranks of the Korvaash battleships. And their own missiles had taken toll of the advancing Korvaash battlecruisers until they had given out. But then the battlecruisers had drawn into energy-weapon range, and their massed laser batteries (specialized armaments were a feature of Korvaash ship designs) had begun to stab at her ships. They had fought back, with weapons enjoying the advantages of Raehaniv engineering. But the battlecruisers, in their ungainly massiveness, could absorb a lot of punishment. And they could mount a lot of weaponry—even crude, inefficient Korvaash weaponry. The brute mathematics of tonnage and firepower, which did not recognize gallantry as a factor, were inexorably wearing her force down.

Avenger had fallen out of formation early, and had by now ceased to communicate. *Deliverer* had blown up with a spectacular effulgence of light. Other ships had suffered various degrees of damage. *Liberator* had gotten off lightly—but not for long. The Korvaasha had now closed to plasma-weapon range, and the slugging match that was commencing could have but one conclusion.

Her eyes met Naeriy's, and no words were necessary. Eric's ships (*Eric!*) were still not even within missile range of the Korvaash battleships. When they did pull into range, they would face the Korvaasha alone.

Things would be different if we had deflector shields like the Terran ships, she thought, oddly calm. *But then we wouldn't have had the drive modifications that enabled us to get here. It was a tradeoff we freely accepted.*

Her eyes went to the viewport. Yes, the Korvaash battlecruiser that showed in all its hideousness on the screen was now visible, like a child's model toy across a twilit lawn. She turned to Rosen and knew that, in some ways, she mourned him more than anyone else. For all the rest of them were Raehaniv, and could not have done otherwise than be here. She felt she should say something. But then he gave his gently ironic smile, and his voice told her not to worry.

"We gave them a good run, didn't we?"

She smiled back. "Yes we did." Then she reached out and grasped his hand, hard. (It would once have been unthinkable for a Raehaniv. He was right; they had changed.) And she spoke a word he had taught her. "*Shalom*, Yakov."

"*Shalom*, Aelanni."

Suddenly, their faces were bathed with light from the screen. An instant later, the tiny Korvaash battlecruiser in the viewport was replaced by a little bit of sun—a point of light which began to grow, and then was all the sky there was. The armorplast darkened just in time to save them from blindness, but spots continued to dance before their eyes as the glare died away, revealing an expanding halo of glowing plasma that had been a battlecruiser.

After a heartbeat, the dead silence in the control

room was shattered as the communicator squawked. "Calling the unknown vessels! Calling the unknown vessels! This is the Free Raehaniv Fleet. Please acknowledge."

In one unbroken motion Aelanni was out of her crash couch, across the control room, and at the comm console, elbowing the communications officer out of the way. "This is Aelanni zho'Morna, daughter of Varien hle'Morna. Please make visual contact."

At this range, neutrino-pulse communications were virtually instantaneous. The comm screen awoke, revealing a man in a highly non-reg version of the wartime Raehaniv fleet uniform.

"Aelanni?" His voice broke in an incredulous squeak. "This is Yarvann hle'Taren. We've been maintaining surveillance of the Seivra displacement point, and we had a quick-response force to react to any developments out here, and . . . and what am I babbling about? Arduin told us your father didn't die as is generally believed, but by now we had become certain that all of you were dead!"

Suddenly, she could barely suppress a giggle as she quoted a saying of Eric's people. "The rumors of our death have been greatly exaggerated." Then she remembered herself, and glanced at the holo tank in which the Free Raehaniv ships were springing into life as the fleets' computers began to talk to each other. "Please continue to match vectors with us and the Korvaasha, Yarvann. We still have a battle to fight. We'll explain everything later. But," she added, beckoning to Rosen, "first of all, there's someone you should meet."

*   *   *

Grashkul stared fixedly at the tactical display and knew the ashen taste of hopelessness.

When the feral humans of the asteroids had set upon his battlecruisers he had ordered the battleships to alter course and attempt to reach Raehan. But the oncoming unknowns had followed, remorselessly continuing to close the range, and a missile duel had erupted that had soon exhausted his depleted magazines. And the victorious Raehaniv ahead had decelerated so as to cross his course, so that now the surviving battleships were about to come into range of their energy weapons. Missiles were still arriving from astern, but he hardly noticed the buffeting of near-misses.

This could not be happening. The Acceptable Knowledge, which had never failed the Unity before, did not allow for it. A universe without the solid and immovable foundation of the Acceptable Knowledge's infallibility was a universe of unimaginable chaos, from which his mind shied away too quickly even to consciously reject it.

And yet it *was* happening.

Kaathgor approached slowly, dragging a leg that had been injured by a falling structural member, threading his way through the damage-control workers. "Scanning reports another incoming spread of missiles, Effectuator. What are your orders?"

For a moment that stretched and stretched, Grashkul was silent, eye staring unseeingly ahead. Kaathgor was about to repeat the question when the Effectuator of Expansion spoke almost inaudibly, to no one in particular.

"Lies. All lies. Nothing but lies."

Before Kaathgor could ask him what he meant, a war-god's mace smote the flagship, and noise and flame became all the universe that was or could be.

*   *   *

"But are you quite certain that this is the way I should put it?" Varien sounded very dubious.

They stood in the midst of frantic activity as specialists established contact with their opposite numbers in the Free Raehaniv Fleet through specially-installed banks of communicators, coordinating the mop-up of the Korvaash remnants.

But Varien had the main console all to himself as

he prepared, before they even rendezvoused with
Aelanni, to broadcast a message that would blanket
the Tareil system.

They had hastily cobbled the message together,
and DiFalco had come into the discussion with the
advantage of a man with a clear idea, and so had
placed a strong imprint on the sheet of hard copy
Varien now held before him, reading over once again
with unabated skepticism.

"I suppose, Eric," he continued hesitantly, "if
you're quite sure . . ."

"Trust me. I know what I'm doing." DiFalco shot
a glance at the chronometer. "You're on!"

Varien cleared his throat and took a breath. "People of Raehan: I have returned . . ."

CHAPTER FIFTEEN

Daeliuv regarded Yakov Rosen and tried once again to overcome a sense of unreality. It wan't that the man across the table was particularly strange-looking—short and stocky on Raehaniv standards, looking older than Daeliuv now knew he was, features and coloring faintly exotic, but overall nothing alarming. It was his very ordinariness which seemed wrong, even though Daeliuv had known about the Landaeniv for some time.

The Free Raehaniv had rendezvoused with Aelanni first, before Varien and his new allies had arrived. By now they had seen other Landaeniv, in all their surprising variety. But Rosen had been the first one they had set eyes on, and to all of them who had been present for that first visual pickup from Aelanni's control room he remained the quintessential Landaeniv, imprinted on their minds with the strength of first impressions.

No, not "Landaeniv," Daeliuv scolded himself. *Terran. Must remember that.*

He dragged his mind back to the subject at hand. "So you found this abandoned base just after entering the system you call 'Terranova'?"

"Yes," Rosen replied in his fluent Raehaniv. "It

was purely by chance—a wildly improbable chance, as I've often reflected in the years since." He frowned and sipped his wine. (The Free Raehaniv had been able to keep limited supply channels open, and the reception the two of them had gotten away from had been an occasion to warrant the breaking out of long-hoarded stocks.) "I gather it was the same with the asteroid—Turanau?—that you Free Raehaniv discovered."

"Precisely. It was only by sheer chance that we learned of this dead civilization that was operating in our part of the galaxy at the time humans appeared on Raehan." Daeliuv paused, then spoke almost plaintively. "And your scientists are *quite* certain that your ancestors evolved on Earth?"

"Oh, yes. That's been established for a long time. There's no break in our world's evolutionary history as there is in yours." Rosen was silent for a long, thoughtful moment, stroking the beard he had grown on Terranova—it was thicker than any Raehaniv could have managed, Daeliuv noted. "But you spoke of a 'dead civilization,' Daeliuv. Are you *absolutely* certain it's dead?"

"What?! Well . . . there certainly doesn't seem to be any evidence that it's presently active."

"No. Not unless you count the fact that we've both been making these highly unlikely discoveries at the same time—which also happens to be the time at which we're coming into contact with each other. Can you imagine what the odds against that must be?"

Daeliuv gave him a long, hard look. Then he smiled. "Don't tell me you Lan . . . Terrans believe in ghosts, Yakov!"

Rosen's intense expression dissolved into a wry grin. "Oh, no. Not to worry. I can't really believe we're all going through the motions as actors in somebody else's . . ." He stumbled to a halt. The Raehaniv for "psychodrama" was beyond him.

"At any rate," Daeliuv said briskly, "we can't let it concern us now. The freeing of Raehan has to take first priority. Speaking of which, it's almost time for the conference.

"So it is." Rosen drained his wine and stood up. "Someday, after all this is over, I want very much to see Turanau. We need to do some very hard thinking about these matters."

"We do," Daeliuv agreed.

Arduin had come out from the asteroids to join the combined fleets, and he and Varien had greeted each other with as much emotion as two Raehaniv of their generation were able to display in public. But the stream of pressurized catching-up had dried to an embarrassed trickle when Varien had inquired as to Tarlann. He had listened unflinchingly to the story of his son's capture.

"His wife and children have never emerged from Gromorgh's headquarters," Arduin had concluded. "Beyond that, our sources have been able to learn nothing about them. We've avoided contacting him, since we're certain that they're being held as hostages and we don't want to put him in an impossible position. He's been keeping a very low profile. Our sources report"—he had avoided Varien's eyes—"he's been walking with a limp."

"He knew the risks," was all Varien had allowed himself to say. Otherwise, he had kept silent, alone with his pain.

Now he and Aelanni sat at the head of the conference table in *Liberator*'s briefing room. He translated English into Raehaniv for Arduin, Daeliuv, Yarvann and Miranni; Aelanni, backed up by Rosen, did the reverse for DiFalco, Golovko, Levinson and Kuropatkin. Captured Korvaash translation devices were being programmed for English, but they were still far from ready.

"Our situation is as follows," Varien began his

summary. "Our light units and transports are proceeding as planned through the displacement point from Seivra, and have destroyed the crippled Korvaash ships there. They will rendezvous with us at Raehan, toward which we ourselves are now on course. We need to decide how to proceed when we arrive."

Daeliuv cleared his throat. "The problem," he began with a didacticism that was perceptible even in translation, "is as follows. The Korvaasha, true to their policy of holding conquered populations hostage, have placed their headquarters and other major installations in four of our chief cities, having razed large areas of those cities for the purpose. We have been able to learn enough about those installations to know that they are *very* strong, particularly the main one in Sarnath. To annihilate them from orbit would require high-yield nuclear ground bursts. To take them by storm would be a costly undertaking."

Miranni spoke up. "Couldn't we simply sit in orbit and wait them out? If we offer them their lives—as much as I hate to do it—they'd surely surrender eventually. They can't squat in their fortresses forever!"

"They wouldn't have to." DiFalco's face was set and grim. "Don't you see? Time is on their side. Sooner or later, a Korvaash convoy or task force is going to pass through Seivra. The skeleton force we've got there now can't possibly prevent at least one of them from getting away and warning the rest of the Korvaash empire. All the Korvaash occupiers of Raehan have to do is hold out until relief arrives."

"Eric's right," Yarvann stated emphatically. He had felt refreshed ever since the initial round of meetings and mutual visits. He *liked* the Terrans!

Miranni ignored him and stared straight at DiFalco. "What are you proposing, then? That we missile the fortresses from space, obliterating our own cities?"

"No," DiFalco answered slowly, giving Varien plenty of time to translate and wishing the Global Wars-era Raehaniv hadn't rejected with horror the kind of precision kinetic-energy weapons that might have spared them this dilemma. But they had, and that was that. "I fully appreciate that that's an unacceptable solution. Your resistance fighters and our Marines will just have to go in and take those fortresses by ground assault. There's no alternative."

Arduin spoke just as slowly. "You realize, Colonel DiFalco, that an all-out ground battle will also wreak horrible devastation on a city? Not as much as a nuclear weapon, of course, but . . ."

"Damn it." Levinson broke into Varien's running translation. "Of course we realize that. But I don't hear anyone offering any better suggestions." He took a deep breath. "Two or three generations ago, Americans—that's my and Colonel DiFalco's people, on Earth—somehow got the idea into their heads that in war nobody is supposed to get killed, and therefore if people *do* get killed it must mean somebody has been incompetent. Like most of the things Americans of that era liked to believe, it was bullshit." Varien supplied a sanitized translation. "Face it: there's no clean, painless, bloodless way you're going to get your planet out from under the Korvaasha and their human storm troopers." He had heard about the Implementers, and the loathing the stories had called up had come from the memories in his very genes.

"We can't argue with your logic," Arduin spoke heavily. "But the fact remains . . ."

"The fact remains," Miranni blurted out, "that it's Raehan, *our* world, that you're talking about. Could you apply the same cool rationality if it were your Earth?"

DiFalco was opening his mouth to answer when Varien held up a hand. "With your permission, Eric, I'd like to respond to that. Aelanni, please translate into English." He turned to the Free Raehaniv side of the table and switched to their tongue.

"I understand what you're feeling," he said, very gently, addressing all of them in the second person plural but looking Miranni in the eyes. "For a long time we Raehaniv have regarded war as a demon that might be summoned up merely by thinking about it in realistic terms. Even you of the Free Raehaniv Fleet still flinch from looking the demon squarely in the face whenever you can possibly avoid it. So did I, until recently. But if we are to end our world's agony, we *must* face it! To prolong war by shrinking from the measures necessary to end it is merely moral cowardice masquerading as moral delicacy. And to impugn the motives of those who advocate those measures is to compound the felony with intellectual dishonesty. Don't resent the Terrans because they're asking you to make the kind of tragic choices we Raehaniv have been able to avoid for so long. On the day we encountered the Korvaasha, our lives became a long chain of tragic choices. Thanks to the Terrans, we may now have the chance to break that chain! You all know by now the risks they've taken to give us that chance. And remember: for them, destroying the fortresses from orbit would be the safe, easy way. In the ground assault Colonel DiFalco proposes, many of his Marines will die so that our cities may live."

Miranni's eyes fell, and there was a long, long silence.

Finally, Arduin spoke gruffly. "You're right, Varien. So are you, Colonel DiFalco. We'll do whatever we have to do." There were low sounds of agreement from Miranni and Daeliuv, and a loud one from Yarvann.

* * *

Tarlann raised his head from the floor to which he had been flung, and looked up, and up, and up. Gromorgh stood before him.

"You know why you have been brought here,"

came the slow, tinny bass from the translator pendant. "You undoubtedly heard the broadcast from the feral inferior being claiming to be your father."

So that's going to be the official line, Tarlann thought dully. Of course he had heard the broadcast; so had everyone on Raehan who had a receiver and had been alerted. The Resistance had been spreading the word that something big and mysterious was going on. He hadn't needed his old close contacts to hear the whispers.

He had listened, and wept, and then sat down to wait. In the old days he would have gone to Dormael's and been spirited to a safe bolthole. But now there was nowhere he could go, nowhere they could not seek out the homing beacon they had implanted in his flesh.

The Implementers had come soon afterwards and taken him to the Korvaash stronghold, where he had expected to at least see Nissali and Iael once more. But he had seen no one; they had locked him in a holding cell and, to all appearances, forgotten about him. Finally, after a time of cold, filth and barely edible slops—he could not say how long a time—the Implementers had returned and taken him to this chamber.

He cautiously raised himself a little—his neck felt like it was breaking, looking up at this angle. "Yes, Director. I heard it. I have no special information concerning it."

"I did not expect you to, given your demonstrated uselessness as a double agent. It is, of course, a palpable fraud, intended to raise morale among the feral elements here on the planet with its fantasies of allies of your own species from beyond the stars, and of technological developments which are logically impossible, being unforeseen by the Acceptable Knowledge. It can have no effect except to incite futile acts of rebellion and delay your race's inevitable incorporation into the Unity. No, your father and sister are dead. The claims in the broadcast are as impossible as its accounts of imaginary triumphs are exaggerated."

Puzzlement grew in Tarlann. Why was the Korvaasha telling him all this, with such un-Korvaash prolixity? It was almost as if . . .

With almost physical force, the realization came. Gromorgh was, indeed, reciting an official line—a line to which he himself needed to demonstrate his adherence, for the benefit of whoever might be listening. The Director of Implementation was actually *frightened!*

The thought was so dizzying in its novelty that Tarlann forgot his inhibitions for an instant. "If this is so, Director, then why have I been brought here?" As soon as it was out of his mouth, Tarlann braced for the impact of a truncheon. But none came, and a heartbeat passed before Gromorgh replied.

"You may be of some use as a hostage, even though we are not, of course, actually dealing with your father. If the feral inferior beings mean to sustain this charade, they will have to *seem* to be influenced by threats to your life."

All at once, Tarlann could no longer keep himself in a crouch. Moving as if in a dream, he rose shakily to his feet and looked straight up into that disturbing eye. Both Gromorgh and the Implementers were, he supposed, shocked into immobility, but that was unimportant. All that mattered was what he now *knew.*

"Yes," he began slowly, "you *need* a hostage, don't you? You and I both know you do." His voice picked up tempo. "And every word in the broadcast was true, wasn't it? And so were the rumors before that." He threw back his head and, for the first time, a peal of joyous laughter was heard within those walls. "Father is back, and Aelanni, and their allies, these *Terrans*, and together we're going to rid the universe of you and your maggot-eaten Unity!"

The spell broke. An Implementer stepped forward and kicked Tarlann's legs out from under him. He tried to stay in fetal position against the rain of blows, but a kick to the kidneys made him arch his back with a gasp of pain. But before the beating could continue, the flat mechanical voice spoke.

"Enough. Take him to the maximum-security level and confine him with his son. Tell Laerav that he is not to be damaged to such an extent as might jeopardize his hostage value."

Tarlann had never realized the extent of the Korvaash fortress. As he was taken down through successive levels, he saw that the brutally intrusive structure in the heart of Sarnath was merely the tip of a subterranean iceberg of weaponry and torment.

The penultimate level was the worst, with its packed cells and much-used torture chambers—no real attempt had been made to clean up the results of their use. He could see why, for the Implementers who worked these levels matched their surroundings. He could detect his guards' disdain. Evidently there was social stratification even among Implementers, and these barely human creatures were the pariahs, the untouchables of that hierarchy of debasement.

But his destination was lower still, the lowest level of all. He wondered if it had been planned that way, requiring the maximum-security prisoners to pass through the regions of nightmare.

The final enormous doors crashed open, and Tarlann was shoved through into a chamber that was on the larger-than-human scale of everything the Korvaasha built, and which also had the characteristic dreary, half-finished look. Piping and cables ran through crudely cut openings in ceiling and walls, and hissing steam escaped periodically from vents, varying the dull metallic clanging and booming that pervaded all Korvaash interiors.

But Tarlann had eyes and ears for none of this. All he heard was the cry of "Father!" and all he saw was Iael's ragged figure stumbling toward him.

For some timeless length of time they embraced in a silence that was too full to hold any words. Finally, Tarlann raised his head and looked around at the chamber's emptiness.

"Your mother . . . ?"

Iael gulped several times, then spoke in a series of disjointed fragments. "They brought us here. . . . She wouldn't talk, or eat. . . . I tried to feed her, but at last she . . ." His features seemed to crumple, and his voice dissolved into an uncontrolable spasm of dry, wracking sobs. Tarlann held him again, more tightly than before.

At last Iael could speak in an emotionless monotone. "They used to come here and yell at us about what would happen to us if you didn't do as you were told. I couldn't understand all of the things they said. Mother never paid any attention to them. It was as if she didn't even know they were here— she just sat and hummed little songs to herself. It made them even madder."

But they couldn't do anything about their anger, of course, Tarlann thought. The captives must be preserved in undamaged condition, lest their later destruction seem but a merciful release from repitition-dulled pain and degredation. He saw no purpose in telling Iael what the boy had been spared by Gromorgh's desire to preserve what he had called "hostage value."

It hadn't saved Nissali, though. She had died of starvation and of her body's sheer lack of will to go on living in a world from whence her mind had already fled.

Farewell, my love. I wanted to see you one more time, but it is as well that I did not. I will remember you as you were.

For a long time, in the dank, echoing chamber, he

clung to the son who was all that he had left, and wondered where was help.

* * *

"Attention on deck!"

The Marines rose to their feet, the handful of Raehaniv ones with the eagerness of newbies and the Americans and Russians with the hangdog fatalism of veterans. The Raehaniv would get over it, Thompson thought as he walked down the center aisle with Kuropatkin and Tartakova. He mounted the podium and faced the packed ready room.

"As you were. We'll begin with the intelligence portion of the briefing."

Kuropatkin stood up and activated the holographic globe of Raehan. Little meteors of light swept slowly around it, indicating the orbital paths of their ships; Thompson had given up trying to understand how the Raehaniv did that.

"The red lights indicate the four cities with major Korvaash fortresses," Kuropatkin began. His English had improved immeasurably. "The orange lights mark those of their missile sites in the hinterlands whose locations we know, either from the Raehaniv Underground or from their own activity since we took up orbit. These will be taken out as our assault is commencing, as they are in relatively empty areas where we can use nuclear weapons. But we are certain that there are others.

"Of the four headquarters fortresses, the central one in Sarnath, the planetary capital, is naturally the strongest." One of the four red lights blinked for attention. "It has therefore been decided to commit the bulk of our powered-armor assets there. The other three will be left for the Raehaniv Resistance, with the aid of one Marine platoon for each. Major Thompson will go into specific unit assignments later. But this is the general pattern of deployment your assault shuttles will follow." Lights crawled around the image of Raehan, and patterns of smaller lights broke off from them, curving down to the planetary surface.

"The landings will, of course be made under cover from the utility shuttles that have been reconfigured as atmospheric fighters. . . ."

Thompson raised his hand. "A couple of questions, Boris." Kuropatkin didn't even sigh. He had long ago given up trying with the Americans. Not even his threat to rob them of their fun by legally changing his name to "Boris" had worked. "How are the Raehaniv Resistance types, who can't possibly have much in the way of heavy weapons, going to be able to take major installations like those with only minimal support? And how are our improvised combat shuttles going to avoid being eaten alive by Korvaash atmospheric fighters?"

"To answer your questions in order, Major Thompson," the Russian replied with pointed formality, "the Raehaniv Resistance is better-armed than you might think. Remember, Varien readied their arms caches before his departure, in collusion with elements of the Raehaniv military. They don't have powered combat armor, of course; we had to recreate that on Terranova out of Raehaniv history, and until we did, it hadn't existed for five centuries. But otherwise they have the best that a personal fortune of almost inconceivable extent could buy.

"As for Korvaash atmospheric fighters, there aren't any, at least not on Raehan. Fighter tactics require a degree of individual initiative which does not come naturally to the Korvaasha, or perhaps is merely disapproved of by their rulers—or, perhaps, centuries of the latter have resulted in the former. At any rate, they don't use them except when necessary to counter a specific threat, which has not been the case in their occupation of Raehan. They do, however, have antiaircraft weaponry which will pose a grave danger to our pilots.

"Major Tartakova will now describe your targets."

Irina Tartakova stood up, as formidably expressionless as ever—nobody *ever* called her "Natasha" to her face—and the globe of Raehan was replaced by a hologram of the central Korvaash headquarters in Sarnath. Then new images began to appear beneath the plane of light that represented ground level, layer after layer of them, down and down like a cancer eating into the flesh of Raehan beneath the skin. "This may be regarded as a minimal representation of extent of Korvaash works," Tartakova began. She went on to describe extrudable weapon emplacements, sliding blast doors, branching tunnels for escapes or sallies, and all the other products of a long-established school of military engineering.

When she was finished, Thompson smiled crookedly. "And now, Major, what's the *good* news?"

"Good news? Oh, I see. You joke. Ha." She reflected a moment. "Well, everything in fortress is built to Korvaash scale. In fact, their architecture uses proportions even larger than they need, doubtless for reasons inherent to their psychology. So corridors, doorways and so forth can accomodate your powered combat armor, which is normally unusable in enclosed spaces."

Thompson turned and faced the room. "Alright, people, you heard the lady. We can kick butt in any and all parts of that fortress. We won't have to wait outside and let the Raehaniv Resistance have all the fun." A chorus of theatrical moans and groans arose. He smiled sweetly. "And kicking *serious* butt is exactly what we're gonna do. You've all heard the stories of what's been going on planetside, about the Korvaasha and their human goons." All at once there was total silence. "Well," Thompson continued softly, "I think this will be one of the times when we get to enjoy our work." Then, all business, "Attention to unit assignments . . ."

*   *   *

Viewed from a distance, the titanic Korvaash

fortress in the heart of Sarnath had always suggested to Dorleann some obscene metal plug violating the world. Tonight, lit up amid the blacked-out cityscape, it seemed even more an unnatural intruder than usual.

He put away his electronic binoculars and descended the stairs of the deserted building. Raenoli was waiting for him at street level.

"Is everything ready?"

She nodded. "Yes. We've gotten as many noncombatants into the slidewalk tunnels as we can." The moving ways had been without power for some time, but the passages where they went under the great city's lowest levels might afford some protection from the destructive energies about to be unleashed upon old Sarnath.

As the Korvaasha had gradually withdrawn from more and more of the city, consolidating their defenses, Dorleann's Resistance units had moved quietly in. Now they were in position, distant from the fortress lest they be caught in the air attack that would preceed tomorrow's landing from the orbiting fleet.

The four urban fortresses around the world would be attacked simultaneously, as the dawn line was about to touch Sarnath. Sunrise would be heralded by another kind of light.

In unconscious unison, their eyes rose to the zenith. It was a clear night, and the orbiting ships could be seen as streaking lights.

"We should try and get some sleep," Dorleann said awkwardly. They were all alone.

"I doubt if we can," Raenoli said. "I know I can't. And . . . we may never have another chance, Dorleann."

Arm in arm, they descended the steps to the basement hideaway, leaving the street empty and waiting.

knew that nothing could save them, for even if one

CHAPTER SIXTEEN

H-hour struck, and Raehan shuddered to a drum-roll of nuclear impacts as the Korvaash missile bases were obliterated. They fought back with countermissiles and lasers, but eventually the defenses were saturated and the bases perished in fusion fire. Before dying, they got off as many of their own antispacecraft missiles as possible, and the Terran and Raehaniv ships grimly raised their own defenses. In vacuum, without a medium to transmit shock wave and thermal pulse, nuclear weapons aren't quite the terror they are in atmosphere. But none of the ships in orbit around Raehan could survive a direct hit.

With the immeasurable advantage of sitting at the top of the gravity well, the human allies were able to stave off serious damage. But they were grimly certain that other Korvaash missile stations hid under other remote regions of Raehan, waiting. And they knew that the missile engagement, for all its frightfulness, was only a preliminary. Already the drop shuttles were falling planetward, commencing this day's real business.

* * *

In the no-frills converted utility shuttle, the jolt when

the grav repulsion took hold was almost like the opening of an old-fashioned parachute. Naeriy loved it.

She brought her fighter swooping around into the proper heading, then ignited the fusion drive. A sword of violet-white flame stabbed out from the stern, and G-forces pressed her back into her seat as the fighter leaped ahead.

Normally, grav repulsion involved tradeoffs between altitude and lateral thrust—and, of course, other factors such as available power, for it was an energy hog. The shuttle had power to burn, and with the statutes against using fusion drives in atmosphere now a dead letter she could use the gravs purely to maintain altitude. The shuttle wasn't designed as a high-performance atmospheric craft, of course, but the generator now installed in the nose deflected the wind with an immaterial shield.

She lost altitude and arrowed eastward over the starlit ocean. Her acceleration had left sound far behind, and she knew the water was boiling in her wake. Seen through her light-gathering optics, the ocean waves ahead were reduced to a blur by her speed. She sighed with pure contentment and silently thanked Aelanni for allowing her this. Her flag captain's position had become redundant now that Aelanni's was no longer an independent command, so she had been able to wrangle this assignment, flying one of the little craft with which she had fallen in love the first time she had test-flown one on Terranova.

There! Up ahead was the coastline. With breath-taking speed it swept under her, and she suddenly needed to pay attention to her altitude. She cut her power—it always depressed her a little—and used the gravs to kill some of of her velocity. Finally she cut the fusion drive altogether and proceeded on gravs alone. They could manage a respectable speed at this treetop-clipping altitude, with the deflector to keep the craft from being buffeted by airflows it was never intended to handle. Very little time passed before Sarnath appeared, silhouetted against the first ruddy glow of dawn.

They didn't detect her until she swept over the outskirts of the city. Heavily-shielded portals opened and underground weapons turrets rose up through the urban wasteland of rubble and twisted metal that surrounded the fortress. Missiles and lasers began to stab at Naeriy's fighter. Her computer riposted with puffs of anti-laser aerosol and clusters of little missiles that homed on the Korvaash fire-control sensors—the equivalent of Terran ARAD. As she got closer, mass-driver artillery tried to hose her down with streams of hypervelocity metal darts. The computer interposed the deflector. All the while—a very short while—Naeriy concentrated nervelessly on the magnified image of the onrushing fortress, with its superimposed target designator.

She released a pair of fire-and-forget missiles, then followed them in, watching them impact and raking the fortress with lasers before pulling sharply up.

Gaining altitude, she committed another criminal offense by doing a slow turn over the city on grav repulsion. Coming around, she did some computer-assisted damage assessment and confirmed that the others were coming in behind her—Taelarr was already starting his run.

Bet that *spilled their wine in there!* She was still very young. *Now to line up to cover the assault shuttles' landings.*

* * *

The rolling thunder died away, and Dorleann and Raenoli cautiously raised their heads and peered over the barricade. They had never seen actual battle, and the gods of war were granting them a spectacular first look by the first light of morning, as the fighters swooped in from the west to meet the dawn.

Even at this distance, the ground had jumped beneath their feet when the attackers' missiles had punched in the walls of the fortress with their shaped-charge warheads of ultra-energetic chemical explosives. Now they looked avidly through their electronic binoculars at the results.

"Can any of them still be alive in there?" Raenali asked, awestruck.

"Remember, its only the above-ground structure that's being hit at all. Nothing can touch the underground portions, short of nuclear weapons. But they *did* make some holes for us and the Marines to enter through." Dorleann paused and checked his chronometer. "Speaking of the Marines"—they had learned the word through their contacts with the Free Raehaniv Fleet—"their assault shuttles must be about to depart. Let's start toward the rendezvous area."

They rose to their feet and turned to their unit leaders, clad like them in the combat dress of the wartime ground defense force that had never been used in the face of an enemy willing to call down nuclear devastation from orbit on any organized resistance. The coverall, with its ablative layer and its plates of metal-fiber composite armor for vital areas, and the HUD-equipped helmet, were more than many of their troops could boast. But at least there were enough of the Saelarien rifles to go around. The weapon was a Fourth Global War design, resurrected during the war. It used a binary-gas chemical propellant to fire either of two kinds of rounds from side-by-side magazines: armor-piercing high explosive or saboted penetrator core, at the firer's choice. It also incorporated an integral grenade launcher. In addition to standard electro-optical sights, it had HUD connection capability for those with helmets that could accept it.

Dorleann had also been able to scrounge enough single-shot portable missile launchers to give at least one to each squad; his special-weapons squads had magazine-fed semiportable ones. Finally, there were a few semiportable railguns which, unlike handheld ones such as those the Implementers favored, could accelerate slugs rather than needles. They and the rocket launchers were the only weapons Dorleann had that would be of any use whatsoever against fully enhanced Korvaash cyborgs—he somehow doubted if the cyborgs would hold still long enough for his engineers to affix the explosive charges they were bringing along to use on the fortress's internal walls.

Orders were passed, and the pick of the Raehaniv Resistance began to converge on the area where the Marines' assault shuttles were to land. As they began to thread their way cautiously through the urban maze, they saw the last of the attacking fighters take a direct hit and spin down like a flaming cartwheel into a distant row of buildings. Dorleann reminded himself that modern Raehaniv did not believe in omens.

* * *

Aelanni checked the latest figures and turned back to the communicator screen.

"All the surviving fighters—over eighty percent of the total—are circling in position to cover the landings in all four cities," she told DiFalco. Behind him, she could see one of *Guadalcanal*'s shuttle holds, and an assault shuttle in the last stages of loading.

"Good," he nodded. "Go ahead and activate the pre-recorded order: 'Land the landing force.'" He grinned boyishly. "Thompson taught me that one. Speaking of Thompson, I'd better go if I'm going to see him off."

Even at this moment, their gazes lingered on each other. Their reunion had taken place in the midst of frantic post-battle cleanup complicated by the whirl of meetings with the Free Raehaniv—all of which had been predictable, but that hadn't lessened their frustration. Their time alone together had been so limited that each of them could remember every stolen hour with the vividness of a dream interrupted by too-early awakening.

It didn't matter, Aelanni told herself. Whatever happened, they'd never be separated again.

"Right," she finally said. "Signing off." She cut the connection, and turned to face Varien.

"Anything new?"

"No," he said slowly. "No more unsuspected missile-launching stations in the hinterlands, it seems. Although they always seem to have just one more in reserve." He frowned in annoyance. The gradual one-at-a-time unveiling of the secret launching sites was not a tactic humans would have used, which made it unpredictable. "Is Eric returning to this ship soon?"

"Yes, as soon as the last of the assault shuttles is away." She frowned. "I can't see why he felt he had to go to *Guadalcanal* and personally supervise the final readying of the assault force. Thompson is quite capable . . ."

"Eric is ordering men down to the surface to face death while he himself waits in relative safety, Aelanni. It doesn't sit well with him. You should know that much of him by now. He needs to involve himself as closely as his position allows with those he's sending into battle."

"Oh, I know. I also know it's one of the reasons men follow him. I sometimes think he wishes he could plunge directly into the fighting himself!" She shook her head irritably, as if to shake away the thought. "But he knows better, of course," nodding for emphasis. She was about to say something else when the computer's voice spoke in tones of cybernetically calibrated urgency.

"Alert! Multiple antispacecraft missile launches fron previously unsuspected site."

"Shit!" Aelanni spoke in English. "How many of these secret missile stations can they have?" She and Varien turned to face the master holographic globe of Raehan. A new orange light was blinking infuriatingly in the far-northern latitudes, where missiles were now roaring up from beneath the tundra. She wondered fleetingly how many Raehaniv slave laborers had been exterminated to preserve that location's secrecy.

"Give me a targeting solution for that base," she told the computer. "And analyze those missiles' flight path." Korvaash tactics called for a missile site to announce its existence with a full salvo concentrated on one ship.

"Acknowledged," the computer replied. Then, without appreciable pause: "The missiles' target is *Guadalcanal.*"

Varien turned his head sharply toward Aelanni. She did not return his look. She was staring straight ahead, mouth slightly open, gazing unblinkingly at nothing that was visible to anyone else in the control room.

* * *

DiFalco could hardly shake hands with Thompson—the powered armor's "hands" were mechanical clamps that could have crushed sheet steel, slaved to the opening and closing movements of the operator's hands. But he looked up and met the Marine's eyes through the viewplate.

"Give 'em hell, Joel," he said, wishing he could think of something more original.

"Aye aye, skipper," Thompson replied, through the external speaker. The other armored giants had filed aboard the shuttle, and the two of them were alone on the hold's deck, which would soon swing open and allow the shuttle to drop toward the planet far below. The transport had a series of such holds, each with its shuttle. The others held regular infantry, clad in non-powered articulated combat armor and limited to weapons that a man's unaided strength could carry.

"And now," Thompson continued, glancing at his HUD chronometer, "it's time for you headquarters types to clear the hold!"

"And get back to where we belong," DiFalco finished for him. He gave a jaunty salute as Thompson walked up the ramp, then turned toward the hatch on the far side of the hold.

All at once a deafening *whoop-whoop-whoop* sounded, and the the intercom awoke thunderously. "Red alert! Red alert! Incoming missiles!" Simultaneously, the hatch began to slide shut as the ship sealed itself off into airtight damage-containing compartments.

DiFalco sprinted for the hatch, getting about halfway there before realizing he couldn't possibly make it. Then, as the hatch clanged shut, a red light began to flash and a new recorded voice added itself to the din. "Stand by for decompression!" And, with a hissing sound, the air began to bleed out of the hold in preparation for releasing the shuttle.

Without conscious thought, DiFalco reversed direction and ran for the shuttle. Damn! The ramp had raised up into the hull, sealing it. And the air in the hold was getting thinner.

Let's see, he thought like an automaton, *I'm wearing a Raehaniv-issue shipsuit, yes, that's right, get that hood out and up and over! But when this deck under me swings open I'll be spilled out into orbit, and the life support doesn't last long. I can't shout from inside this hood, even if it would do any good, which it wouldn't. Got to get into the shuttle's visual pickups, maybe they'll see me and . . .*

The deck seemed to jump under his feet as *Guadalcanal* took a near-miss, and the ship's pain belled through the hull. DiFalco was thrown to the deck, head spinning. Just as things started to steady, the deck began to tilt—and he knew that wasn't his head, for he began to slide along the smooth expanse, and a little crack of star-filled blackness appeared, and grew. . . .

The clamps grasped his upper arm with superhuman strength. He found a split second for amazement that Thompson could manage such fine control of the servomechanisms as to not break his bones, as the Marine lifted him up, almost pulling the arm out of his socket, and deposited him on the partially lowered ramp.

"Inside," Thompson snapped unceremoniously, and as he was thrust into the shuttle DiFalco glanced down and saw the hatches that had been a deck yawn wide, with the blue curve of Raehan beyond. Then he was in and the ramp was up and sealed.

"*Now* can we release?" the pilot called out querulously.

"Go!" Thompson barked. The pilot slapped his control panel, cutting the power to the magnetic clamps that held the shuttle to the hold's overhead. With a dropping sensation that seemed to send DiFalco's stomach up into his throat, the shuttle fell into infinity.

As soon as the artificial gravity took hold, DiFalco stumbled forward and looked over the pilot's shoulder at the view-aft. *Guadalcanal*, showing her wounds, was rapidly dwindling in the screen. Then something seemed to flash in from the side, and the glare of the direct hit dazzled his eyes before the screen could automatically compensate.

He peeled back his hood and turned to Thompson. "The others . . . ?"

"All the shuttles got away," the Marine reported. "We were the last to leave—had a little delay," he added, all blandness.

DiFalco flushed. "Oh, yeah, I almost forgot: thanks for saving my bacon."

Powered armor couldn't reproduce a nothing-to-it shrug, but Thompson's face did it for him. "Several lifeboats also made it," he continued. "The captain of *Guadalcanal* knew the ship had had it after that near-miss. At least sixty percent of the crew must have survived."

"Thank God for that."

"Amen. And now . . ." Suddenly, Thompson's face took on an expression that defined the term "shit-eating grin," and he gestured toward the after bulkhead where the spare suit of powered combat armor was stored. "Having chosen to join us," he asked archly, "would the Colonel care to make himself useful?"

"I'm more the ornamental type," DiFalco grinned back. "But now that you mention it, I *was* getting tired of feeling like a midget in here with you grunts!"

*   *   *

Neither Varien nor anyone else in *Liberator*'s control room felt like violating Aelanni's silent misery.

They had heard the report of *Guadalcanal*'s death, and as the lifeboats had checked in she had overridden the comm officer to ask each of them if DiFalco was aboard. He was not, and no one had seen him during the evacuation. That the missile base that had claimed *Guadalcanal* was now a radioactive crater was clearly of no comfort to her at all.

Finally, Varien felt he must say something, however awkward. "There may be other lifeboats, you know. They may not have all made contact."

"Perhaps you're right," she sighed. Neither of them believed it for an instant, but it was a ritual in which each had to play out a role that included the pretense of belief. And now it was over.

Varien tried again. "No one in the lifeboats actually saw him killed or injured," he began, attempting briskness. Aelanni smiled her gratitude to him, but shook her head slowly. He shut up.

After a moment, she spoke. "Do you know what I was thinking while speaking to him for the last time?" She chuckled joylessly. "I was thinking that we'd never be separated again. . . ."

The communicator emitted a scream of static, over which a voice barely rose. "Assault shuttle G-4 calling *Liberator*! Come in please. And please establish visual contact."

They looked at each other. No. That static-distorted voice *couldn't* be . . . Without a word, Aelanni sprang to the console and switched on visual.

The image was a match for the voice signal,

streaked and repeatedly disappearing altogether. But it unmistakably showed the open viewplate of a suit of powered combat armor. and the face. . . .

"*Eric!* What are you doing . . . ? And what is that . . . ?"

"No time, Aelanni! We're starting to enter atmosphere, and the ionization is already playing hell with this signal." A screech of static came as if on cue, to confirm it. "I was a little rushed when *Guadalcanal* was hit. This shuttle was my only way off. So now I'm headed down with Thompson. I'll be in touch as soon as possible. I love you. I'll . . ."

The static rose to a shriek, then died down to a low, steady roar, and the screen was all snow.

For a moment Aelanni was silent, emotions chasing each other across her face. Then she yelled at the screen.

"*You did this on purpose!*"

Then she collapsed into the chair, weeping with all the tears she had been holding since the first word of the attack on *Guadalcanal* and could now release. Varien stood behind her, massaging her shoulders and smiling a gentle smile.

CHAPTER SEVENTEEN

Afterwards, it occurred to DiFalco that he should have thought of the fact that he was setting foot on Aelanni's world. But at the time, his only impressions as he came down the shuttle ramp in the smoke-dimmed early morning sun were of ravaged cityscape, the fighters swooping overhead as they expended their last missiles covering the landing and, above all, the sounds of battle.

A small group of Raehaniv in combat dress came out from behind wreckage, one of them carrying the transponding beacon that had guided them to this particular part of the landing zone. Another—the leader, if DiFalco remembered his wartime Raehaniv rank insignia—stepped forward.

"Major Thompson?" he asked with a heavy accent.

"Here," Thompson said, motioning forward one of his Raehaniv Marines to translate. "But this is Colonel DiFalco. He's the senior man here."

"It's your show, Major," DiFalco demurred. "I'm just a flyboy who's out of his element and knows his limitations." He turned to the Resistance type. "And you are . . . ?"

"Dorleann hle'Toral, commanding. We weren't

expecting you to come here personally, Colonel DiFalco." He looked almost embarassingly impressed. "All my units are in position by now, although we had to fight our way here. As you know, the Korvaasha have tunnels running from the fortress to various locations in the surrounding areas of the city. As it turns out, they have more of them than we thought. They've been using them to mount flanking attacks on us as we advanced to this landing zone. But all we've encountered so far have been Implementers. They must be holding their Korvaash cyborgs of the warrior elite in reserve and expending their cannon fodder. At any rate, we've taken losses, but we beat off all the attacks."

Even in translation, Dorleann's pride in his people was evident—they had met their first trial by fire and not broken. DiFalco and Thompson looked at each other wordlessly, knowing that the Implementers were as new to actual battle as the Resistance, and that the real test was still to come.

"All right, Dorleann," DiFalco spoke diplomatically. "It sounds like your people could use a breather. As we advance toward the fortress, I suggest that Major Thompson's Marines take the flanks. . . ."

* * *

The immense doors slid open with a grinding clang and Gromorgh entered the vast chamber where a crowd of Implementers waited, flanked by Korvaash cyborgs.

"Is there some problem?" Gromorgh adjusted the voder's volume to fill this space. "I understand you have expressed reluctance to face armed opponents. Does terrorizing helpless civilians represent the limit of your capabilities?"

There was much furtive exchanging of glances among the Implementers, and finally a Senior Assault Leader shuffled forward.

"Director," he began, still cringing out of habit, "we've followed your commands, and launched all ordered attacks against our fellow inferior beings of the Resistance. But now these *Marines* have landed from orbit. The word is that their elite units have got powered combat armor straight out of the Fourth Global War!"

"What of it?" Gromorgh's translator produced its usual expressionless Raehaniv. Inwardly, he was astonished. These worms were so terrified that their normal cravenness was in abeyance, overshadowed by something they feared more than the neurolash.

"Director, we're willing to face the Resistance, as we've shown. But if you send us out there now we'll be slaughtered! Send *them!*" He pointed at the cyborgs who flanked Gromorgh, bulking even huger than normal Korvaasha, the chamber's dim light reflected from their dully gleaming metal surfaces.

Gromorgh made a small gesture, and one of the cyborgs snapped up an arm that ended in a short tube tipped by a now-clenched grasping mechanism. Faster than sight, with terrible force, the tube telescoped itself out to three times its at-rest length and punched through the Senior Assault Leader's chest.

The Implementer tried to scream, but his opened mouth produced only a gout of blood. The cyborg rotated the tube, a kind of wet crunching sound was heard, and then the tube was yanked out, clutching the Implementer's heart in its metallic grasp.

The cyborg held the heart on display for an instant, then flung it into the crowd of Implementers. It smacked one of them in the face before falling to the floor.

"Are there any further complaints or suggestions?" asked Gromorgh in the mechanical tones of his voder.

He waited until the chamber was clear—about five seconds—before turning and making his way to the elevator that took him down to the command center. The rest of the ruling council was there, observing the progress of the battle on a battery of screens.

"Well, Director," Lugnaath greeted him, "have you resolved the problem of your Implementers' insubordination?"

"I believe they are now sufficiently motivated, Third Level Embodiment. But, as we realized from the first, their usefulness has limits. I will continue to expend them, of course, but it may soon be necessary to commit the cyborg units in a frontal counterattack. As you can see"—he indicated the main city map, with its color-coded lights—"the feral inferior beings have by now found the termini of almost all our tunnels and are in the process of sealing them with explosives. Soon it will no longer be possible to launch surprise flanking attacks. It was the prospect of having to frontally assault the new elements that have arrived from orbit that discouraged the Implementers."

"Vermin!" Sugvaaz spoke venomously. "I have always felt that you rely far too heavily on them. But is a counterattack necessary at all? You have repeatedly assured us that this fortress is impregnable to ground assault."

"And so it is, Conservator," Gromorgh assured him, carefully not adding the defeatist thought that it could have been made even more impregnable by the simple expedient of setting—and making known—a nuclear device to obliterate the fortress and the city around it if an attack were to succeed. "We could simply sit here and crush any attempts to gain entry. But that would leave us in a stalemate with the inferior beings effectively controlling most of the city. The purpose of the counterattack is to smash their ground-assault capability, not merely stymie it. This is especially important in view of the fact that matters are not going well with the other three urban headquarters." He indicated readouts from around the globe. "Not unexpected, of course; this fortress is stronger than those by orders of magnitude, and all the cyborg shock units are here. So it

is vital that we impress upon the inferior beings the
futility of attacking us here, placing them back in
their original dilemma of having to either destroy
us—and their capital city—with nuclear weapons or
try to wait us out before relief arrives from the rest
of the Unity."

Sugvaaz was silent. "Very well, Director," Lugnaath
said. "So ordered."

*   *   *

Naeriy stumbled again as she made her way
through the wreckage-strewn streets. She cursed in
the English that was so much more suited to the
purpose than Raehaniv. The sun was getting higher,
and sweat trickled down her inside the shipsuit. Still,
she couldn't complain. It was a minor miracle that
she had been able to ease her wounded fighter down
to within a few meters of a vacant lot before the
gravs had died and she'd fallen the rest of the way.
The landing had shaken her up, but nothing was
broken. Now she proceeded cautiously toward the
sounds of battle.

Coming to the end of a block she peered around
the corner of a building, then jerked her head back
quickly. The men she had seen had a look about
them that suggested a group of deserters rather than
a patrol. But they were unquestionably Implementers; they hadn't discarded enough of their gear to
disguise that fact. She slowly reached for her laser
sidearm.

Suddenly her upper arms were grabbed from
behind with brutal strength. "Hey! Over here!" her
assailant shouted. "Look what I've found!"

The other Implementers—ex-Implementers?—trot-
ted around the corner. "Well, well," one of them
leered, watching Naeriy's futile struggles. "A flier—
one of these new arrivals who've fucked everything
up for us!" He turned to the others. "We can't stay
around here too long, but there's no reason we can't
take a short break for a little fun."

He stepped forward and ran a hand over Naeriy's shipsuit, lingering to squeeze a breast with vicious force. Her gasp of pain brought a smile to his face. "Let's see—how do you get one of these suits open? Well, there's one way." He drew a knife. Naeriy recognized a monomolecular-edged blade. "Of course, the suit isn't all this is gonna cut. . . ."

A *crack!* sounded, and the Implementer's head exploded in a pink-and-gray mist that caused her eyes to blur. A wall down the street crumbled outward as the first of the towering suits of powered combat armor came crashing through it. The other Implementers started to bolt, but the Marine had switched his railgun to full-automatic now that he didn't have to carefully avoid hitting Naeriy, and he scythed them down, their bodies blossoming out in a shower of gore as the hypervelocity slugs tore through them. Naeriy's captor held onto her—hoping to use her as a hostage?—but she kicked backward sharply. As his grip faltered she wrenched her right arm free, grabbed her laser pistol, and thrust it up under his jaw before pressing the firing stud. For a moment the stench of cooked brains and evacuated bowels overcame her. The next thing she was aware of was the deep, concerned voice.

"Naeriy, is that you? Are you okay?"

She looked up and recognized the dark face behind the powered armor's viewplate. "Yes, Major Thompson, I'm all right—thanks to you. My fighter was hit and I was trying to find your troops."

"Well, it looks like you've found us," he said cheerfully. "Now we need to get back to the main body ASAP. These flanking actions seem to have died away, and we're getting ready to assault the fortress itself." He reached down with one arm and scooped her up. "If you'll permit, we can travel faster this way. And none of us have been able to figure out a way to get fresh from inside one of these tin suits!"

Her laugh had an edge of released hysteria, but at least it was a laugh.

*   *   *

The counterattack came as they were nearing the
fortress. Behind a wave of Implementers, blasted
down almost contemptuously by the Marines, came
the cyborgs, supported by weapon turrets that only
now revealed themselves, rising up through the
wreckage and belching death from heavy weapons to
which powered combat armor meant little more than
ordinary combat dress, or naked flesh. Their fields of
fire were limited as long as the cyborgs were
deployed, of course. But DiFalco knew that if they
defeated the counterattack it would only be to face
unrestricted fire from those massive plasma guns and
mass-driver artillery when they assaulted the fortress.
And he had to force down a rising suspicion that this
was going to be tougher—a *lot* tougher—than they
had suspected.

"We've got to send the Resistance troops back,
Joel," he yelled into his communicator, above noise
that even the armor's soundproofing couldn't keep
out.

"Why?" He could barely make out Thompson's
voice.

"Because it's murder to send Dorleann and his
merry men against the cyborgs, damn it! They'll be
eaten alive—they're just simply playing out of their
league, and you know it!" He took a breath. "I said
this was your show down here, Joel, but if I have to
make this an order . . ."

"No need, Skipper; you're right. But let me keep
a couple of Resistance special weapons squads on the
front line. They've got some stuff that can make the
cyborgs say 'Ouch.' And they're willing—*God*, but
they're willing!"

"Permission granted. I'll do the same. Signing off."
As he spoke the last words, the cyborg squad broke
upon them with the blinding speed that seemed to
belie their bulk.

Semiportable mass driver guns manned by Marines

in nonpowered combat armor fired back in a continuous crackle as their slugs broke mach. Those hyperdense rounds, accelerated at such a velocity, would have stopped a main battle tank of Earth, DiFalco reflected as he got his plasma gun up; the cyborgs would keep coming for a little while through a burst of them. Marines in powered armor fired back with their various arms (each was, in effect, a walking special weapons squad) and the sheer concentration of firepower became more than the heat-containing urban battlefield could seemingly hold.

A heavy weight crashed down on DiFalco's armored back and he went down, rolling over with the cyborg that forced itself on top with a strength exceeding even that of powered armor and tried to maneuver a forearm weapon mount of some kind against DiFalco's viewplate. The American made an activating motion with his jaw, and a foot-long blade of aligned crystalline steel sprang out of its powered sheath under his left arm. He drove it into the wiring at the base of the cyborg's "throat," and was rewarded by a crackling noise accompanied by sparks. With the cyborg momentarily "stunned," he pushed himself out from underneath and gripped one of its arms in his clamps with crushing force, and, with a tremendous heave, yanked the arm out. There was no blood, only the sparking of torn electrical circuitry. All lower-ranking Korvaasha were "cyborgs" in some degree, but one of these things was little more than a robot with an organic central processing unit that had once been a living being's brain.

In the instant it took the cyborg to assimilate the loss of the arm, DiFalco grasped his plasma gun, specially designed to be handled by the suit's clamps—his right arm's integral laser weapon would have taken too long to burn through that tough metal hide. The cyborg had just staggered erect when he got off an insanely short-range shot while lying on his side, and in a senses-overpowering blast the cyborg ceased to exist save as a charred, sparking stump above its legs. DiFalco felt singed despite everything the armor's temperature control could do, but at least the radiation shielding held—no warning squeal awoke in his ear.

As he performed the difficult maneuver of getting to his feet in powered armor, he saw that his troops had taken losses but were in possession of the field. He wondered how Thompson was doing.

"Damn it, Naeriy, I thought I told you to go to the rear!"

The young Raehaniv pushed back her borrowed combat helmet and looked up at Thompson defiantly. "I've attached myself to a special weapons squad— the Resistance people are showing me what to do. You've *got* to let me do something, Joel!"

"Oh, what the Hell!" Thompson closed up his viewplate and spoke through the outside speaker. "Get back to your unit, Marine!" he barked, and turned away before she could smile dazzlingly at him. "What a war!" he muttered to himself as he strode off. And he'd thought Colombia had been weird!

He continued his inspection of the perimeter, approaching a semiportable plasma gun emplacement. "What's the word, Suvarov?" he called out, recognizing the crew chief.

The Russian raised the faceplate of his nonpowered armor. "Quiet, Major. We seem to have stopped the counterattacks. At least we haven't seen any more cyborgs since . . ."

A nearby structure that held another strongpoint took a hit that showered them with debris, and Suvarov frantically closed his faceplate as he ordered the plasma gun swivelled in search of targets. They must be close, Thompson reflected, since they had gotten off a shot without benefit of the laser target designators that, as they must have learned by now, only alerted the Marines to the fact that they were being targeted. And they must also be doing without the heat sensors that the Marines' armor, with its IR cloaking feature, could defeat. So where *were* they?

Then they were visible, darting in and out of cover with that impossible speed. Thompson, whose plasma gun had long ago shorted out—at least it *seemed* long ago—put his mass driver gun on full auto and hosed one of them down, cutting the relatively vulnerable legs out from under it. Legless, it continued to try to hump itself forward with its arms. Fighting off a sensation of nightmare, Thompson put a burst through it lengthwise, from the top of the head down. It shuddered and jerked convulsively, as if from a heavy jolt of electricity, and finally lay still.

Suddenly, Suvarov's plasma gun, which had been laying down a barrage of lighning bolts and thunderclaps, blew up with a force that threw Thompson off balance. As he tried to right himself, a mass-driver slug crashed through the armor of his left arm with shattering impact, sending his own weapon flying and spinning him around to crash to the ground. His suit's biomonitor reacted instantly with a painkilling injection, but the sudden chemical influx left him barely aware of the cyborg that was approaching, training its weapon on him. He closed his eyes.

It was as well that he did, for he missed the explosion. His sound pickup automatically tuned out the deafening noise, and he kept his eyes shut as flying debris rattled like hail on his armor. When he opened them, there was only wreckage where the cyborg had stood. From behind a pile of rubble, Naeriy stood up, still shouldering the missile launcher that looked too heavy for her.

Thompson, at the threshold of unconsciousness, managed a smile. "Lady, you are somethin' else!" he breathed.

She went to her knees beside him and fumbled with the access hatch. "Quick!" she called to the Resistance troops that were busily setting up weapons emplacements. "Help me get him out of this powered armor! And get a medic over here!" Her voice was a little unsteady.

Thompson smiled again and let the darkness take him.

*   *   *

The first missile impacts of dawn had been audible even down in the maximum-security level, and Tarlann and Iael had awakened, wide-eyed, to the dull *crumps* and the shouting of the Implementers that had, as time had passed, taken on an unmistakable tone of panic.

It was, Tarlann decided, time.

They had, of course, scanned him thoroughly and taken away anything that could possibly be used as a tool or weapon. But they had left him his clothes, including his shoes. Now, as Iael watched unblinkingly, he twisted off the left heel. Its interior, of what was to any Korvaash scanner exactly the same plastic as the right heel, fell out. He reaffixed the hollow shell of the left heel.

The research laboratories of the conglomerate Varien had left to him were on the leading edge of many new technologies, including electrically active plastics that could be encoded to respond to certain stimuli in certain ways. As Tarlann tapped the heel repeatedly against a pipe, crouching over to shield it from any surveillance pickups, it began to change shape. Iael's eyes got even bigger as it took on the form of a very small knife. Tarlann tested the edge. It wasn't crystalline steel, of course, but it would cut.

"Father . . . ?"

Tarlann gestured him to silence and slipped the plastic blade into a pocket. He gave Iael a long look. "We can only wait," he said noncommitally. The boy's lips tightened and, with a steadiness beyond his years, he nodded.

He is so young, Tarlann thought. *His youth is only one of the things the Korvaasha have destroyed.*

Will anyone ever again have a youth like mine was?

After some interminable time, the door clanged open and three Implementers entered. The leader turned and pressed his thumb to the wall scanner, closing the door behind them. Then he swung around, and Tarlann saw a face burned into his memory as if by corrosive acid.

"Yeah, it's me," Laerav slurred. "Working down here's usually a punishment detail, but I volunteered—me and these boys." He was drunk. Like his subordinates, he had a mag needler slung over his shoulder. He also held a monomolecular-edged knife with which he gestured at one of the other two, who grasped Tarlann's left arm and pulled it painfully up behind him.

Laerav thrust his face within inches of that of Tarlann, who had become the current focus of a lifetime's impacted, festering hate. "The Director wouldn't let us hurt you," he spat. "Just like he wouldn't let us have any fun with your crazy bitch of a wife—she wouldn't've been as much fun as the little cunt anyway. But now everything's turning to shit and noboby's paying attention. I'm gonna cut you up real slow. But first you're gonna watch what Durlien does with your spoiled little prick of a son. He *likes* boys!" Laerav grinned drunkenly. "And then you're gonna watch us cut *him* apart before we start on you! You're gonna pay for . . . for my whole . . . for *everything!*" His voice had risen to a scream, and he was shuddering convulsively. Then he took a deep breath. "Durlien, get started!"

The Implementer holding Tarlann forced him to his knees and pointed him toward the corner where Durlien had trapped Iael and was forcing him to the floor, grinning idiotically. He had laid his mag need-ler on the floor.

Desperately, Tarlann fumbled for the plastic knife with his free hand while his captor watched Durlien eagerly. His fingers finally closed around the smooth hard coolness of the grip. With all the strength he could muster in this position, he stabbed backward.

With a roar of startlement and pain, the Imple-menter released Tarlann's arm to clutch with both hands at his stomach, from which the plastic handle protruded. Before Laerav and Durlien could come out of their haze of alcohol and anticipation, Tarlann lurched up and slammed a shoulder into his erst-while captor, shoving him against Laerav. He cut himself open on the Assault Leader's almost infinitely sharp knife, screaming and lurching in convulsive agony and sending the blade flying out of Laerav's hand.

Durlien started to rise, then glanced back and had time for a split second of horror as he saw that Iael had grabbed his mag needler. The weapon's recoil was small, but it was enough to throw the boy's aim off and send a stream of hypervelocity needles arcing across the chamber. But the tracery of death crossed Durlien's chest, ripping through his heart. Blood squirted from the little holes and gushed from his mouth.

With frantic clumsiness, Laerav started to unsling his own mag needler. But Tarlann, drawing on hys-terical strength and quickness, dived for Laerav's dropped knife, scooped it up, swung around and up, and plunged the blade into Laerav's abdomen up to the hilt, slamming the Assault Leader up against the wall.

For an instant, they stood locked together in a silent tableau, with only a small trickle of blood com-ing from beneath the hilt that pressed tightly against the orange coverall. Laerav's eyes protruded and sweat poured from him. But he didn't move.

"Yes, that's right, don't move," Tarlann whispered. "You know what this blade can do. If you move, you'll just slice yourself on it."

Involuntarily, Laerav moved a little. It brought a gasp of agony and a renewed flow of blood.

Tarlann nodded. "Now, Laerav, I want you to reach over to the thumbprint scanner and open this door. I'll guide your hand. Afterwards, I'll leave you with the knife still in; if you don't move, maybe help will reach you."

Eyes glazing over, Laerav obeyed. The door sensed his living thumbprint and slid grindingly open.

With a quick motion, Tarlann brought the knife down, the one-molecule-wide edge slicing effortlessly through everything it encountered and exiting through Laerav's crotch.

Laerav's eyes popped and he shattered the silence with a horrible, gurgling shriek as he watched his guts bulge out and fall with a plopping sound into a greasy, steaming pile on the floor.

"I lied," Tarlann admitted genially.

Laerav's screaming died down to a kind of agonized rasping as he fell forward. Tarlann turned to Iael.

"Collect their needlers. We'll get others from the Implementers on the levels above while we're freeing the prisoners." Iael sprang to obey while Tarlann stepped ouside the door and studied a schematic of the fortress, its writing in Raehaniv for the benefit of the Implementers.

By the time they departed, Laerav's noise had ceased.

* * *

They brought what was left of Dorleann back to the command post.

The Resistance leader had insisted on taking part in the latest futile attack on the ruinous-looking fortress that loomed up tantalizingly ahead. Once again they had been flung back.

"And that's the story," DiFalco concluded, speaking into the ground-to-orbit communicator. *Liberator* was currently over this hemisphere, and he had brought Aelanni up to date. "Our intelligence badly underestimated the defenses of this place. We can't put a dent in those heavy-weapons turrets, and we can't make any headway against them. If we could just reach that fortress, I'm convinced we could take it. But we can't cross the killing ground around it."

"The fighter-configured shuttles . . . ?"

"Our fighters are a spent force. The ones that are left can keep circling over Sarnath indefinitely on grav repulsion, but they've expended all their missiles. Their lasers are attenuated by all this smoke down here—the turrets laugh at them."

Silence fell in the little command post. Raenoli, now in command of the Resistance, sat quietly, face graven with unshed tears. Thompson—DiFalco had ordered the medics to bring him around with stimulants—lay back, left arm encased in Raehaniv instacast spray. He would lose the arm (hypervelocity projectiles inflict no small wounds) but it was only temporary; the Raehaniv could force-grow a cloned replacement and graft it on. And he would live, at least if Naeriy had anything to say about it. She had not left his side, and she was still there.

DiFalco wiped his brow and knuckled his eyes again—he had never realized what a sybaritic luxury that was, for none of their training exercises on Terranova had ever overloaded the air conditioning systems of powered armor suits like the one he had just climbed out of. The suits had ingenious facilities for dealing with the body's other wastes, but nobody had ever thought of the sweat that ran down the inaccessible brow into the eyes. All you could do was blink a lot. *Note for future reference: issue tennis headbands to powered-armor troops.*

Golovko's voice—he was also in on the hookup—

came from the communicator. "Eric, it's no good. You've got to abort the operation."

"*NO!* We've come too far to stop now, damn it! I will not *let* these bastards stop us now!" DiFalco startled himself with his vehemence.

Thompson tried to sit up, and Naeriy grasped his hand protectively. "The Skipper's right," he got out, gasping for breath. "We've paid in blood for this ground! If we cut and run now, a lot of good people will have died for nothing. I don't think we'll ever be able to mount a second assault." He actually grinned. "Hell, Colonel Golovko, we couldn't break off this engagement if we wanted to! Without fighter cover, they'd shoot us out of the air as our assault shuttles lifted from this landing zone!"

"But, Eric," Aelanni asked, voice charged with urgency, "*how* will you get into the fortress?"

DiFalco's head hung for an instant, then he straightened. "You'd better put all the heavy-duty intellects up there to work on that, Aelanni. We're open to suggestions! And," he added quietly, "ask Yakov to mention this problem to God, will you? I think we need a miracle."

* * *

"Well, Director," Lugnaath spoke languidly, "despite the failure of your counterattack, you appear to have been as good as your word concerning the invincibility of this fortress."

Gromorgh carefully didn't reveal his relief. He had experienced some bad moments when the counterattack had been stopped—who could have imagined that these *Marines* would be able to stand up to the cyborgs? But it had been merely a disappointment, not a disaster. The fortress was still inviolate.

"Indeed, Third Level Embodiment," he said unctuously. "We can continue smashing these pathetic attacks indefinitely. Nothing can penetrate our defenses here. Nothing!"

Behind him, the scanner lock beeped and the
entrance to the command center slid open. Gromorgh turned, annoyed. No one should be entering
now. . . .

No! It wasn't possible!

A disarmed Implementer was thrust in, and the
ragged human scarecrow behind him pumped a
burst of electromagnetically accelerated needles into
the nearest Korvaash guard. More freed prisoners
crowded in, cutting loose with their captured
weapons. And Gromorgh recognized their
leader. . . .

The ruling council rose to its feet as one in
consternation, just in time to be mown down. Sugvaaz,
with an inarticulate cry, raised his arm with its
implanted laser mount. An adolescent human
male—Gromorgh thought he looked vaguely
familiar—fired a long burst from his mag needler, and
the Conservator of Correctness staggered backwards,
his eye seeming to explode and his brains spattering
the wall behind him. Lugnaath was down, bleeding his
life out from a dozen little holes, and Gromorgh knew
he was next. . . .

"No! Not him!" the leader shouted. He came forward, mag needler in one hand and
monomolecular-edged knife in another, walking with
a slight limp.

Tarlann made sure the command center was
secured and sentries posted before turning to where
Gromorgh waited under the mag needlers of two of
those whose torments he had decreed.

"Gromorgh," he began, "I won't make any promises that you're too intelligent to believe. But you
can prolong your life if you tell me where the power
controls are."

The Director of Implementation didn't even reply.

Tarlann smiled and quoted. "I see that you need
more incentive."

He turned to one of the fallen security guards and took the neurolash from its belt holder. It was heavy, and designed for Korvaash hands, but he could manage it.

As he approached Gromorgh, he thought he could detect odd motions, almost tics. Was this what Korvaash fear looked like? If so, it answered the question of whether this device affected the Korvaash nervous system.

At the touch of the lash, Gromorgh stiffened convulsively—alarming in a being his size. His pendant was silent, for it didn't translate meaningless noise. But Tarlann could distinctly hear a sound like a distant, very deep foghorn.

Interesting, he thought with scientific detachment. *The Korvaasha can make a noise that's audible in the human range, if it's loud enough and high-pitched enough.*

"Well, Gromorgh?" he asked, withdrawing the lash slightly. "And I think you know better than to lie."

Still trembling, Gromorgh pointed to a console. Tarlann rushed to it and depressed a series of Korvaash-scale knobs. The pervasive hum died in a descending whine.

All at once, the command center was illuminated only by the red lights of emergency life-support power. And the din that filled the fortress began to subside as armored turrets ceased to move up and down into their protective pits and high-energy weapons fell silent.

"Colonel! They've ceased firing!"

"I see they have," DiFalco acknowledged the lookout's report. He looked at Raenoli, standing beside him at this forward fire base where they were organizing their next desperate attack. She met his eyes, and no translation was needed.

"It *could* be a trick, you know," DiFalco felt obligated to say. The Raehaniv Marine translated for

him, but Raenoli's only reply was to heft her
Saelarien rifle.

*Oh, Hell, we probably can't stop her and her peo-
ple anyway. Might as well go along and try to keep
'em out of trouble.*

Rationalization completed, DiFalco activated his
suit's communicator and spoke to his unit commanders. "This is DiFalco. Forget the countdown.
Commence attack . . . *now!*"

In a human wave whose lack of coordination
would have brought tears to the now-sedated
Thompson's eyes, Marines and Resistance swept
toward the barn-door-wide holes that the fighters had
blasted in the aboveground structure, streaming past
the silent heavy-weapons turrets.

Tarlann rose from the console and turned grimly
to his fellow ex-prisoners. "All right, let's get that
doorway barricaded. We're going to have company
very soon."

The floor of the corridor jumped under their feet
as the shaped-charge blastpack punched through the
massive blast door.

"All right, let's go!" DiFalco yelled into his communicator, and they were through and into yet
another corridor of Hell. Raenoli, he noted, was still
with him.

There had been few Implementers, and most of
them were trying to surrender—sometimes successfully, as long as it was Marines they tried to
surrender to. But the Korvaasha fought on. Few
cyborgs were left, but a lot of ordinary security
guards had appeared from branching corridors, and
their advance down into the depths had been
through nightmarish carnage.

A grenade exploded in their faces as they
approached a turn of the corridor. DiFalco heard a
scream from behind him, but his armor shielded

Raenoli from the fragments that whined off it. She hit the dirt, or whatever, just as the Korvaash security guards came around the corner. DiFalco blasted one apart and Raenoli opened up with her Saelarien. She was using APHE ammo, and the guards' torsos exploded in blood that was a lighter red than humanity's and guts that were more grey than pink.

He stole a glance at her. She clenched her teeth tightly as she held the trigger down, and the tears that she was finally letting out made runnels in the blood and soot that covered her face. She must be going deaf in here, and she would require antirad treatment after this was over. Unarmored personnel had no business in this combat environment, but DiFalco hadn't brought it up, mindful of the First Principle of Military Leadership: "Never give an order you know won't be obeyed."

Then the firefight was over, and they resumed their advance through the darkened fortress, down a ramp to the next level below. DiFalco activated his holographic HUD and consulted the schematic Intelligence had provided.

Let's see . . . can't be much further to the command center.

The blast was deafening in an enclosed space, even one as vast as the command center. When Tarlann raised his head and peered over the console, he saw that the improvised barricade lay scattered. Then he ducked his head again, pulling Iael to him, for a shower of grenades was preceeding the Korvaash security guards into the center. The series of explosions seemed to roar on forever. Afterwards, for just an instant, there was quiet. Then the Korvaasha loomed in the smoke.

Tarlann stood up and opened fire. But the Korvaasha could carry weapons that made nothing of the consoles and command chairs his people sought to shelter behind. Just to his left, a hypervelocity slug

crashed through one of the consoles, and an ex-pris-
oner was hurled against the wall behind them. He
sagged to the floor, leaving a smear of gore on the
wall.

Then one of the terrible projectiles smashed the
mag needler from Tarlann's hands, breaking fingers.
Another ripped through his thigh, shattering the
femur. In an excess of pain, he crashed to the floor.

With a cry, Iael flung himself atop his father, trying to shield him with his boy's body. Tarlann smiled
faintly, and awaited death.

Gromorgh stood forth from behind the pillar that
had sheltered him. He spoke to the guards, but his
translator continued to translate, not having been
told otherwise. "Take those two alive. They must be
saved for extraordinary punishment. . . ."

There was a sudden uproar from the corridor outside, and the guard nearest the door turned to
investigate, only to be flung back into the command
center in flaming ruin as a plasma gun spoke. Suddenly, the entrance held a figure that caused Tarlann
to wonder if the pain had cracked his sanity: a towering suit of powered combat armor from out of
history's worst nightmares of slaughter, blackened
with smoke and splashed with blood. Tarlann's neck
hairs prickled, for his primitive ancestors would have
known themselves to be in the presence of the god
of death.

For less than a heartbeat, the tableau held. Then the
newcomer's plasma gun flashed and thundered again,
and Gromorgh's upper half burst asunder in a ball of
flame. Others entered, some armored and others—like
a Raehaniv woman who darted recklessly ahead,
Saelarien rifle yammering—in ordinary combat dress.
They all poured fire into the stunned guards.

But the guard who had wounded Tarlann kept
coming, and with Gromorgh's order now in abeyance
he swung his weapon toward them. And Tarlann
knew that nothing could save them, for even if one

of the rescuers fired and killed the guard, he and Iael would be in the line of fire.

With surprising speed, the power-armored figure who had first entered bounded toward them. With a metallic *snick*, a long blade sprang from under the armor's left forearm. Just as the guard started to turn to face him, the newcomer swung the blade back-handed in a long sideways cut with all the force of which powered armor was capable, and the guard's head thudded to the floor. For an instant the body stood. Then, fountaining blood from the stump of its long thick neck, it toppled over toward Tarlann and Iael, drenching them with the warm stickiness.

Abruptly, the firefight ended, and in the sudden silence the armored figure approached and opened its viewplate. The man within looked down at them and smiled.

DiFalco wondered what a boy—he looked four-teen or fifteen, tops—was doing here. (Hell, what were *any* humans doing in this chamber, fighting a battle?) And the man was badly wounded; he'd have to send for a medic. He opened his mouth to try to speak to them, then decided to stop kidding himself about his aptitude for languages. He called a Rae-haniv Marine over to translate.

"I'm Colonel DiFalco, leader of your Terran allies. We and the Resistance have taken this installation, and you're safe now."

The man smiled through his obvious pain and began talking.

Then, leaping out of the stream of rapid-fire Rae-haniv, came the syllables "Tarlann hle'Morna."

"*What?!*"

The Marine grinned. "That's right, Colonel. He's Varien's son!"

"Ah, tell him we'll get him medical attention soon. And . . . tell him he and I have a lot to talk about!"

*   *   *

The sun was high in the sky, a red ball shining faintly through the smoke of the many fires, by the time they stumbled up out of the depths of the subterranean abattoir that was the fortress and emerged into the light.

Got to get Raenoli to put her people to work on fire control before all the blazes coalesce and we get a firestorm, DiFalco thought in his fatigue-sodden brain as he was assisted out of the powered armor's access hatch. He was just remembering that it had already been done when a shuttle came over the ruined buildings around the landing zone and set down in a swirl of dust.

As the hatch opened, a rift parted in the smoke and glorious golden sunlight seemed to ignite the flame-like colors of the woman who stepped out and ran toward him.

No, DiFalco thought, weariness and horror lifting from him like an insubstantial fog. *Her fire comes from within, not from the sun. She brings the light with her, and the darkness cannot stand against her.*

Then they were in each other's arms, oblivious to those around them, even to Varien, who walked slowly down the ramp and set foot on the world of his birth.

CHAPTER EIGHTEEN

They stood in the ancient chamber, gazing across the ages into that inexplicable stone face that had been carved out of the stuff of this asteroid a light-millennium from Earth in an age when Earth's humanity had gotten no closer to spaceflight than a thrown flint hand-axe.

"The maps in the Terranova system. This face here at Tareil." Aelanni's voice was hushed. "In both cases, the same perfectly logical explanation for why they were left behind: they were relief sculptures, part of rock walls. And yet . . . no maps here, no faces there. Why?"

DiFalco shook his head slowly and continued to study the face. It could have passed for Raehaniv, which meant it was within the range of Earth's races and mixtures of races, though not really like any of them. *And who really knows what Cro-Magnon's facial features looked like, beyond basic bone structure?*

Aloud: "I don't know, Aelanni. It's as if they were two parts of a puzzle."

"But it still doesn't add up to a complete picture, does it? We're still mystified. Are there, perhaps, other parts?"

"There must be." DiFalco was grim. "I'll tell you

this: when we get back to Sol, I'm going to advocate a *thorough* search of the asteroids and the outer-planet satellites for more of these bases, or whatever they were."

"But that would be an overwhelming task! Remember, the two we know of were only discovered by blind chance."

"Yeah—at almost exactly the same time. That's another thing that bothers me." He shook his head irritably. He *hated* mysteries. "Anyway, we have to start somewhere. For now, shall we get back?"

At her nod, he reached up and took off his virtual-reality headpiece. Aelanni was doing the same, here in their suite in the Provisional Government's headquarters in Sarnath. By now he had gotten used to the way the universe, as reported by his senses, abruptly changed.

They regarded each other in silence for a moment and then, by unspoken mutual consent, walked out onto the balcony. The building—secondary government offices before the war—stood on a hill with a fair view of the city, and Sarnath lay before them under lightly-overcast skies, its wounds visible but the pulse of life somehow perceptible. Already the work of rebuilding had commenced.

DiFalco thought back to the first days after the liberation, when the populace had come hesitantly out of the places it had taken shelter. As the shock had worn off, a long-pent-up reaction had erupted with irrepressible force—even after all he had seen during the battle, he still shuddered at the memory of what the crowds had done to the ex-Implementers they had hunted down. He and Thompson—*sans* left arm, but with the replacement growing nicely in the tank—had tried to protect the ones who had surrendered by posting a heavy Marine guard on the prisoner compound. Then they had toured the lowest levels of the fallen fortress, and listened to tales of what had been done there from those who had been freed. Afterwards, he and Thompson had exchanged a long look—and Thompson had given his troops the afternoon off.

Finally the cathartic insanity had run its course, leaving the Raehaniv drained, stunned by the realization of what they were capable of. Rosen had speculated that centuries of social harmony had left them without antibodies against mob psychology. At any rate, the habits of civilization had returned, perhaps even deeper for no longer being taken for granted, and the Provisional Government was having an easier time of it than DiFalco would have expected.

It was headed by a troika of Arduin, Tarlann and Raenoli. (Varien had firmly refused any formal position.) Some had suggested that they establish their headquarters in some relatively unharmed city like Norellarn, but Arduin had set his face against it: Sarnath had always been the capital, and so it would remain, as a gesture both of continuity and of defiance.

DiFalco and Aelanni clasped hands as they gazed over the city, drawing on its quickening life. *I've been able to see some of Raehan over the last few weeks*, he thought, remembering his hurried visits to various parts of the planet. *This lovely world—Aelanni's world—will live, and heal. That is enough.*

The door chimed for admittance and DiFalco spoke a command, as he could do by now without having Raehaniv computers turn up the noses they didn't have at his accent. Levinson entered, dressed like DiFalco in service dress blacks. (During the years on Terranova they had gotten around to standardizing uniforms, and the Russians wore the black too. At the same time, all the Marines wore dark-green uniforms with Russian-style shoulder boards; it was one of the concessions Thompson had had to make in exchange for calling them "Marines." And the system of rank insignia showed historical Raehaniv influence, courtesy of Miralann.)

"Well, as much as I hate to break this up," Levinson

drawled, "it's time for our final meeting before departure. Of course, you realize they'll try one more time to talk us into staying longer. And they'll probably load us down with some more honors—especially you, after all your dirtside feats of derring-do." It was a subject on which he still hadn't forgiven DiFalco and, as usual in moments of agitation, he reverted to vintage American popular culture. "The CO landing on the dangerous planet and plunging into high adventure! Gimme a break! Who do you think you are? Captain Kirk?"

"I keep telling you, Jeff, I had no choice! It was the only way I could get out of *Guadalcanal* before she blew."

"Yeah. Right. I believe that about as much as your wife does!" Aelanni smiled demurely.

"I swear it's the truth," DiFalco insisted. "Thompson corroborated it." But he knew *that* wasn't much help. The Marine had taken a sadistic delight in recounting the story with complete truthfulness . . . and with the intonation of a man under orders to lie like a trooper. *He'll pay*, thought DiFalco, not for the first time.

Suddenly, Levinson's mercurial face went serious. "Of course it's the truth," he said gently. "It may even be what history will record. But you and I both know what legend will say. Legend and, eventually, myth."

Acutely uncomfortable, DiFalco looked to Aelanni for rescue. But her face wore exactly the same expression as Levinson's.

"Aw, Hell," he said roughly. "If people are looking for a hero, Tarlann's their man. If it hadn't've been for him, we'd all be up shit creek without a paddle! Speaking of Tarlann," he continued, relieved to change the subject, "it's time to go meet with him and the others."

* * *

"Are you quite sure you must leave now?" Varien

asked, fulfilling Levinson's prophecy. "There is much left to do in preparing our defenses against the inevitable Korvaash return."

They were seated around a large oval table in a conference room redolent of the light airiness of classical Raehaniv architecture. Varien sat beside Tarlann, who still needed artificial aids to walk but whose face had lost the grayness that had come with his premature plunge into the work of the Provisional Government. Arduin and Raenoli were at Tarlann's other side. Beyond them sat Yarvann, who in his capacity as military C-in-C had been persuaded to adopt a less flamboyant and more nearly regulation version of the old Raehaniv space fleet uniform.

"I know there is, Varien," Difalco replied. "But you don't need us for it. Isn't that true, Yarvann?"

"Yes," the Raehaniv said reluctantly. He needed no interpreter; Korvaash translator software had by now been adapted, and a device resembling an old-fashioned hearing aid repeated his words into DiFalco's ear in English. "Colonel Golovko should be in position at Seivra now with most of our combatant ships—he departed just after this planet was secured—so the displacement point leading to Korvaash-occupied space is *very* well-guarded. And our strength is already increasing as we turn out more and more ships and weapons, using"—a wintery and ironic smile—"the industrial plant that we've inherited. The Korvaasha must have an inkling by now that something is wrong at Seivra, but it will take time for them to mount an attack."

"Very true," Tarlann affirmed. "By its very nature, their system is incapable of quick reactions."

"Still, we can't sit on the defensive like this forever!" The translator conveyed Yarvann's eagerness. "Given enough time, they'll be able to mount an attack in overwhelming force! We've got to launch a counteroffensive as soon as possible, liberate the old Raehaniv-explored systems and go beyond that, into their own territory. Now that we have their navigational data, we can use the continuous-displacement drive to do repeatedly what Aelanni did to them here!"

"And so we shall," Arduin reassured him. "But there is much to do first. We must consolidate here and build our strength. And, of course, we need to cement our alliances."

"Exactly," DiFalco put in. "That's the primary reason for our immediate departure. The peoples of Earth *must* be told what's happening out here. As Varien knows, we joined him because our world is starting to turn its back on space just when such a move holds the prospect not just of stagnation—it always held that—but of disaster. Remember, once we begin the counteroffensive against the Korvaasha it's only a matter of time before a ship equipped with continuous-displacement drive falls into their hands. From what Tarlann has told us about them, they'll be able to rationalize adding the drive to their technological repertoire, on the grounds that it's just another application of gravitics and is therefore covered by the 'Acceptable Knowledge.' And on the day that happens, our world's security is gone; it won't be able to hide behind Sol's lack of displacement points. Earth's only safe course will be to ally itself with you Raehaniv, adopting your technology and joining with you to put an end to the Korvaash threat for good. And I *know* we can convince them of that."

Varien smiled and thrust shrewdly. "Can't you at least wait for your son? It's been a while since you've seen him."

DiFalco and Aelanni winced in unison. A courier vessel had gone with Golovko's fleet to Seivra, and was now enroute to Terranova to bring the news to the colony there. It would return to Tareil as a spacegoing nursery, bringing Jason and the other Terranova-born children of those who had departed into unknowable danger.

Slowly, Aelanni shook her head. "No, father. I want with all my heart to see him again, while he still remembers us. But this is too urgent. The sooner we can get to Earth, the better our prospects there will be."

"Yeah," DiFalco said grimly. "Believe me, things there are going to get worse before they get better. There's no time to lose." He brightened. "Besides, it's going to take time for Jason to get here. We should be back not too long after he arrives. Now that we've refitted *Andrew Jackson* so she can keep up with *Liberator* in continuous-displacement drive, it won't take us long to get to Sol after arriving at Alpha Centauri via the Lirauva Chain. Aelanni and I should be able to bring *Liberator* back soon after that, leaving Daeliuv and Miranni and the rest of the diplomatic mission with *Andy J.*, for which we've made up a crew of people who've decided to return to Earth."

"Well," Varien said, "I can see that the two of you have thought this through and that there's no dissuading you. So let me take this opportunity to make an announcement of my own." He looked around the table. "I have decided to retire to Terranova. I will probably depart after my grandson has arrived and I have provided for his care to my own satisfaction."

DiFalco broke the stunned silence. "But Varien, I . . . I'd kind of assumed that you'd be going to Sol with us. I mean, forging an alliance with Earth's governments was your original reason for going there. Now's your chance to finish the job!"

Varien smiled. "That's not precisely correct. I went to Sol seeking allies to help us liberate Raehan. And in that I succeeded, albeit in a manner which was, like so much else in life, unexpected."

"But . . . but *why*, Varien?" Arduin was almost inarticulate with shock. "Why do you want to leave Raehan? We need you here, now more than ever!"

"No, you don't," Varien stated flatly. "Tarlann has been running the family enterprises for some time, and is quite capable of continuing to do so." Tarlann nodded; he had been the only one who had known in advance. "And as for why—well, at the risk of repeating myself, Raehan is liberated, I know the fate of my son and grandchildren"—joy chased sorrow across his features—"and I feel a sense of . . . completion. It's time to move on to something else." He darted defensive looks around the table. "Well, I'm not *that* old, after all!"

"But," Arduin persisted, "why Terranova? From the descriptions I've heard . . ."

"Yes, I know, it sounds barely habitable. But it grows on one. For some inexplicable reason, I actually came to like the place. And I want to work with the Terran scientists there on some wholly new possiblities in the field of gravitics that our work on the deflector only suggested. Some of them are very brilliant people, and they've come to the field without preconceptions. I find them stimulating." Yarvann nodded as if he could understand that.

"Furthermore," Varien continued, "Raehan holds too much sadness for me. So much has been destroyed, and will be rebuilt in ways that are strange to me. Don't misunderstand; I have the highest expectations of the new Raehan. But it won't be *my* Raehan, if you take my meaning. Everything I've known must change now. If I remain here, I fear I shall be running a genuine risk of becoming a disagreeable, opinionated curmudgeon!"

He managed to maintain an air of dignified incomprehension through the storm of guffaws that broke over him.

* * *

"Approaching displacement point," the navigator reported crisply. DiFalco and Aelanni saw it confirmed in the holo tank in *Liberator*'s control room, suspended just ahead of the slowly moving lights that represented *Liberator* and *Andy J.* in response to the flow of data from the nav computer.

There were two ways to locate a known displacement point. One was to have the nav computer compare, on an ongoing basis, the apparent relative positions of the stars (and, for greater precision, the local planets, if the data was available) with what they *should* be at the displacement point's precise location in space at the precise time in question. When the two coincided exactly, the displacement point had been reached. Given Raehaniv computers, this was quicker than the other method, which was to search with grav scanners for the telltale gravitational anamoly in precisely the same way a new system was surveyed for hitherto-unknown displacement points (but limiting the search to a known vicinity).

Customarily, the first method was used with the second as a backup. Thus it was that they watched in the nav tank as Tareil's fourth displacement point grew nearer.

DiFalco marvelled anew at the sophistication of Raehaniv computers. Genuine artificial sentience remained as elusive and controversial a possibility as it was on Earth, but the really complex ones could fool you. (And, he gibed at himself, what did *that* say about relative sentience?) He had asked *Liberator*'s nav computer what date it was on Earth—he himself had long ago lost track. The computer had performed the multifaceted operation with contemptuous ease, and he now knew that if the voyage went according to plan they would arrive in mid-April.

Springtime in the Rockies. I cannot ask for more. He gazed at the tank hungrily. Beyond that displacement point lay the Lirauva Chain, and home. Impulsively, he put his arm around Aelanni's shoulders and squeezed. She smiled, knowing what it was to watch one's own home change from star to sun.

Then, out of the corner of his eye, DiFalco noticed movement at the scanner console. Loreann was fiddling with the controls, visibly annoyed.

"What is it, Loreann?"

"Well, Colonel," the Raehaniv said, straightening up, "I was just running the routine scan of the displacement point, to confirm the nav computer's conclusions. But I can't seem to get any return from it. It's as if there was no displacement point there at all."

DiFalco frowned. "Something must be wrong with the grav scanners. Run a diagnostic check."

"I just did, Colonel," Loreann replied. "Everything seems to check out."

"Well, check 'em again," DiFalco ordered irritably. "And get somebody out there on the hull to . . ."

"Colonel," the navigator broke in, "we're coming very close." His tone, and his entire body, eloquently conveyed just how little he thought his computer needed any confirmation from grav scanners. DiFalco was inclined to agree. He looked at Aelanni and she nodded.

"Okay, cancel that EVA; no time. We'll go on through according to plan."

The seconds ticked by, and DiFalco gave the order to execute. The stars wavered as the gravitic pulse distorted space around them. . . .

And then they stopped wavering and resumed the familiar patterns of Raehan's night sky. And the little golden spark of Tareil continued to glow in the view-aft screen.

"What the Hell?!" DiFalco rounded on the engineering station. "What happened?"

Loreann, who had been in muttered consultation with the engineer, looked up. "Unknown, Colonel. But," she added, pointing to a screen, "whatever it was, it also happened to *Andrew Jackson*."

It was true. *Andy J.* was still with them, and the two dissimilar ships plunged on into the outermost reaches of the Tareil system in formation.

"Raise Colonel Levinson," DiFalco ordered comm, then turned to Aelanni and spoke *sotto voce*. "What

could have happened? Could we have entered the
displacement point at the wrong heading?"

She shook her head dubiously. "That was also
under computer control." She spoke to the nav
computer in Raehaniv and frowned at the display
that was fed into her optic nerve. "Right now, all
we know is that it's going to take us a *very* long
time to come around and line up for another run."

"Don't I know it!" DiFalco groaned. He might not
have her kind of computer linkage, but he knew his
ballistics. "In fact, given our present vector it would
be a lot easier to return to Raehan. . . ."

Levinson's face appeared on the comm screen.
"What happened, Jeff?" DiFalco began without preamble. "Did you see that we weren't successfully
transiting and just decide to stay with us?"

"Negative," Levinson replied grimly. "We *tried* to
transit, and as far as we could tell everything was on
the green—except that during the approach we
couldn't get the displacement point to register on
grav scanners."

DiFalco and Aelanni looked at each other for a
long, long time. The control room was very quiet.

"Perhaps," Aelanni finally said in a completely controlled voice, "we *should* return to Raehan."

DiFalco nodded emphatically. "Yeah. Before we
risk these ships we need to find out just exactly
what's going on here."

During the long, tense trip back they listened to
the uproar in the interplanetary comm channels as
ship after ship reported failure to transit Tareil's
other displacement points.

CHAPTER NINETEEN

"I think I know what happened!"

Varien had to shout to make himself heard above the tumult in the conference room. It was the same room they had met in before their departure, but this time it was full to overflowing. The oval table was surrounded by a tightly packed crowd, mostly Raehaniv but including a number of Terrans. Their mood mirrored that of the entire planet—a choppy sea of tense uncertainty with whitecaps of incipient panic.

But Varien had their attention, and the noise level gradually dropped, leaving an expectant silence.

"As you all know," he began, "displacement points owe their existence to the arrangement of stars in the galactic spiral arms, which produces gravitational interrelationships of incredible complexity. We have known this for a long time. We have known for an even longer time that that arrangement is constantly changing, that the so-called 'fixed stars' are, in actuality, in motion with respect to each other. For some reason, it never occurred to us that the latter might have an impact on the former, and that the displacement network may be no more immutable than anything else in nature."

"Wait a minute, Varien," DiFalco spoke up. "If

you're saying what I think you're saying, then Tareil's displacement points not only don't work any more . . . they don't *exist* any more!"

"Not only Tareil's, I should think. I would imagine that the problem is more extensive than that, probably affecting this entire region of the spiral arm. Of course, this cannot be verified without . . ."

"But Varien," Rosen cut off the maddeningly calm voice, "as you yourself said, the stars are in *constant* motion, so their relative positions are constantly changing. So if your theory is correct, then why isn't the displacement network in a constant state of flux? We know it isn't. Granted, you Raehaniv have only been using it for a short time; but the Korvaasha have been expanding via displacement points for centuries! And I don't think there's any indication in the records we've captured that anything like this has ever happened to them." He glanced at Kuropatkin, who nodded in confirmation.

Varien pondered for a moment. "Remember, centuries or even millennia are mere eyeblinks of time on the cosmic scale. But I believe the real answer to your question lies in the sheer number of stars and the slowness of their motion relative to the distances between them. The pattern of which we're speaking is one of almost inconceivable vastness, and an enormous number of factors go into defining it. It must possess tremendous . . . inertia? Resiliency? Yes, that's it. A great deal of random stellar motion can take place without disrupting it. But eventually the cumulative effect of such motion exceeds the pattern's capacity to accomodate it. Then a disruption *does* occur, and it occurs *all at once*. Remember, gravity is propagated instantaneously. And, given the interrelatedness of the displacement points, any such disruption is likely to be widespread due to what I believe you Terrans call a 'domino effect.' "

"How widespread?" Miranni asked in a small voice.

"There is, of course, no way for us to know. Likewise, until we've been able to observe the phenomenon for a very long time we'll be unable to even guess how frequent such events are. Perhaps their occurrence is completely random. Or perhaps they run in epicycles—which, if true, might help to account for the fact that the Korvaasha have never experienced one; we could only now be entering into a period when the intervals between them are shorter."

Arduin spoke slowly, his engineer's practicality asserting itself. "Varien, this is all very interesting, but if I'm understanding you correctly, shouldn't there be a *new* pattern, based on the new interrelationship the stars have shifted into?"

"Indubitably!" Varien nodded vigorously. "And such a pattern should stabilize as instantaneously as the disruption of the old pattern. It should manifest itself at once. I propose that we survey this system exhaustively for new displacement points. Of course, we should not be too hopeful of locating any; only a minority of stars have these phenomena associated with then, so the odds are against us. But the fact that Tareil previously had *four* displacement points suggests that perhaps this star is located in a kind of crucial region—a nexus, as it were, resulting from an unknowable concatenation of factors. If this is the case, then perhaps . . ."

"Wait a minute! Wait a minute!" Levinson took a breath and spoke into the startled silence he had created. "Excuse me for interrupting this fascinating bull session, but just where does all this leave *us*? How do we go about getting back to Earth?"

Varien had the embarrassed look of a man abruptly reminded of something he should have thought of but hadn't. "Ah. Well. That poses a problem. You may recall the discussion we had before departing from the Solar system, when we had learned that the Lirauva Chain was denied to us. Well, it is now denied to us with even greater finality. In point of fact, the Lirauva Chain no longer exists. I pointed out at that time that we could not even locate Tareil in realspace. Well, the same applies in reverse now; we have only the vaguest, most inferential notion of where Sol might be located."

"Hold on, Varien," DiFalco said, sternly commanding his voice to steadiness. "I know you only have general approximations of Sol's distance and bearing from here. But you've never tried to do better—you've never had to! Can't we use those approximations to narrow the search to a certain segment of the sky, and then narrow it down further by process of elimination? I mean, we know Sol's spectral class, and what bright stars are nearby . . ."

He trailed to a halt, silenced by what he saw in Varien's face: compassion without a trace of condescension or complacency.

"We can certainly try," the old Raehaniv spoke. "And we *will* try, as a partial interest payment on the debt we owe you. But I don't think you fully grasp how many stars that 'segment of the sky' contains. And remember, at our departure from Sol we destroyed every scrap of information, including and especially everything related to descriptive astronomy, that might have enabled the Korvaasha to find Sol had our enterprise failed. If we still had that information, the methods you suggest might well succeed, given time. But as it is, we simply lack the data to build on.

"And even if we *could* locate Sol," Varien went on with the same quiet finality, "how would you use the information? Our conclusions as to the impracticality of voyaging from Sol to Tareil under continuous-displacement drive apply with equal force to any attempt in the opposite direction."

"Hey, look," Levinson began, almost stammering, "there's *got* to be *something* we can do! Like . . . well, we know where Terranova is in the sky, damn it! We can go there via continuous-displacement drive, and . . ."

"And what?" Varien asked gently. "Oh, I suppose it's not absolutely impossible that Terranova's displacement point, and the Altair Chain beyond it, are still as we remember them. But it would be unwise to invest much hope in it."

DiFalco barely heard them. He had already passed beyond the denial that still held Levinson in its grip and was letting his consciousness adjust to a new fact, so enormous that it must henceforth form the backdrop to his entire life. He eventually grew aware that Aelanni was gripping his hand tightly.

In search of something to say, he looked around and noticed Rosen's faraway expression. "Yakov, we haven't heard anything from you lately."

Rosen turned to him with an ironic little smile. "Oh, I was just thinking of a conversation that is supposed to have occurred in the last century, between two very brilliant men. You may have heard the first half of it; it's one of Albert Einstein's most famous quotes. He said, as nearly as I can recall it, 'The good Lord is subtle, but He is never malicious.'"

DiFalco nodded. "Yes, I've read that."

"Ah, but you may not have heard Enrico Fermi's rejoinder: 'Albert, stop telling God what to do!' "

*　　*　　*

The orbital tower had been built before the days of artificial gravity and this geostationary terminal station had been designed to rotate, producing a forged gravity that equaled one Raehaniv gee at the outer edge. So in the older areas the stars seemed to march in an unending circle in the viewports. But this was a newer addition, and the firmament held steady in the lounge's wide-curving transparency. And in the center of the floor, a circular well surrounded by small tables sloped down to a lens-like transparency in which Raehan's night side, almost thirty thousand kilometers down, was like a black shield bejeweled with lights. The outlines of seas and oceans could be traced by the shining necklaces of coastal cities.

The tower, and its antipodal twin, had survived both occupation and war. The economic usefulness of virtually cost-free orbital interface had been as clear to the Korvaasha as to humans; and when they had withdrawn to their urban strongholds, the possibility of booby-trapping had deterred the liberating forces from using them. So the towers stood unharmed, and DiFalco was glad of it. He had been able to see an engineering feat far beyond the capabilities of Terran humanity, riding up with Aelanni in the kind of passenger module he had previously experienced by computer-generated proxy.

Now they had this lounge to themselves, waiting to catch a glimpse of the incoming ship before it docked and they went to greet their son.

It had made its way from Terranova to Seivra just before space had shifted shape. The captain, mindful of her precious cargo of children, had waited there with Golovko's fleet until the courier had arrived by continuous-displacement drive from Tareil. Afterwards, Golovko had made the decision to abandon Seivra, whose now-nonexistent displacement points had always been its only points of interest or significance. He had divided his forces, taking to Tareil those ships for which the long voyage was practicable. The others, mostly Terran ones carrying Americans and Russians (and, in some cases, their Raehaniv spouses), had returned to Terranova. Some of the children had gone back with the second group, but others had continued on with Golovko, and had now entered the Tareil system with his and were on their final approach.

Fortunately for both of them, the age of space had brought with it a return to a kind of patience that had passed away with the age of sail.

The thought of the children, and their parents,

who by now were on Terranova reminded DiFalco of the infant colony. Aelanni had clearly been thinking of it too.

"Will they be all right on Terranova?" she wondered aloud.

"Sure they will," DiFalco stated positively. "They—we—have a solid foothold there by now. And they won't really be isolated, even though they're over a hundred light-years from here. We can keep in contact by means of the ships that have the powerplant modifications to make the trip, as more and more ships will. They'll be okay. And," he grinned, "once they have the time to spare for it, Terranovan politics should be lively." Aelanni laughed, knowing exactly what he meant. The noncombatants had been left there under the leadership of a council whose most prominent members were George Traylor and Liz Hadley.

"Am I interrupting anything?"

Varien stood in the entrance, silhouetted against the light beyond. With a rustle of his long traditional cloak he stepped forward into the lounge's dimness and joined them.

"No," Aelanni told him. "We were just thinking about the colony on Terranova. The courier we sent there should be returning soon, so we'll know for certain how they're faring, and whether their system has any displacement points now."

"Yes—Terranova." Varien's voice trailed off into thoughtful silence. Then he straightened and spoke briskly. "I hadn't mentioned it, but soon after Jason arrives I intend to go forward with my plan to relocate there"

"What?" Aelanni looked at him sharply. "But father, you made that decision when Terranova was one displacement transition and ten light-years by continuous-displacement drive from here. Now it's . . ."

"Yes, I'm fully aware of the changed circumstances," Varien cut in just a bit testily. "Undeniably,

Terranova is more isolated from the Tareil system than it was. But it is still accessible, albeit less conveniently. And all the arguments in favor of my decision still have as much validity as ever."

"Well," DiFalco spoke awkwardly, "as you know, we're staying here. There's a lot to do; we're still getting the search for Sol organized. Of course, for a while it will have to take a back seat to the work of rebuilding here on Raehan. But," he continued stoutly, "once we get a breather and can concentrate on it . . ."

"Of course." Varien nodded politely. "You can be sure I will be giving much thought to the problem." He paused, seeming to hesitate. "I knew the two of you would be staying here. But I have come to feel that I can leave with a certain degree of confidence. You see . . ." He hesitated again, then plunged in.

"As you both may be aware, I originally was not altogether in favor of your relationship. I had," he added quickly, turning to DiFalco, "always recognized that you were not without many excellent qualities, if perhaps a bit . . . ahem!" He pulled back and regrouped. "Nevertheless, I felt that you were perhaps not the best possible choice Aelanni could make. I was . . ." He tried unsuccessfully to continue, then took a deep breath and began again. "I was . . ." He seemed to be experiencing some obstruction of his ability to speak, and Aelanni began to look concerned. Varien visibly gathered himself for a supreme effort. "I was . . . wrong."

After a long, speechless moment, DiFalco grew aware that his mouth was hanging open. So was Aelanni's. *Always a first time for everything*, he reflected. *The Hell of it is, nobody will ever believe us. If only we had witnesses!*

"At any rate," Varien went on, palpably relieved that it was over, "I have no hesitancy about retiring. I meant what I said before about a sense of completion—and I meant more than just the success of our joint enterprise. It is time for me to go, and I do so, content."

He turned and walked along the curved transparent wall. Then he stopped and turned to face them, and for an instant that DiFalco would remember to the end of his days he stood silhouetted against the star-blazing blackness, his features only dimly visible, gazing at the two of them—at them and into them and through them. Then he spoke a phrase he had picked up from Rosen.

"Bless you."

And Varien was gone.

After a time of silence, Aelanni sighed deeply.

"What do you suppose will happen now?"

DiFalco straightened. "We'll continue to do what we can. One good thing: we don't have to worry about defense against the Korvaasha, at least for the foreseeable future. The displacement connection between us and them has been severed. And," he continued grimly, "I don't think the universe will have to worry about their Unity any more. It was overextended even before this happened. Now its component parts are strictly on their own. The ones that can't figure out how to function in the absence of centralized control will die like all life forms that lose the ability to adapt. The ones that *do* adapt will change in the process. The Korvaash race will survive, but the Unity is dead."

"From what Tarlann has told us, it's been dead for a long time. A rotting corpse in armor, polluting the galaxy." She shuddered. "I wonder if we'll ever encounter any of those 'component parts' after we start exploring through the new displacement point in earnest?"

They were silent. Like everyone else in the system, they were still adjusting to the news that one of the survey ships had found a displacement point in a region of Tareil's outer system where none had been before—a telling confirmation of Varien's theory. A well-armed squadron had cautiously transited it, to find an unoccupied system, heretofore unvisited, with two more displacement points leading no one knew where.

"We'll find out," DiFalco finally said. "Of course, given the small percentage of stars that have displacement points at any given time, the odds are against it. And, of course, we have to get back on our feet here on Raehan before we can launch any extensive exploration program." *A program which will drain resources and talent from the search for Sol*, he did not add. Aloud: "I think we'll want to proceed cautiously in displacement point exploration from now on. We'll never really be able to trust them again, or let ourselves get too dependent on them. Your father's right; we don't know whether the new displacement alignments will last ten millennia or ten weeks."

"Still," Aelanni insisted, "we must explore these new displacement connections. If there *is* a surviving fragment of the Korvaash Unity at the other end of a displacement chain, we need to know it. And . . . one of those chains might lead back to the vicinity of Sol."

He looked at her sharply. He hadn't considered that. "Yeah. Who knows? Maybe Sol itself has one or more displacement points now. Maybe *they'll* find *us* eventually! And maybe . . ." He held her eyes with his and spoke the thought that no one else had been allowed to hear.

"And maybe it doesn't really matter very much. All of us have begun building new lives here or on Terranova. I wonder if the inevitable return to Earth was ever anything more than an assurance we needed to give ourselves, a kind of justification for what we were doing? I, at least, had to present it to myself as a way of saving my country from itself." He paused and, with a kind of purgative rush, pushed relentlessly on with thoughts he had not shared even with her, nor even with himself. "Maybe I was just whistling in the dark about that. Oh, Earth will endure, in the long run. But as for my country . . . I don't know. I can see now that I came to manhood in its Indian summer, which I mistook for springtime. If it survives to play a part in the future, it won't be in any form I'll recognize. There'll be just enough familiarity to hurt." He gave a wry grin. "Listen to me! I sound like Varien!"

She smiled at him with the gentleness of strength under the guidance of loving wisdom. "But we'll keep searching for Sol, of course. We have to try. For you to not try would be self-betrayal. And yet . . . you're right. It doesn't really matter very much. For you *have* saved what was best of what your country once was—yours and Sergei's. You've saved it by bringing it here. It isn't dead; it's scattered among the stars for all time! Nothing can kill it now! It will live regardless of what your people manage to do to themselves on Earth."

For a long time he gazed at her in the starlit dimness, wishing he could put into words what was in his heart but happy in the knowledge that he didn't need to. All he said was: "I hope you're right. And, yes, we have to try."

Suddenly her eyes blinked and she took on the attentive look that he had learned heralded the arrival of a message via her implant communicator. Then her features awoke in pure joy.

"The ship is about to dock!"

They looked outward through the transparency, seeking a glimpse. But for an instant DiFalco's eyes strayed downward to the central well and the darkened world below. And as he looked, Tareil broke blindingly over Raehan's edge, flooding the lounge with light.

Arm in arm, they stood watching the ship approach, its silvery flanks reflecting the light of their home sun.